Little Black Dress Reader

Thanks for picking up this
of the great new titles from
romance novels. Lucky you
romantic read that we know

Why don't you make your Little Black Dress experience
even better by logging on to

www.littleblackdressbooks.com

where you can:

- Enter our **monthly competitions** to win
  gorgeous prizes
- Get **hot-off-the-press** news about our latest titles
- Read **exclusive** preview chapters both from
  your **favourite** authors and from brilliant new
  writing talent
- Buy **up-and-coming** books online
- Sign up for an essential slice of romance via
  our **fortnightly email** newsletter

We love nothing more than to curl up and indulge in an
addictive romance, and so we're delighted to welcome you
into the Little Black Dress club!

With love from,

The *little black dress* team

Five interesting things about Marisa Mackle:

1. Marisa speaks six languages but this can often increase to eight after a few drinks.

2. In biology lessons, Marisa learnt all about the reproductive system of a cockroach. This information has had no benefit on her life whatsoever.

3. People often suggest Marisa should be a stand-up comedian, but due to her tiny stature she prefers to sit down.

4. Marisa believes Mr Right is just around the corner – if only she knew which corner.

5. Marisa is owned by three ungrateful cats.

By Marisa Mackle

The Mile High Guy
Confessions of an Air Hostess
Chinese Whispers
Living Next Door to Alice

Living Next Door to Alice

to Alice

Marisa Mackle

little
black
dress

First published in 2008
by LITTLE BLACK DRESS
An imprint of HEADLINE PUBLISHING GROUP

A LITTLE BLACK DRESS paperback

1

ISBN 978 0 7553 3991 4

Typeset in Transit511BT by Avon DataSet Ltd,
Bidford-on-Avon, Warwickshire

Printed and bound in Great Britain by
Clays Ltd, St Ives plc

HEADLINE PUBLISHING GROUP
An Hachette Livre UK Company
338 Euston Road
London NW1 3BH

www.littleblackdressbooks.com
www.headline.co.uk
www.hachettelivre.co.uk

I would like to dedicate this book to my mother,
Daphne Mackle.

Acknowledgements

I would like to thank my parents for their continuous support and Roxanne Parker for being such a good friend. I'd also like to thank Cat Cobain and my patient, hardworking editor, Leah Woodburn at Little Black Dress. Most of all I'd like to thank God for everything He has done for me.

Tanya Thomson was getting married. Finally. To the man of her dreams. Yes, Eddie was about to propose. She could feel it in her bones. The fortune-teller had been right. Last year he had told Tanya that she'd be involved in a minor car crash, that she'd win some money and get engaged. Of course Tanya had shrugged the whole thing off till a man in a BMW who was talking on his mobile phone ploughed straight into the back of her red Nissan Micra when she'd stopped at the traffic lights. Luckily nobody had been hurt but after the shock of it all, Tanya began thinking that the fortune-teller, who had swiftly pocketed sixty quid of her hard-earned cash, might not have been such a crook after all. Four weeks later she'd won a hundred quid on a scratch card, and now, two months after all that, Eddie had announced that there was something very important he wanted to discuss with her.

He'd phoned her that afternoon when she was at work in the beauty salon but she'd been busy giving a particularly hairy woman a leg wax and couldn't speak.

'I'll call you later,' she hissed into the phone before returning to Ms Gorilla-woman to administer more punishment by pouring hot wax on to her left lower leg.

'Okay, but I want you to keep tomorrow evening free. I've booked us a table at Town and Grill for eight o'clock. I've something very important I want to ask you, Tanya.'

'Ouch,' squealed the woman as Tanya ripped off the waxing strips. She was yelling so hard, Tanya wouldn't be surprised if a passer-by called the police. Honestly! Some people had no pain threshold. Didn't she understand the meaning of 'no pain, no gain'?

Finally the dirty job was done and the ungrateful woman left the salon without even leaving a tip. The next appointment had cancelled and Tanya was glad of the rest. She'd been working flat out all day and her colleague Rose had phoned in citing the flu. But as she'd been on a hen night the night before, Tanya had her secret suspicions that this so-called flu was probably a hangover from hell. Rose didn't seem to know the difference between a few sociable drinks and downing cocktail after cocktail until she practically collapsed, usually into the arms of some unsavoury male character.

Tanya washed her hands and took refuge in the tiny kitchen above the salon. She boiled the kettle to make her first cup of coffee of the day. She needed something to pick her up and a dose of strong caffeine never failed to do the trick. But no matter how tired she felt, nothing could beat the warm glow she felt inside at the prospect of getting married to the man of her dreams.

She had almost given up on men before she met Eddie. Eligible men in Dublin were thin on the ground at the best of times but recently there had seemed to be an all-out drought in the capital city. Tanya had been happy enough to be single before her twenty-eighth birthday but now she was thoroughly sick and tired of getting hammered on vodkas with the girls. Fruitless nights spent in city-centre bars, entertaining idiots in suits, and falling out of cabs at four in the morning no longer held any appeal. There had to be a lot more to life than spending good money having your hair done just to get drunk and stumble home the worse for the wear a few hours later having met nobody at all suitable.

She'd first seen Eddie at the bar in Café en Seine with a group of lads. He'd stood out immediately because of his height and broad shoulders, but it was only when he'd turned around, caught her eye and winked, that something inside her had melted. It was like a scene in a movie, only instead of watching it on the couch wearing a comfy tracksuit and scoffing a box of Quality Street as she normally did, she was now the star and he was her hero. This is it, she thought, this was one of those life-changing moments.

He raised an eyebrow and she daringly raised her glass and winked back. She felt great, having had her roots done the day before and having got the all-over fake tan done by Rose before she'd left the salon that evening. Wearing a stunning red number from Chica boutique and Jimmy Choos from the Shoe Room in Brown Thomas that had cost almost a month's salary, she was now ready to take on the world. Or at least the Cary Grant lookalike at the bar. God, but he was great-looking. Almost too gorgeous if she was being perfectly honest with herself. Handsome men were always more trouble than they were worth but she was sick of living like a saint. Anyway, just because you went out with an ugly guy, it wasn't a guarantee that they would treat you like a queen. Sometimes the plainer men had chips on their shoulders and were so insecure about themselves that they constantly tried to take you down a peg or two in order to make themselves feel more important. Tanya reckoned you were as well being treated unfairly by a hunky rather than a chunky dude. Anyway, life was all about taking risks so she flashed the gorgeous guy another winning smile and within seconds he was over to her. Goodness, this was actually easier than she'd anticipated.

'Excuse me, but do I know you?' the vision before her enquired.

She stared into his ice-blue eyes and felt herself blush. Had she completely misread his signals?

Oh God, how embarrassing was this? Maybe he didn't fancy her at all. Maybe he just thought she recognised him or something. Maybe he was married. Perhaps he thought she was a friend of his wife. A quick check of his wedding finger, however, confirmed the absence of a gold band. Well, thank God for that anyway.

'Er . . .' she struggled. 'Do you live in Blackrock? Your face is very familiar.'

He smiled, showing picture-perfect teeth. 'That would be a no.'

At least he spoke with a nice Dublin accent anyway, Tanya thought. At least he wasn't just a tourist in town for the night looking for a bit of action. Lots of guys came to Dublin on stag parties but Tanya wouldn't even entertain those kinds of fellows. She had far too much self-respect.

'I'm sure I know you from somewhere,' she lied. She knew for a fact she didn't know him. God, who would ever forget a face like that? To her surprise and her delight he slid into the seat beside her.

'Maybe you saw me in a dream,' he teased.

Hmm. He wasn't half big-headed, was he?

'Or maybe a nightmare?' she offered cheekily.

He noticed her empty glass. 'Can I tempt you for another?'

He could indeed. And for another one after that. And another two or three or was it four? She'd lost count by the time they'd both stumbled into Lillies Bordello club several hours later. Her friend Sandy had gone home citing an early start in the morning as an excuse. Although to be honest, she'd probably decided that playing gooseberry for the rest of the evening wasn't going to be much fun. Tanya snogged Eddie at the end of the night. Only briefly, though. And when he'd suggested a party after Lillies she'd stared at her watch in mock innocence. 'At four in the morning? Sure, what kind of a party would that be?'

He'd duly taken her number and then she'd had to spend an agonising three days checking her mobile phone every ten minutes for any sign of a missed call or text. And when a casual 'How are you?' finally arrived in her inbox just as she was about to lose hope, she made him wait a full day before replying 'I'm fine'.

And so the games had begun. They were a necessary evil, she supposed. Although Tanya hated games, she also knew that most guys who claimed to hate games too played them the most. So she just had to play along.

The casual texting went on for a little longer than she would have liked. Three weeks, to be exact. And when he still hadn't suggested another meeting at that stage, Tanya texted him to say she was going away to Tenerife for a week of madness with the girls. It wasn't an exact lie. After all, she was heading off for a week in the sun. But she was being accompanied only by her mum and the height of their madness would probably be two brandies in the hotel bar during Happy Hour. Still, it was no harm to have him guessing she'd be dancing on tables in the clubs of Playa de las Americas every night attracting sexy Swedes and dishy Danes.

It worked. Eddie was desperate to meet up with her before she got on that plane. And so they hooked up for drinks in Bruxelles off Grafton Street and chatted for hours over pints of Guinness.

He invited her back to his place in Sandyford and she refused which seemed to keep him very interested. She still lived at home and knew that her mother never slept properly till she heard Tanya put her key in the front door of the family home. So she was a good girl and played it cool. And the next morning when she was rewarded with flowers from Eddie, she couldn't keep the smile off her face. Oh yes, the game was well and truly on and already she was winning.

2

Alice had been dreading her thirtieth birthday. On the morning itself when she woke up she didn't feel any different. She certainly didn't feel as old as she'd thought she might feel. But when she got up the first thing she did was look in the mirror and scrutinise her face for any sign of fine lines. Luckily, thanks to the great genes of her mother and her grandmother before her, she definitely looked younger than her age. But she was well aware of time passing her by. Thirty was way over the hill in LA and LA was home to her now.

She'd been living in Santa Monica for two months with the love of her life, Bill, in his impressive condo with an outdoor heated pool and elevated whirlpool. His place was enormous with plush cream curtains and deep carpets that you could sink your bare feet into after lounging around the pool all day doing nothing. And that's exactly what Alice seemed to do every day now: nothing. She took out her jar of Crème de La Mer from the huge bathroom mirrored cabinet, rubbed a blob of it between her palms and then patted her face carefully. She had to make sure she looked after her face now as though her life depended on it. It was the only thing she had left. It was her ticket to greater things. Hmm. Maybe she should give up sunbathing altogether. After all, sizzling under the sun all day was just inviting trouble. You always read about the ageing effects of the sun in magazines. But then again, she really did love lying in the heat, feeling warm, reading trashy paperbacks and drinking cocktails. That was something she relished; it was so different to home.

She couldn't wait to leave Dublin with its grey winter skies, hellish traffic and small-minded people. In Dublin other women had always been very jealous of her. It had started way back in school when she'd suddenly grown head and shoulders above the other girls during puberty. She'd even gone and bagged her own boyfriend at the age of thirteen, and had then traded him in for a better-looking one at the age of fourteen. At fifteen she'd completely lost all her friends when she had started dating the captain of the rugby team at one of Dublin's most prestigious schools. All the girls had fancied him and they were so envious of Alice that some of them started calling her names such as 'beanpole' because of her height. They'd stop talking when she entered the room and excluded her from their birthday parties. Things of course became a lot worse when she was approached in Stillorgan shopping centre by a model scout who'd told her she had what it took to make it as a top model. Alice's mother had at first refused to let Alice try out modelling, but after much sulking in her room and moping around the house listening to her headphones and not studying, her parents finally agreed that Alice could do the odd modelling job, provided she also promised to study for her exams.

A week later the modelling scout rang her and booked

her for a hair show. Alice had to endure her hair being backcombed and practically drenched by a can of hairspray before the show but it had all been worth it in the end. To this day Alice would never forget the first time her picture appeared in the paper. She had been photographed at a hair show with another girl and underneath the photo, her name was clearly printed. Alice loved the idea of so many people seeing her picture. She couldn't wipe the smile off her face. That would teach the bitchy girls in school who'd slagged her off behind her back. That would give the nasty nuns who always said she'd never be anything something to put in their pipe and smoke. That would show her cocky medal-winning boyfriend that he wasn't the only one to get his mug into the papers. And instead of studying harder like she'd promised her parents, she became more determined than ever to become a modelling sensation. One day, she told herself, one day in the not too distant future, Alice Adams would be a household name. In fact, she'd even drop the Adams bit and just like Naomi, and Giselle, become known by her first name, Alice. Of course she would be invited on to *The Late Late Show* to discuss her life with the country, all the paparazzi would chase her down the street every time she went out, but she'd deal with it. Even better, she'd have enough money to buy anything she wanted. Yeah, baby! She was going to be a super bitch and get away with it.

Alice had made her dad buy ten copies of the paper the day her picture first appeared. She wanted to post copies to aunts and uncles abroad so that they could all see it. Then she bought a scrapbook at the local newsagent and cut out the newspaper photo and pasted it on to page one. By the end of the year, she vowed to herself, the entire scrapbook would be full of her clippings. And then it would be time to fill another one.

Going into school the following morning she had expected that she would be treated a bit differently at least. Maybe her fellow pupils would start being nicer to her now that she was in the papers. But no. Funnily enough, nobody said anything, except at lunchtime when Caroline, the school nerd, briefly mentioned that she'd seen her in the paper. And then another girl from the year ahead whom she didn't know very well told her she'd also spotted the picture and thought Alice looked nice. Apart from that, nothing. It was a huge anti-climax. Well, she fumed; obviously the other girls were too consumed by envy to compliment her. And to make things even worse, in all the excitement of her new-found fame, she'd forgotten to bring her blasted hockey stick into PE the following day and the battleaxe of a gym teacher from hell had given her an hour's detention.

She came home in a fit of rage having had to write an essay in detention entitled 'Why I'm no better than any-body else'. It had made her sick having to write something so degrading. She *was* better than everybody else in school. She'd show them. It wasn't her fault that the PE teacher was five-foot-nothing with a moustache and a deep voice. Huh, she probably fancies me, thought Alice in disgust.

However, instead of being put off modelling, Alice had been bitten by the bug and was now more determined than ever to get more work. She'd show the jealous girls in school that they couldn't keep her down. She'd been paid sixty quid for the hair show – three times more than her weekly pocket money and she wanted to earn more. She could hardly contain her excitement when the casting agent rang and booked her for a press call in Grafton Street the following morning for a bikini shoot with three of the country's top models.

Alice was over the moon. She had seen those other girls on TV and in magazines. In fact, they weren't even girls; they were real women, unlike the silly twits that she was in school with. All those losers ever did was smoke in the toilets and think that was a cool thing to do. Pathetic!

Alice was determined to eat as little as possible the day before the press call. In fact, all she had was an apple for lunch which she ate painfully slowly. Her stomach hurt from the lack of food but she ignored its loud rumbles of protest. She was a woman on a mission, after all, and that mission was to be a rake. She wasn't going to prance around Grafton Street sporting a jelly belly and have people laughing at her. God, no.

The following day she put on her uniform and pretended to her parents that she was going to school as usual. But she didn't go, of course. She reckoned she could always forge her mother's signature the following day and pretend she'd gone to the dentist or something. She got the bus into town and met the other girls in the Westbury Hotel where she changed into the skimpy white bikini that had been handed to her by the PR person. She'd never felt so self-conscious in her life, but she had to banish any feelings of insecurity now because she was a model and this is what models did for a living. She pulled on a wrap dress over her bikini and made her way down to Grafton Street with the rest of the girls. As it was an outdoors shot it was freezing. The wind bit cruelly at her ankles but she tried to ignore the cold. When she took off her wrap dress to reveal her bikini she ignored the wolf whistles from passers-by who suddenly started taking their own pictures with their mobile phones. Goose bumps appeared from the tops of her shoulders right down to her toes. It was pretty miserable and not at all glamorous. The client, a middle-aged man in a grey suit and wearing glasses, who seemed to think he was pretty important, stood in the middle of the girls as the hired photographer snapped away. Alice thought it was all very unfair. If he wanted to be in the photo then he should be wearing swimming trunks too! The photo call probably only lasted less than half an hour but to Alice it seemed endless. By the time the photographer announced he was happy with his shots, her skin was almost blue with the cold and she couldn't even feel her toes as they were numb. She pulled her wrap dress back on and gratefully ran back to the Westbury where she ordered a coffee to try and heat up. As she gradually began to feel normal again, she had to ask herself what she was letting herself in for. Standing in bikinis with stuffy corporate types putting their arms around her was not the glamorous life she'd once dreamed about. Still, she had to start somewhere, she supposed. And what was the alternative? Doing a secretarial course and licking ass from nine to five, Monday to Friday? No thanks.

Finally, when she'd convinced herself that modelling really was the way forward to leading a good life, she got the bus back home and told her parents that she'd been given a half-day off school because one of the nuns had died. They believed her till the following day she was well and truly caught out when her practically naked form was splashed all over the papers. Alice found herself grounded for a month.

Just before Tanya left work, she made sure to put copies of both *Irish Brides* and *Confetti* magazines into her bag to read on the bus home. Normally she never flicked through those bridal magazines, instead preferring to catch up on all the gossip in *Heat* or *Hello!*. But things were different now, she thought with a secret smile on her face. She was going to be one of those bridezillas, obsessed with their weddings. She just knew it.

She locked up the salon and braced herself for the cold night air. She hated these dark evenings and working in the salon entailed late nights to deal with customer demand. Usually when clients came through the doors enquiring about the bridal package, Tanya would secretly wonder why they were prepared to spend an absolute fortune on looking perfect for their big day. From now on she'd be a lot more understanding. She stuck her hands deep into her pockets and walked briskly along the road towards the bus stop. Of course there was so much planning ahead. Her hen party, for example. She supposed she'd have to organise something or else her friends would be very disappointed. Personally, if Tanya had her way, she wouldn't be bothered having a hen party at all.

They were usually ghastly affairs with people's interfering aunts coming along. Well, certainly, if she was going to have a hen party it would have to be a classy affair. No L signs or strippers or chocolate willies or anything like that. A nice meal in a decent restaurant with her closest friends would do nicely. Oh God, she supposed she'd have to invite Eddie's mother and aunt along. Hmm. Eddie's mother and aunt could sometimes become loud and raucous after a few drinks. Maybe the best thing to do would be to book dinner at a restaurant with a very long table so that Eddie's relatives could be at the far end and she could be with her friends at the other. Yes, that would be best. Then Peggy and Breda could be as vulgar as they liked and nobody would hear them.

The funny thing was, Tanya had never set out to be a beauty therapist but after school she hadn't really fancied spending years as a penniless college student. At least training as a beauty therapist would lead to getting a job and earning her own money straight away. She'd got her first interview immediately and had been waxing and preening ladies and the odd man basically ever since. People always asked why she worked on the other side of town when there were so many beauty salons within walking distance of where she lived. But Tanya had a very good excuse for wanting her work to take her far away from home. She couldn't bear the thought of having the girls she went to school with popping in for a bikini wax or an eyebrow pluck. No, that would just be too humiliating by far. At least in the salon where she worked, every customer was a stranger and that was the way she liked it.

That evening, when she eventually got home, all she wanted to do was make herself a cup of tea, retire to bed and get her beauty sleep for tomorrow. She went into the kitchen and put the kettle on to boil. The house was empty and cold. Nobody had switched on the heating. Tanya decided she'd make herself a hot-water bottle, and go to bed with a book. She couldn't wait to finish Melissa Hill's latest.

She was about to go upstairs when one of her oldest friends, Dianne, rang her mobile.

'Whatcha up to?'

'I'm just in from work and I'm shattered. Just dreaming of my bed now.'

'Well, stop dreaming,' Dianne ordered. 'And come and join me at the Dylan for one.'

'But it's never just one with you, Dianne; you know that only too well.'

'Come on. I *need* to go out. So do you. You're only young once. I'll pick you up in fifteen.'

And before Tanya had the chance to protest further, Dianne had hung up.

Wearily, Tanya changed into a pair of jeans and a black top. She had very little interest in venturing out but a part of her wanted to meet Dianne and tell her the good news. Her pal would be over the moon for her. She'd always said she thought herself and Eddie made a great couple. The only trouble was that Dianne had a big mouth and found it impossible to keep secrets. Could Tanya trust her on this one?

Fifteen minutes later Dianne hooted her horn outside Tanya's family home. That was the one good thing about her friend – she was always bang-on time. Tanya put on her coat, slammed the front door shut and slid into the passenger seat of her friend's silver Ford Fiesta. 'I can't believe you're forcing me out,' she grumbled amiably.

'I'm going to ignore that comment of yours.' Dianne laughed. 'You've got to be more positive. The Dylan is where it's all at now. You never know who you'll bump into there. Celebrities and all drink there.'

Dianne had been single for over a year now but was refreshingly always optimistic that Mr Right was just around the corner. Tanya marvelled at her enthusiasm. She was so glad that she herself was no longer single. Just the idea of putting herself out there in the hope of meeting a suitable partner in one of the many clubs and pubs dotted around Dublin was enough to send an uncomfortable shiver down her spine. She didn't mind admitting that she couldn't wait to get married. Tanya couldn't wait to be Mrs somebody instead of just another Ms. It'd be great referring to Eddie as 'my husband'. And it would be very nice indeed to get that solitaire for the ring finger on her left hand at long last. Finally, finally that time was about to come. She'd been with Eddie for two years now. It was time to move on to the next stage.

The Dylan was a fabulous five-star boutique hotel in the heart of Ballsbridge. Achingly trendy with low lighting and super-cool furniture, it attracted all sorts of well-heeled customers. Dianne and Tanya found a nice quiet corner and ordered two exotic-sounding cocktails from a stunning-looking Polish waitress.

'You look happy,' Dianne commented as they clinked glasses and toasted each other's health and happiness.

'Well, I've good reason to be,' Tanya said, blushing slightly.

Dianne's radar shot up. 'So? Tell me why. I'm your best friend. I need to know.'

Tanya grinned and took a sip of her cocktail. 'Um, I don't know whether I should say . . .' she trailed off mysteriously.

'*I* know what's happened.' Dianne's eyes suddenly lit up with excitement. 'Eddie has proposed, hasn't he?'

Tanya looked away coyly. She'd never been good at hiding her true feelings through her facial expressions. An Oscar-winning actress she would never be.

'Yes, well, don't tell anyone, okay?' she said in hushed tones.

Dianne let out a terrific squeal, attracting the attention of two businessmen sitting at the next table. 'I *knew* it,' she gushed. 'Oh my God, this is so, so exciting. Have you decided on a bridesmaid yet? Not, of course, that you have to choose me . . . I wouldn't dream of putting you under pressure . . .'

'But of *course* I want you,' Tanya insisted, her cheeks flushed with excitement. Now the cat had been let out of the bag, there could be no holding her back. 'You're my best friend. I couldn't think of anybody I'd rather have. I'll have you and my sister, of course. You girls can even choose your own dresses.'

Dianne drained her cocktail and looked around to see if she could spot the Polish waitress to reorder. 'This is incredible. I've never been a bridesmaid before. Maybe I'll even catch the bouquet! Do you know you're my first friend to get married? I can't believe you'll soon be somebody's wife.'

'God, neither can I.'

'So, tell me all the details. How did Eddie propose? Did it just come out of the blue? Did he get down on one knee? Come on, this calls for a major celebration. Do you want another cocktail? Where's that waitress gone to? No, hang on, I'll order champagne. Let's do this in style. After all, it's not every day of the week that my best friend gets engaged!'

'Hush,' said Tanya, beginning to panic. Dianne was almost shouting now and the last thing she needed was anybody to overhear their private conversation. 'Now, listen to me, Dianne, you've got to swear to secrecy. Eddie hasn't popped the question yet but he will tomorrow night. I'm so sure of it. He's asked me to meet him for dinner and he sounded all mysterious on the phone and, well, nervous almost. Very unlike Eddie. Oh God, he's just so sweet. He's probably already asked Dad for my hand in marriage but you know my father, he'd never let on.'

'So you haven't told your folks yet?'

'No, that's why you need to be very careful and not breathe a word to anybody. My mother would just die if she thought I'd told you before her. You know what she's like. She's so emotional, Lord love her.'

The waitress appeared again and Dianne ordered a bottle of Moët.

'You're dreadful,' Tanya said, shaking her head. 'I hope you're not going to try and get me drunk.'

'Let's make the most of this evening,' Dianne said, her eyes shining. 'Sure, once you get married our girls' nights out will be few and far between so we've got to make the most of now. I'm gonna leave my car parked outside and

I'll collect it first thing in the morning. Do you think Eddie has bought a ring yet?'

Tanya paused for a moment. 'I dunno . . . I hope not. I wouldn't really trust Eddie to choose me something I'd really like. I'd rather the two of us went ring hunting together, you know? I mean, I'll have to wear the thing for the rest of my life so I *have* to love it.'

'The rest of your life . . .' Dianne echoed dreamily. 'How romantic it must be when a man decides that you're the woman he wants to grow old with. I wonder will he want to start a family straight away?'

'Now, Dianne, you're making me nervous. I haven't even thought about children. Maybe in a few years, though . . .'

'I wouldn't leave it too long. It'd be nice to be young parents. I really think your children will be beautiful. Yourself and Eddie are such a good-looking couple.'

The waitress came back with the champagne and poured it into two flutes. The girls clinked glasses giddily. 'To a wonderful happy future with Eddie,' Dianne said, beaming.

'Ssshhh, keep it down. I hope nobody we know comes in,' Tanya said, looking around her nervously. 'They would want to know why we're drinking champagne mid-week.'

'Let them wonder whatever they like. Who cares? It can be our secret.'

The girls continued to drink happily. In a way Tanya was glad that Dianne had persuaded her to come out. If she hadn't, she'd probably just be at home reading a book trying to keep her feet warm with a hot-water bottle. Why shouldn't she celebrate? Eddie, the man she loved with all her heart, was finally going to make a decent woman of her. Never again would she have to go out on the tiles again as a single woman being subjected to cheesy chat-up lines by sleazy men in suits just looking for a one-night stand. She envisioned cosy nights in front of the fire watching DVDs, drinking decent wine and cuddling on the sofa. While her single friends were still out there searching and waiting on taxis outside Renards club in the rain, she, Tanya, would be fast asleep, safe in her gorgeous husband's arms. The wedding couldn't happen fast enough as far as she was concerned. She wouldn't miss being single a bit. Not one single bit.

'I think we should go to Lillies,' said Dianne once she'd got stuck into her second glass of champagne, 'and dance the night away.'

'Oh God, do we have to?'

'Now, listen here,' said Dianne, pretending to be cross and draining her glass purposefully. 'Just because you're all loved up and are about to get hitched doesn't mean you can just forget all about your single friends. *I'm* still on the lookout, you know.'

'I know,' said Tanya gently, suddenly feeling a surge of sympathy for her friend. Poor Dianne always had the worst luck when it came to men. And it was nice of her to be so enthusiastic about her wedding to Eddie. God knows, if the shoe was on the other foot and Dianne was getting engaged instead of her, Tanya didn't know if she'd be big enough to hide her disappointment. It had always been Tanya's biggest dread that all her friends would get married before her and that she'd end up the spinster friend always being asked to babysit. She knew she was lucky and therefore, much as she didn't want to hit a nightclub this evening, she would do it for Dianne's sake.

'Okay then, you've twisted my arm. You really are such a bad influence on me. But listen, I'm not going clubbing in these clothes. I look like a nun.'

'Ah, it doesn't matter now that you're no longer on the pull,' Dianne teased.

Tanya wagged a finger accusingly at her friend. 'I won't let myself go just because I'm no longer looking for a man,' she insisted. 'I really can't understand women who let their looks go once they get a ring on their finger. It's one thing getting a husband and quite another thing keeping him. I don't want Eddie in a few years' time looking at younger, slimmer women and wondering if he's pulled the short straw.'

'Right, then. We'll get a taxi back to yours and you can tart yourself up if you like.' Dianne grinned. 'Anyway, it's about time I said hello to your folks. I haven't seen them for ages. How's Elaine? Is she still in UCD?'

'Yeah, I think she wants to end up as a fashion journalist or something.'

'I can't say I blame her. If I was to do it all again, I'd do something glamorous myself instead of going into hotel management. The hours are desperately unsociable, and as for the pay? Don't make me laugh!'

Tanya couldn't help but feel for her friend. Not having been particularly academic in school, Dianne had wanted to become an actress, but her conservative parents wouldn't hear of it.

'You'll only end up in the gutter,' her mother had sternly warned, and her parents had enrolled her in a four-year hotel management course down at Shannon. Dianne had travelled the world working in various hotels from New York to Switzerland and now she was a hotel manager in one of Dublin's top hotels. But as for meeting men through work? Well, that seemed to be a total no go.

'Most of the male staff are gay or foreign or both. And as for business clients checking in for the night? Don't even go there,' she'd often moan. 'If they're looking for a bit of female company, well, there are escorts out there who provide such "entertainment"!'

The girls hopped into a taxi on Baggot Street and were soon in the Thomson home. All the family were now in the house, the heating was fully on and the TV was blaring. Not realising the girls were already pretty merry at this stage, Mrs Thomson innocently opened a bottle of wine and offered the two friends a glass each which was duly accepted.

'We haven't seen you in an age, darling.' Mrs Thomson gave Dianne a warm kiss on the cheek. 'How is our third daughter getting on these days?'

'Oh fine, not a bother.' Dianne beamed, delighted with all the attention.

'Any men on the horizon? I'm sure you must be beating them off with a stick!'

'Oh God, don't I wish? No, still single, I'm afraid, unlike our Tanya here,' Dianne giggled, ignoring the warning look that her friend shot her.

'Well, we live in hope that Tanya will give us a big day out soon.' Mrs Thomson sighed wistfully while her other daughter, Elaine, dressed in jeans and a hoody, giggled, seemingly amused by the conversation.

'That might be sooner rather than later,' Dianne guffawed, taking a large gulp of white wine from her goldfish-bowl-sized glass.

Mrs Thomson looked confused as Tanya's heart hit the floor. All the alcohol must have gone to poor Dianne's head. Please, please, don't let her spill the beans, Tanya begged silently.

'Don't listen to her, Mum,' she said.

'I wouldn't say Eddie is the type to rush into marriage,' said Elaine pragmatically, tossing her long dark hair over her shoulder and tucking her feet under her on the sofa. 'He's a real Jack the lad, isn't he?'

Tanya felt a surge of annoyance seep through her. Why was Elaine making comments like that? She didn't know anything. She'd only met Eddie a couple of times so she had a bit of a cheek making rash judgements!

'Eddie is very stable,' she answered coolly, not wishing to be drawn into a family argument over her future fiancé. 'In fact, out of all the guys I've ever dated he's probably the most likely to settle down.'

'Exactly,' Dianne chimed in. 'By the way, Elaine, if – and it's a big *if* of course – Tanya were to get married and you and I were to be bridesmaids, what colour dress would you like to wear?'

Elaine looked at her incredulously as if she'd gone and grown a second head. 'Where is this going? Tanya is no more going to get married than I am. That's a joke if ever I heard one. In fact, I'd almost lay bets that *I'll* walk down the aisle before Tanya will.'

Tanya could feel her blood boil. Elaine needn't become a smart arse about the whole thing. After all, she was a decade younger than Tanya and should respect her elders. Obviously her college education was giving her a swelled head and making her cockier than she had any right to be.

'For your information, Elaine . . .' she started, but then thought better of it.

Too late. Her whole family had turned towards her with interest.

'There isn't something you'd like to share with us, is there, pet?' asked Mrs Thomson, her voice full of hope.

Tanya stared at the ground. Should she tell them? Would that not possibly jinx everything? You could almost cut the atmosphere with a knife.

'Dad?' she turned to her father who till now had been pretending to watch the news rather than admit listening to the conversation.

'What is it, love?'

'Has Eddie been around here recently?'

'No. Not that I know of. Why?' he asked, sounding puzzled.

'I mean to chat with you . . . man to man?' Oh God, she could feel herself digging deeper and deeper.

'Well, no,' he said, sounding a bit miffed. 'But if he's planning on asking my eldest daughter to marry him, then it would be the right proper thing to do.'

'*Tell* them,' Dianne urged, polishing off her glass of Chablis and then gratefully accepting Mrs Thomson's offer of a fill-up. Tanya groaned inwardly. Why, oh why, had she allowed Dianne to come home with her? Announcing her engagement in the *Irish Times* would have attracted less attention.

'Tell us what?' Mrs Thomson's eyes nearly popped out of their sockets with all the excitement.

Tanya decided she might as well come clean. It was no big deal, she told herself. After all, tomorrow night they'd all have to be told, anyway, after Eddie's proposal. And it *was* pretty rare to have all her family in the same room at the same time. Elaine was usually in the UCD library studying in the evenings and her parents always had something on, such as bridge or dinners at the golf club. Maybe it'd be just as well to get it over and done with.

'Okay then.' She relented. 'Since I'm really feeling the pressure here, it's best just to come out with it. Eddie has asked me out for dinner tomorrow in Town and Grill because he has something very important he wants to ask me. I wanted to keep it all a secret but thanks to blabbermouth here' – she shot a look at Dianne, who at least had the good grace to look guilty – 'I can no longer keep it quiet.'

Mrs Thomson let out an almighty shriek. Then she sprang from her position on the sofa, ran over to Tanya, and enveloped her in a great big bear hug. Her daughter struggled to breathe. She was afraid her mother would suffocate her!

'Oh darling,' Mrs Thomson gasped, almost hyperventilating with excitement. 'This is the most wonderful news ever. It's marvellous. Oh Gosh, my baby . . . imagine, my baby girl is growing up! Oh, we'll have to ring Granny straight away. She'll be over the moon!'

'No!' Tanya practically shouted. 'Can we not wait till tomorrow? Too many people know already and Eddie won't be a bit pleased if he finds out most of my family know the news before he's even got the chance to tell his own parents.'

Mrs Thomson looked injured. 'But poor Granny never gets any good news. This'll give her something to look forward to. It's a big deal to have your first grandchild getting married. You wouldn't deny a poor old woman that much, would you?'

Overcome with sudden guilt, Tanya relented. 'Okay then, you can tell Granny. I'm sure she won't tell anybody else. But that's it, then, do you hear?'

'Sure,' agreed her mother before rushing out to the hall to call Granny in the old folks' home. She came back moments later, a big grin plastered all over her face. 'Mummy is thrilled,' she announced. 'You've really given her something to look forward to, Tanya. She wants to know if it'll be a summer or a winter wedding so that she can start planning her outfit.'

'Well it'd better not clash with my exams or I bloody well won't show up,' said Elaine gruffly, speaking for the first time since the big announcement.

'It won't be that soon. Probably a year from now so we'll have plenty of time to get organised,' Tanya mused. This was all happening so fast she hadn't even thought about when they'd actually have the big day. She wondered if herself and Eddie would get married in Dublin or whether they'd opt for a country wedding instead. There would be so much to plan, so many relatives to please . . .

'If it's a year from now, that gives us plenty of time,' agreed Mrs Thomson. 'Mummy said she's going to ring Uncle John in Australia straight away so that he can make plans to come home. Flights are cheaper when you book them well in advance.'

'She's ringing Uncle John?' Tanya shrieked in horror. 'Mum, I told you to tell her not to tell *any*body.'

'But Uncle John won't tell anybody,' her mother insisted. 'Sure, isn't he holed up in hospital with a broken leg at the moment?'

'Yeah, maybe, but he has a phone so he'll be ringing around all the other relations. Oh Jesus, that's all I need. All the cousins and everybody will know by the morning.'

'Now, dear, don't be getting yourself worked up. It's only natural for us all to be excited. It's just because we love you. Have another glass of wine, or should I open a bottle of bubbly? I mean, if we can't drink champagne on this occasion, then when can we drink it?'

But before Tanya could protest and explain that herself and Dianne had already consumed a bottle in the Dylan Hotel earlier, Mrs Thomson had rushed out to the hall to get the bottle that she and her husband had won last Christmas at the tennis club's annual Turkey Tournament. She duly came back into the sitting room, looking scarily like that Bucket woman from *Keeping Up Appearances*, with five Waterford Crystal flutes on a silver tray. Everyone accepted a glass, even Elaine. Tanya could feel her head beginning to spin. This all felt like a bad dream. Imagine if poor Eddie could see her family right now. He'd probably get so freaked by the whole circus-like situation he'd call the whole thing off.

'To Eddie and Tanya!' Mrs Thomson raised her glass and everybody drank to that. Tanya suddenly felt dizzy. She remembered that she hadn't eaten a thing since lunchtime. No wonder she was feeling light-headed. She wasn't in the mood for clubbing now either. She glanced over at Dianne who had practically fallen asleep on her dad's shoulder with Petra, the family pooch, curled up on her knee. Good, well at least that was something. Honest to God, a night on the tear was the last thing she needed now. After tonight's drama all Tanya wanted to do now was fall into bed. Anyway, Dianne was so indiscreet that if they ended up going to Lillies she'd probably end up forcing the DJ to announce the forthcoming wedding from his box and then all of Dublin would know.

She went over to her friend and shook her gently. 'Come on, Dianne, I'll put you in the spare room and wake you early in the morning so you can collect your car.'

Dianne groggily agreed and soon all the Thomsons headed for bed.

After giving Dianne a clean, warm nightie and tucking her up in bed, Tanya made her way into her own small but comfy bedroom. It was still as pink and girlie as it had been since she was a teenager although the Madonna posters had all been taken down to make room for the Laura Ashley wallpaper that Mrs Thomson had bought a few years ago in the January sales. The curtains matched and so did the lampshade on her bedside table. Tanya loved this room and would be sorry to move out of it once she got married. She'd never done the whole 'sharing with friends' thing as Dublin rents were atrociously high these days. Although she was twenty-eight she had never felt the urge to flee the nest as she'd always got along fine with her parents. Even living with Elaine was almost tolerable now that Mr Thomson had put a lock on Tanya's wardrobe door to stop her sister from nicking her clothes. She hoped her parents would leave her room the way it was so that she could come back and stay here sometimes. Her mother had always said that if she ever moved out she'd turn the room into an ironing room but it would be a shame if that happened. Tanya didn't like too much change. Just as she was about to turn out the light above her bed, she received a text message. Her face lit up when she saw it was from Eddie.

'Remember we're meeting 2moro at 8,' the message read.

Tanya almost laughed when she saw it. Remember? That was a good one all right. How could she possibly forget?

Alice enjoyed everything about LA. She loved the beaches and the weather and the way that people dressed casually but still looked fab. She liked the bars and the restaurants and the laid-back way of life. People came here from all over the world hoping to make the big time. They came to make their dreams come true. LA was full of opportunities. It was an optimistic place to live in. Alice felt she fitted in here. Now that she was thirty and had endured years of begrudgery back home, she was glad to be far away from the madness of it all. Even the man on the street had become jealous of her success. Over here people applauded ambition. There was nothing wrong with it. People had travelled from one-horse towns across the globe to come to LA. Anything was possible here.

Back in Ireland Alice had finally realised there was no future for her. She had reached the top of her game, landed countless ad campaigns, had seen herself on numerous billboards. She had even trodden the boards alongside Jodie Kidd and Naomi Campbell when they'd come to Dublin to take part in a huge charity fashion show. She'd dated Ireland's top movers and shakers and apparently dated others whom she hadn't even met, according to some scurrilous papers that she'd gone on to successfully sue. But they'd got her back by writing more crap about her and hounding anybody she dated for a picture. She was convinced that all the press attention surrounding her scared decent men away. The whole media circus thing had become so tedious in the end. Every so-called glittering red carpet event she turned up to was full of the same old tired faces, and eager young wannabes who wore too much fake tan, false eyelashes and hair extensions and wanted to look just like her. Everything had become so, well, jaded. She had con-templated moving to London for a change of scene but accommodation in Central London was terribly expensive and she wasn't prepared to live out in the sticks some-where or to share with strangers. No, she was far too set in her ways to even contemplate such carry-on. Anyway, in London she wasn't well-known and Alice had come too far to go back to being a nobody again. So what was she going to do? Where was she going to go next? Would she ever meet her Mr Right who would whisk her away and treat her like a princess? Was there even anybody left?

She had all but given up men when she'd bumped into Bill, literally, on Grafton Street. At the time she'd been making her way to the Brown Thomas car park after a fashion show. Her face was smothered with heavy make-up and she had so much hairspray in her hair that it resembled a bird's nest. Still, that didn't stop the tall, handsome, deeply tanned guy in the sharp suit doing a double take as she swanned past.

'Excuse me,' he called out to her.

She swung around and came face to face with him. He

had a strong, masculine jaw and the bluest eyes she had ever seen. What a fabulous-looking guy, she thought. And he had a slight American accent so he wasn't from around here.

'Yes?' She arched an eyebrow.

'I don't suppose you could give me directions to the Shelbourne Hotel, could you?'

'Sure I could.' She gave him a winning smile, worrying that with all the heavy make-up, she now looked more like a transvestite than Ireland's top supermodel. 'You continue on up the street, turn left, pass one set of traffic lights, and you'll come across it. You can't miss it.'

'Thank you so much.' He grinned. God, with a smile like that he could have given Brad Pitt himself a run for his money. Then again he probably had an Angelina Jolie-type girlfriend back wherever he came from.

She was about to walk on ahead, albeit reluctantly, when she heard him speak again. 'I don't suppose you'd like to come with me and join me for a coffee or some-thing?'

Alice stared at him. 'I can't,' she answered abruptly. 'I'm really sorry.'

'Could I tempt you to go out for dinner instead?'

Alice bit her lip. She wasn't used to being put on the spot like this. 'I'm sorry, but I'm busy.'

'Well, that's a shame, but if you change your mind, you could give me a call later.'

The guy whipped out his wallet and, much to Alice's surprise, he handed her his business card. She stuck it into the back pocket of her jeans without even looking at it. 'Well, goodbye,' she said curtly.

'Goodbye, and hopefully we'll hook up later. I'm Bill, by the way,' he said, holding out a big tanned hand. She shook it firmly.

'Alice,' she said.

As soon as she got home Alice Googled Bill's name. It said on his card that he was an entertainment lawyer, whatever that meant. And that he lived in a nice upmarket part of Los Angeles. Santa Monica, to be precise. When she Googled his name to see if he was authentic she was deeply impressed by all the information that came up. Bill was indeed a hot-shot lawyer with many celebrities as clients. Suddenly Alice felt honoured at having been asked out by such a good catch. She decided to take a shower and try and rinse out all the gunk that had been put in her hair for the fashion show. Once that was done she decided she would text him. Why wouldn't she? His offer was the best she'd had from anybody in a long time. And anyway, he was American, so nobody would know him here. That meant that if anybody spotted her out with him, it wouldn't get into the gossip sections of the papers. Or if it did, they'd have to describe him as Alice's mystery man. That had actually happened once after she'd brought her dad along to a film premiere. They'd described her poor old man as 'a distinguished-looking admirer'. As if! Well, at least herself and her bemused father had both had a good laugh about it over breakfast that Sunday morning.

Alice stepped into a hot shower and scrubbed her hair till it felt clean again. It was a great feeling. After wrapping a fluffy towel robe around herself, she sat down on her large double bed and sent a text to Bill. His reply came back immediately. He wanted her address to send a car to pick her up. Alice smiled as she read his text. Now *that* was a first. So many men these days didn't even bother collecting you, preferring to meet you in the pub or whatever, the lazy sods. Alice blamed the Irish Mammies for their behaviour. Those fusspots had Ireland's male population spoilt rotten.

At 7.45 p.m. Alice stepped into the waiting limousine feeling like royalty. This guy must have serious dosh if he'd organised this. To her delight the uniformed chauffeur pointed out the minibar and told her to help herself to a glass of chilled champagne.

'Well, if you insist,' she giggled and poured herself a glass. This was the life indeed. If my friends could see me now, she thought. Not, of course, that Alice had many friends. She sure as hell hadn't kept up with anyone from her schooldays and although she was friendly enough with a couple of the models, she wouldn't go so far as to call them true friends. The modelling scene in Ireland was very small, insular and competitive. It was dog eat dog as far as she was concerned and all the girls were after the same few castings.

She knew she wasn't the most popular model around but who wanted popularity? As long as the clients liked her and kept hiring her that was the main thing. And she always made a point of keeping the paparazzi sweet too. She knew them all by name and, what was more, she made a point of knowing their wives' and girlfriends' names too. It made them feel very important. Oh yes, Alice had learned early how to play the pap game well. It was very much in her interest to do so. After all, they of the long lenses could make or break a girl's career. When the limousine pulled to a halt outside the plush city-centre hotel the doorman stepped forward to open the car door. Alice noticed a couple of passers-by crane their necks to see who was getting out of the door and she smirked to herself. Maybe she should have gone the whole hog and worn dark sunglasses! She sauntered into the foyer and spotted Bill immediately. He'd changed out of his suit into blue jeans and a simple white shirt with the top buttons opened to show off his deep tan. She reckoned he must be in his late thirties due to the faint creases around his eyes. His hair was lightly streaked blond and she wondered if it was naturally that colour. It was very LA, anyway. Wearing a short, fitted black lace Dolce & Gabbana dress and six-inch Manolo heels she felt, and hopefully looked, a million dollars. Bill gave her an appreciative peck on the cheek. 'You look different to earlier on.'

'In a good way, I hope,' she answered flirtatiously.

'You look better than earlier and I didn't think that would be possible.' Bill offered her his arm as they made their way into the restaurant.

Once inside, he pulled out a seat for her and she thanked him graciously. God, he would certainly be able to teach Irish men a thing or two. And to think she'd thought the age of chivalry was dead and gone!

The waitress offered them both a menu and asked if they'd like to see the wine menu.

'Yes, please.' Bill's smile seemed to have put some sort of magical spell on her. He turned to Alice. 'Would you prefer red or white?'

'I'll have whatever you're having.'

He chose an Australian red – the second most

expensive on the list, Alice noted approvingly. She really did like generous men. She was so sick of tight bastards who invited you out and then expected you to go Dutch. Or else grudgingly paid for dinner but expected you to fork out for the drinks for the rest of the night and pay for the taxi home. Alice had a good feeling about Bill's generosity. She'd even decided to leave her purse at home for the night. After all, if things didn't go well, and she had no way to get home, her dad could always collect her. He was always so protective of his only child and she thought nothing of regularly phoning him from Lillies or Krystle at 3 a.m. He never ever complained. He'd read too many stories of young women like Alice being attacked over the years. And besides, there were so many foreigners in the country now that even the police didn't know who anybody was any more.

Alice scrutinised the menu. Hmm. She didn't want to put on too much weight so she had to be careful while ordering. Tomorrow Bill might be on the plane home for LA never to be seen again, yet those dreaded extra calories would remain on her hips for ages. There had been a time, of course, where she could have eaten what she liked and got away with it. But the years had caught up with her and gravity with it. Now, unfortunately, every morsel had to be considered.

'I think I'll skip the starter,' she announced. 'I had a big lunch,' she added. A lie, of course, but Bill didn't seem to mind.

'I won't bother with a starter either then,' he said. 'Have you decided on a main course?'

'Mmm, not yet.'

She wondered if Bill was watching his weight too. He probably was, given that he lived in LA. They were all obsessed with their looks over there, weren't they? Mind you, he did look fit. She wondered whether he was a gym freak, in bed every night at ten and up at six every morning to work on his abs.

Eventually she decided on the salmon. Bill went for the wild mushroom risotto. Alice sipped her wine thoughtfully. It was going down a treat. She hoped Bill was enjoying himself. 'So, are you in Dublin on business?' she asked casually. She was sure he must be in town on business. Bill didn't look like the type of guy who would be walking around Trinity College with a map of Dublin in his hand and a camera around his neck.

'Yes, business,' he said, choosing not to elaborate. 'And thankfully now that you're here, a little bit of pleasure.'

Alice sat up straight in her chair. She wasn't sure how to take that last comment at all. If he thought there would be any hanky-panky up in his hotel room after dinner he was very much mistaken. Alice wasn't that type of girl. Well, not any more. She was done with shagging rich men. You never got any thanks for it anyway.

'Is this your first time in Dublin?' she asked him, swiftly deciding that this was not the time to be thinking about unsavoury men from her past.

'It is. I'm only here for two nights, unfortunately. It's a pity, because I'd like to travel a bit outside Dublin. I hear the Irish countryside is quite spectacular. Do you know Galway?'

Alice gulped. She did. Oh God, why did he have to go and mention Galway now? Even the thought of her childhood summers there still filled her with dread. She'd spent most of her teenage summers cooped up in a small caravan just outside Salthill. As far as she could remember, it had rained nearly every day and her parents hadn't let her make friends with any of the other kids staying in the campsite because they considered the other kids too rough. Both teachers, Alice's parents had encouraged her to read books instead of watching TV. Some people thought she was lucky that her parents were teachers because they got to go on long holidays together as a family, but Alice found it hard to see what the advantages were. Her summers were boring beyond belief and no fun at all. She'd envied the lucky kids who were sent to summer camps and Irish college instead of being stuck in a claustrophobic caravan with two old stick-in-the-muds for company.

Her mother had made her read all the classics and she remembered one year ploughing through the depressing Dickens novel that was *Bleak House*. How she'd ever finished all nine-hundred-odd pages of it was a miracle. But it was either that or look out the window watching other kids enjoying barbecues and having careless fights with water pistols instead.

Once, when her parents had gone to the shops to get some groceries for the week, she'd taken a tenner from under her mother's bed where she knew she kept all her dosh and sneaked out. She'd run straight for Salthill which was full of amusement arcades and people having fun. Alice had gone into one of the arcades and changed the ten-pound note into coins and had spent a glorious two hours of freedom putting coin after coin after coin into the slot machines. She had felt so grown-up. It was only when a squad car had pulled up outside the arcade just when she was down to her last pound that she sensed the game was up. The uniformed officer had asked her for her name before himself and the female garda had escorted her out to the squad car and made her sit in the back seat. Everybody on the street had stared and Alice had felt herself going a deep shade of red as though she was a common criminal. This was by far the most embarrassing thing that had ever happened to her before in her life. What was the big deal anyway? She'd only taken a tenner. She knew girls in school who stole a lot more than that. She knew girls who regularly went into town at the weekend and nicked all kinds of stuff from the shops. They'd even once tried to get Alice to nick a choc-ice from the corner shop but she had refused. The thought of getting caught and getting expelled from school was enough to put the fear of God into her. So she'd always been a good girl. And had played by all the rules. Only once had she ever done anything bad and that was taking that miserable tenner. And she'd gone and managed to get herself arrested. Well, not arrested exactly, because of course no charges were brought. Her father had looked immensely relieved when the squad car had pulled into the campsite, much to the interest of all the other holidaymakers staying there. Her mother had burst into tears and had sworn aloud to St Anthony that she'd be putting fifty pounds in his poor box next Sunday at Mass. Alice had been quite bemused with all the fuss made about her disappearance. But then once the family were behind closed doors, her mother had suddenly stopped the crocodile tears, had drawn back her hand, and slapped her only daughter hard across the face. Alice had been stunned to say the least. What about St Anthony and Mass and thanks be to the Lord now? She had put her hand to her cheek where it stung. Ouch.

'Don't you ever do that to your father and me again,' her mother had shrieked like a fishwife. 'We have been out of our minds with worry. We thought you had been abducted, you ungrateful little thief. How dare you steal from me? You have never wanted for anything in your life. I can't believe how little thanks you've shown us. We are now the laughing stock of this place.'

Alice glanced at her dad desperately for support but instead of sticking up for her, he'd simply put on his coat and wordlessly left the caravan.

Alice had finally found her voice although it shook a lot. 'The laughing stock of this place, Mum? Do you think we aren't the laughing stock already? Everyone here thinks we're weirdos. The kids point at us any time we leave the site which is almost never. Nobody invites us to their barbecues and they never invite you and Dad for drinks because you're both pioneers. You think we're all superior to everyone else here but we're not. We're pathetic and miserable and just once when I try to have a bit of fun you punish me. I should call the guards back and tell them about this abuse. I'm having a shit summer and everything about this holiday is shit. I would rather be holed up in a bloody prison cell than be stuck here.'

Alice had burst into tears at finally being able to stand up to her controlling mother. Mrs Adams had simply stared at her teenage daughter through cold grey eyes.

'Go to your bunk,' she said icily, 'and don't come back here till you've apologised.'

'I won't apologise,' Alice said defiantly.

'Right, well, don't come out then.'

She'd sat on her bed for God knows how long before the hunger pangs finally became too much. Then she'd thought she might as well say sorry, even though her mother should have been the one apologising. Still, it was just a word and it needed to be said. Alice didn't mean it, of course. She was only sorry that the police had arrived as early as they had and that she hadn't got to put that last pound in the slot machine.

Apology over and still refusing to look her mother in the eye, she'd asked if she could go over to the communal TV room beside the laundrette on the other side of the caravan site. Her mother glanced at her father. 'Could you go over with her, Frank?'

Frank was about to stand up and do the honours when Alice spoke again. 'No, it's fine, Dad. Don't come with me. I'm thirteen. I don't need to be escorted over to the TV room. None of the other parents carry on like that. It's embarrassing. I'd rather stay here, thank you very much.'

Her father had looked so hurt that Alice immediately felt guilty. It wasn't her dad's fault that he'd married somebody who'd turned into the battleaxe from hell. 'It's nothing personal, Dad,' she said, blatantly ignoring her mother. 'It's just that I'd rather not have everyone here laughing at me again.'

Mr Adams looked helpless. He turned to his wife. 'I don't suppose it would be too terrible if we let her go over for half an hour and make some friends.'

Alice looked at her mother, not expecting her to budge, but to her absolute amazement her mother had nodded curtly. 'Right. Half an hour. And if you're not back in that space of time you won't be let out again for the duration of the holiday.'

Alice could hardly believe her luck. She looked at her watch to make sure she got the timing perfectly right. She was determined to come back early just to prove to her parents that she could indeed be trusted. She was so excited about this new-found freedom that she bounded across the caravan park towards the communal area where the television was. Of course she had absolutely no intention of sitting down with those grubby children trying to make friends. God, no. You see, Alice had spotted a shelf earlier on in the corner of the room laden with books. Not the awfully boring classics that her mother forced her to read in her room, but exciting-looking books with pictures of stunning-looking models pictured on them wearing bright red lipstick and dripping in diamonds. Alice couldn't wait to get her hands on one of the books. She walked into the TV room and ignored the other kids who turned around and stared at her. She walked straight over to the shelf and picked out a thick Jackie Collins novel. It had obviously been read a few times and was pretty dog-eared but that didn't matter. Alice sat in the corner with her back to the TV and the other kids, opened the book at page one, and then immersed herself in a world she knew nothing about but was fascinated by. She read about rich, randy men who owned lavish yachts and the beautiful women who seduced them. She devoured the chapters describing powerful, well-connected people who threw amazing parties and wore designer clothes. Her favourite character was a model who was able to reduce men to their knees with a single look. Alice thought she sounded fabulous. Imagine being able to use your looks to make money and get power, she thought wistfully. And just before the half-hour was up, she hid the book backwards under a heap of other books so that nobody else would borrow it. By that stage she had made up her mind that she, Alice, was one day going to be a model.

'Hey, Alice, I seem to have lost you to another world there,' said Bill with a charismatic smile.

'Sorry, you must forgive me. Sometimes I zone in and out. I've had a long day. What were you saying again?'

'I mentioned that I'd like to visit Galway some day. I've heard a lot about it.'

'Oh.' Alice's smile remained frozen on her face as she turned her attentions to her plate. Her granny who had been as thin as a whippet had always told her that a good rule of thumb was to only ever eat half your plate, so Alice had always taken heed. After much tossing of her food and listening to Bill chatter on about life in LA, she put down her knife and fork and dabbed her mouth with her serviette. 'That was absolutely delicious, Bill. How was yours?'

'Delicious too,' he agreed, setting down his own cutlery. Alice noticed he hadn't exactly licked his plate clean either. Yes, the more she thought about it, the more she was sure that he watched his figure. And she bet it was a nice figure too. He looked toned underneath his light cotton shirt and he had nice broad shoulders. Suddenly she began to imagine him without his shirt, and then without everything else.

'What are you thinking?' he asked suddenly.

'Oh nothing,' she lied, feeling herself blush slightly. She wondered if he'd guessed her thoughts.

'Do you fancy a coffee?'

'An Irish coffee would be great,' she said boldly. 'But let's have it in the main bar where we can people watch,' she suggested. The restaurant had fairly cleared by this stage and Alice, knowing she was looking her best and with such fine arm candy for company, wanted to be seen.

'Good thinking,' Bill said, and then, having paid the bill, he offered Alice his arm and led her into the main bar which was heaving with middle-aged, well-dressed men and women. Alice quickly scanned the room. She didn't recognise anybody which was unusual, although she was sure people recognised her as they always did. But at least when you hung out in five-star hotels people didn't come up to you annoying you for autographs or asking you if you were really you. Mind you, Alice wouldn't have minded a bit of attention tonight just to let Bill know how important she was in town. He might not believe her otherwise.

'Do you come here a lot?' Bill asked after he'd returned from the bar with two Irish coffees.

'Not all the time, no,' she said, shaking her head. 'I alternate between here and the Dylan, Doheny and Nesbitts, the Bailey and Cocoon at the weekends. I just tend to stick to the same old places.'

'Do you ever fancy a change of scenery?' He looked her straight in the eye. 'Do you ever feel like just leaving it all behind and starting off somewhere new?'

Alice threw her eyes towards the ceiling. 'Are you kidding me? I've been thinking about it a lot recently. This is a small place and I've reached the top of my career here.'

'You'd do very well in LA, I reckon,' Bill said quietly.

'Would I really?' Alice's eyes widened. She'd never really thought of hot-footing it over to LA to pursue her career. It just seemed like such a faraway place to be when you didn't know anybody. Of course life over there seemed so fabulous with the nice weather and celebrities hanging out at every street corner but in some of the trashy books she'd read about Hollywood, it seemed that there was also a much seedier side to the place. She didn't want to go over there and end up working in a bar or a shop like so many hopeful young 'models' and 'actors'. She wondered whether Bill was just trying to flatter her or if he was being serious. 'But aren't the girls out there all-American-looking with blond hair, blue eyes and fake tits? Where would I fit in with my dark hair, brown eyes and non-existent chest?'

'You're different and because of that difference I reckon you'd get loads of work. Think about it.'

'I will,' Alice mused. And she would too. Maybe this was fate? Winter was settling in now and the thought of spending the next few months in this cold godforsaken town was enough to sink her into a deep depression. Alice was convinced that she suffered from SAD, seasonal affective disorder. She'd read up about it on the Internet and she seemed to have all the symptoms. She couldn't bear the cold and felt it more than most, especially since she had no puppy fat to shield her from the biting Atlantic winds. Also, Alice was a Cancerian star sign. She'd been born in July and she'd read somewhere that summer babies felt the cold more than most people. No wonder she was always freezing then!

The Irish coffee was going down a treat. Alice felt relaxed and Bill looked like he was thoroughly enjoying her company. She wondered how the evening would end. The night was still young, of course. They could head to a club later and go dancing maybe. As Alice drained the last of her drink, she noticed that Bill's glass was already empty. He stood up and she expected him to go to the bar to order another two. But to her absolute astonishment, he came over to her side of the table, bent down and kissed her lips. The sensation of his lips on hers just blew her away. She wanted to melt in the moment. But then he just looked at his watch and announced that he'd better get an early night so that he'd feel refreshed for his long flight the following day. Alice stared at him unblinkingly. What? Was he serious? Didn't he want to kiss her again? For a bit longer? Did he not want to go dancing? Did he find her boring? Not attractive enough? She suddenly felt herself riddled with insecurities, something which hadn't happened to her for quite a while. Did he not realise who she was? Did he not know that half the male population of Dublin would give anything to trade places with him right now? Did he think he was too good for her or something?

'I'll call the limo now and the driver should be here in five minutes or so,' Bill said, whipping out his mobile phone. Five minutes, huh? He obviously couldn't see the back of her fast enough, Alice thought crossly. She barely uttered a word as they stood outside the front of the

Shelbourne waiting for the car. When it finally pulled up, Bill took her hand and kissed the back of it. Alice was stupefied. He must be gay. He *must* be. Of course that was it. She should have guessed sooner. He was far too good-looking to be straight. And far too well-dressed. So that was it. All he'd wanted was a bit of company. She could have been just anyone.

'Thank you for a lovely evening.' He smiled at her.

'You're welcome,' she said, just about managing to smile back gracefully. She wasn't about to let him know how disappointed she was. If he'd been a gentleman at all he would have at least given her the opportunity to turn him down.

Just as she was about to slide into the back of the limo, a very tall, dark, attractive man in a suit walked quickly past. Forgetting her feeling of rejection momentarily, Alice swung around and so did the guy. They clocked each other's eyes and the guy halted in his tracks.

'Hi,' said Alice in amazement.

'Hi there,' he replied, looking equally as stunned.

God, there was a blast from the past if ever there was one. So Eddie Toner was back in town. She gave him a delicate little wave and then slid into the limo as Bill held the door open for her.

'Who was that?' he asked, not seeming quite as cocky now.

'Oh, him? Eh, nobody,' she lied with a grin spreading over her face. 'That was nobody at all.'

W hen Tanya woke up she could have sworn that somebody was standing in the bed above her repeatedly hitting her skull with a hammer. She opened her eyes to make sure that there wasn't. Then she closed them again. Why oh why did she have the mother of all hangovers? And then suddenly she remembered. Eddie was going to ask her to marry him tonight. Oh God! She sat up straight in the bed and pressed the back of her hand against her forehead. She was going to look awful. Dammit! She should have gone to bed early last night so that she'd be looking well for the proposal instead of agreeing to meet that little rascal, Dianne.

Reluctantly she dragged herself from the comfort of her warm duvet, put on her slippers and dressing gown, and tiptoed across the hall to the spare bedroom. She'd better wake poor Dianne or else her car would surely get clamped outside the Dylan.

To her surprise the bed in the spare room was empty and had been left neatly made-up. Tanya shook her head in wonder. Dianne never failed to surprise her. How on earth had she managed to rise so early? She wandered downstairs to find her father and mother hunched together in front of the computer in the corner of the kitchen.

'How's the bride-to-be?' Her mother beamed from ear to ear.

Tanya groaned inwardly. Oh, please don't let them start all over again.

'I'm going to learn how to surf,' Mrs Thomson continued, ignoring the fact that her daughter hadn't answered her question.

Tanya felt her heart sink. Her mother was way too old to be taking up water sports. She had taken up rock climbing last year with disastrous results, ending up with a sprained ankle. Why hadn't she learned her lesson at this stage?

'Oh Mum, do you think that's such a good idea? Surfing is a dangerous sport. And besides, we don't exactly have a suitable climate for surfing in this country.'

Her mother threw back her head and laughed raucously. 'Oh Tanya, dearest, I'm not going to be anywhere near the sea. Your father is going to teach me how to surf the Net. It's about time I learned how to do it. I'm going to start emailing people and everything so that I won't get left behind in this age of modern technology. You and I can email each other all our news from now on.'

Tanya shook her head in exasperation. She still lived at home, for goodness' sake, and spoke to her mother at least a couple of times a day. Why on earth would they need to email each other?

'I'm going to look up all the wedding sites so we can get as much information as possible. The first thing we need to do is to start looking at hotels, and Dad says he knows somebody in the tennis club who can get us a good deal on a Rolls-Royce. His own daughter got married last year so he's been through it all before. He rang the man earlier and he was out but he left a message with his wife to call us back as soon as he can.'

'Oh God, you didn't go and do that, Dad, did you? Now everyone in the tennis club will know before I've even had the chance to tell my friends.' Tanya looked anxiously from her mother to her father. 'Will you please, please keep this to yourselves at least till tomorrow?'

Her parents reluctantly agreed and Tanya breathed a sigh of relief. She wandered over to the kitchen presses and retrieved a box of All-Bran, took some skimmed milk out of the fridge, and then sat down at the table to enjoy her breakfast. Thank goodness she had the day off. God only knew how Dianne always managed to drink as much as she did and still get up for work every day. Tanya took her hat off to the girl, she really did.

'So what are you wearing tonight?' her mother wanted to know. 'You can borrow anything of mine if you like.'

'Thanks, Mum, but I already have something in mind.' Tanya didn't, in fact, but she doubted she'd be taking her mum up on her generous offer since they had completely different tastes in clothes and were different dress sizes anyway. Her mother was a size fourteen and for as long as Tanya could remember she'd been trying to slim down to a size twelve – Tanya's own size. Every now and then she'd go on these crazy diets such as the grapefruit and coffee diet, or the cabbage soup diet, or the South Beach diet, but she always seemed to succumb to chocolate on day three. Besides, her mother enjoyed her wine too much and there wasn't a diet around that allowed for copious glasses of vino in the evening.

'I think I'll go and get my hair done,' Tanya announced. 'At least that might make me look alive again.'

'Good idea,' her mum agreed. 'There's nothing like a blow-dry for a good pick-me-up. Speaking of hairdos, do you think you'll wear yours up for the wedding? I suppose it all depends on whether you'll be wearing a veil, doesn't it? Will you be wearing a veil, do you think, Tanya?'

Her daughter shot her a significant look and Mrs Thomson immediately backed down. 'Okay, okay, I promise not to interfere. I'm just so excited, that's all. My own baby is getting married,' she added emotionally, tears welling in her eyes.

Tanya quickly got some All-Bran and a cup of coffee into her and then made her way into town. She couldn't put up with any more home drama. As she sat on the bus she stared out the window at the passers-by all lost in their own little worlds, listening to their iPods. Life would never be the same again once she got married. Still, she was ready for a change. She knew Eddie was the one and couldn't even imagine spending her life with anybody else. Although she'd instantly fancied him from the start, she clearly remembered the exact moment she'd actually fallen in love with him. They had been walking along by Stephen's Green when she'd spotted an injured pigeon in the middle of the road. It had obviously been hit by a truck and one of its wings was flapping. Tanya had shrieked and pointed out the pigeon to Eddie. Instinctively, he had walked out on to the busy street and held up his hand to stop the traffic. Then he'd taken off his jacket to wrap it around the pigeon. Both of them had brought it to a vet in a taxi where Eddie had paid for the frightened bird to be attended to till it was fit to be released into the open again. That day Tanya realised that Eddie was so kind and special, one in a million, and she knew that she would never find anyone like him ever again. She couldn't wait to be married. With marriage would come the security that she so badly craved. Mrs Toner. Mrs E Toner. It was like music to her ears. Lots of women didn't change their name when they got married these days but Tanya would be more than happy to change hers. Tanya Toner. She liked that. It had a nice sound to it. Eddie and Tanya Toner. Perfect. God, she couldn't wait for their first Christmas together so that she could start writing their joint names on the cards.

She hadn't made an appointment at the hairdresser's but being a weekday they weren't all that busy and gave her an immediate appointment. Karen was assigned to her. Tanya didn't like the look of Karen much. She had very short pink hair and a ring in her left eyebrow.

'Nice and straight?' Karen barked without smiling.

'Yes, please.'

'It's not in very good condition, is it?'

'What?'

'Your hair. It's in a terrible condition.'

'I know,' Tanya said, feeling about two feet tall. 'But I've been dyeing for as long as I can remember, so—'

'Do you blow-dry your hair a lot?'

'No.'

'Do you use straighteners?'

'No.'

'Do you use treatments?'

'No, not really.'

'We've a really good treatment for sale here at the salon,' suggested Karen. 'Would you like to buy some?'

'No. Honestly, no thanks, I'm broke at the moment.'

Karen wasn't giving up. 'Your hair will fall out if you're not careful,' she said.

'Well, if it falls out it falls out, and so be it.'

God, there was a time when going to the hairdresser was a relaxing experience. You got your coffee and your magazine and the hairdresser kindly asked you if you were going out that night or off on holidays soon. Now it was about as pleasant as a Ryanair flight the way they were always trying to sell you something you didn't want.

Tanya sat for the next forty-five minutes in relative silence reading the last chapters of her book as the hairdresser got to work on her barnet. She then left the salon looking reasonably normal, even if she wasn't quite feeling it yet. After that she wandered around town in something of a daze finding herself at one stage standing outside a bridal shop and gazing wistfully through the window. One day very soon she'd be putting on one of those fairy-tale white dresses herself and saying her vows. It was so exciting it hadn't even really sunk in yet. She wasn't sure which style of dress she wanted for her big day. Definitely not a meringue-type dress for sure. No, she'd prefer something simpler. And something that wouldn't cost the earth either. It was scandalous the amount of money that brides paid these days for some-thing that would only be worn for a few hours. It would be better to spend that type of money on something more useful, like a kitchen, say. Tanya wondered where she and Eddie would end up living. His one-bedroom apartment in Sandyford was definitely too small and the walls were so paper-thin that you could hear the neighbours flushing the loo. Besides, she needed something with two bedrooms at least, in case somebody came to stay. And she also needed a spare bedroom where she could take refuge when Eddie started snoring. Not that he snored all the time, of course, but after a few pints he had the horrible habit of sounding like Connolly train station at peak period. Tanya, being the practical and realistic girl that she was, needed a peaceful place to sleep in when the noise levels reached unbearable levels.

She popped into Clery's department store and had a leisurely browse around as she let her mind wander. She hoped Eddie would get that promotion he was after before the wedding. He'd been working as a junior solicitor in a big firm for a few years now so it was time he got some sort of recognition. Dublin was a ridiculously expensive place to be trying to buy property in these days, and her wages as a beautician wouldn't go very far towards a mortgage. Perhaps her parents and Eddie's parents would help them with a deposit but she didn't want to be putting anybody under pressure. After all, none of them were minted. She presumed herself and Eddie would spend the next few months seriously looking for a suitable home and discussing their finances. It would all seem terribly grown-up. Some of Tanya's friends had mortgages so she already knew the sacrifices that came with owning your own home. There would be fewer meals out in fancy restaurants, no more last-minute city breaks or going crazy with the credit card at Brown Thomas. Still, she wouldn't mind not being too extravagant, however, as long as she was married and had Eddie. They'd be in this together and to be honest, cosy nights in with her gorgeous husband sounded a lot more appealing than frittering away her hard-earned cash on cosmos with the girls in the bars and clubs around town. And at least working in the beauty industry had its advantages and she could still treat herself to massages, manicures, leg waxes and sunbed sessions all for free. Now if there was only a way she could manage to blow-dry her own hair without looking like Worzel Gummidge's sister!

By the time she got home, she was famished but settled for a small bowl of soup just to keep the hunger at bay. After all, the last thing she wanted to do was stuff her face now and have no appetite for later. She was definitely looking forward to her meal in Town and Grill. One of the trendiest eateries in the city, it always had a buzzing atmosphere and the food was simply to die for.

Just as she was about to pour the soup into the saucepan, her mother startled her.

'Darling, I've learned how to surf!'

Tanya swung around almost expecting to see her mother wearing a wetsuit. She couldn't help but laugh at Mrs Thomson's pleased-as-Punch facial expression.

'Well done.' She smiled.

'I've also been thinking . . . you know my cousin Father Tim who's a missionary in the Philippines? Well, I think it would be a very nice gesture to invite him to say your wedding Mass. What do you think?'

'I, well . . .'

'I could send him an email,' she continued excitedly. 'I know he sent us a Christmas card last year with his email address on it but of course I wasn't able to use the computer back then. Will I send an email off this afternoon to see if he's free?'

Tanya looked at her incredulously. She was like a woman possessed. God, if she was like this now, what would she be like on the run-up to the actual day? Tanya was now deeply sorry she'd gone and opened her big mouth. If her mother continued acting in this demented way, she'd just have to persuade Eddie to go to Las Vegas with her and elope with Elvis as a witness.

'Mum,' she said irritably, pouring her soup into the pan, 'can we please just slow down and not lose the run of ourselves? Sure, I think it's a lovely idea to invite Father Tim home to Ireland to do the honours, but we can't ask him when we haven't even set a date yet. Everything all in its own good time.'

'I just feel we should be doing *something*,' Mrs Thomson sighed, wringing her hands. 'We don't want to be leaving everything up to the last minute and then panicking. I really want to be a hands-on mother of the bride. I was just in Fennella's Flowers there on the corner and Fennella herself was in the shop. She said she'd be delighted to do the flowers on the day and she even showed me samples of what's popular these days. White lilies, for example, are extremely—'

'Mum! I told you not to be telling everyone. Can't you just be quiet?' Tanya could feel her blood pressure begin to boil. Honestly, this had gone beyond a joke now.

Her mother looked wounded. 'But Fennella won't be telling anybody. Customer confidentiality and all that.'

'Don't give me that. Dublin's way too small. Her snooty daughter Ingrid lives on the Northside and is a regular in the salon. She's the biggest gossip around. I certainly don't want that cow quizzing me on my wedding the next time she comes in for a pedicure.'

'Okay, well, I suppose we can always tackle the flowers issue later. So what are you wearing tonight? Have you decided? Your hair is very nice by the way.'

'Thanks,' Tanya muttered, stirring her soup.

'Is Eddie calling for you?'

'Yes, I presume he is.'

'Well, why don't the two of you come in for a little aperitif before your dinner?'

Tanya could think of nothing worse. 'Ah no, Mum. Eddie won't want to drink and drive. He'll have a glass of wine at the restaurant but that's it. The laws are so strict these days. Anyway, I wouldn't trust yourself or Dad not to say something inappropriate.'

Oh no, that wounded animal look again. Tanya poured her soup into a bowl and sat down at the kitchen table. She sipped thoughtfully as her mother busied herself watering the kitchen plants, humming to herself. She still had a few hours to kill before meeting Eddie but she couldn't decide what to do. Tomorrow, lots would have to be done. For a start she would have to go on to her Facebook site and change her relationship status to 'engaged'. Then herself and her mother would carefully choose the wording for their engagement announcement in the *Irish Times*. She would have to phone all her friends personally, of course, because they would just kill her if they read about the engagement in the paper along with everybody else. She really would have to set a date soon though. If her mother was right about one thing, it was that the waiting lists for weddings at the best hotels were endless. You had to book almost a year in advance at the top establishments and put down a crazy deposit of a few thousand euros. Then the guest list would have to be decided on. Would she go for a big swanky bash or just have an intimate wedding with close friends and relatives? It would all depend on Eddie. After all, she didn't really know his thoughts on this. Somebody would also have to be commissioned to make the cake. Would she go for a traditional fruitcake or a sponge? Would it be a three-tier? Would they make a video of the wedding or just have a photographer? Did it really matter? Would she and Eddie like to record the whole thing so that one day they could sit down with their kids and show them the day when Mummy and Daddy got married?

Tanya sighed. She decided to go upstairs and have a hot bath and read in order to relax. She had finished her book earlier on her bus journey and was ready to start a new one. Once in the bath, with her hair firmly covered by a shower cap, she settled into a brand-new Patricia Scanlan novel, and finally began to relax.

'Say cheese.' Mr Thomson snapped the disposable camera as he still hadn't managed to figure how to use the digital camera he'd got for Christmas last year.

'Cheese.' Tanya and her mother grinned.

'Now I'll take you and your father, there beside the piano,' Mrs Thomson offered.

'Okay.'

She clicked away for what seemed like for ever. 'I'll just take a couple more to be sure,' she fussed. 'I think your father may have blinked in a couple of the pictures. Now, that's better. Chin up, Tanya, shoulders back.'

Just when Tanya thought she could bear it no longer, Mrs Thomson shouted for Elaine.

'Elaine! Get down here at once.'

Tanya's younger sister strolled into the sitting room in a tracksuit and bare feet looking completely disinterested. 'What is it now?' she yawned.

Mrs Thomson handed her the camera. 'Now, take a good few shots. Give us three before you click.'

'Did you really drag me away from my studies for this?' Elaine grumbled.

'Listen, if one day somebody proposes to you, Missy, you'll want to celebrate too. Now at least pretend to be happy for your sister.'

Elaine dutifully snapped and then without a word went back up to her room to bury herself in her books.

Mrs Thomson shook her head at Elaine's departing back. 'Knowing my luck I'll probably be stuck with that girl for ever. Sure, who'd have her? What man in his right mind would want to marry such a sourpuss?'

'I wouldn't worry about Elaine,' Tanya said immediately, jumping to her younger sister's defence. 'With her killer good looks she'll be fighting them all off in no time. She's just stressed about her exams, that's all.'

It was true though. At five-foot-ten, Elaine towered

over the rest of her family who all seemed to have drawn the short straw in the growth department. Tanya had always teased her little sister saying that there must have been a mix-up in the hospital when she was a baby and that their mother had brought home the wrong child. With a flawless milky complexion, high cheekbones, huge baby-blue eyes and long tumbling locks of dark, shiny hair, Elaine could have her pick of any man. She just wasn't all that bothered. Secretly Tanya envied her take 'em or leave 'em attitude. Elaine never seemed to wait by the phone anxiously for some fellow to call her or fret if she didn't meet somebody nice on her nights out. Men, she seemed to think, were just a complete waste of space.

Mrs Thomson finally put the camera down on top of the piano. 'Well, that should be enough for now,' she said, sounding satisfied with herself. 'Of course if you and Eddie pop back after the dinner, we can take a few more of the both of you.'

'We won't be coming back here, Mum. I'll be staying at Eddie's tonight. It's nearer town.'

Mrs Thomson grimaced and didn't respond. She didn't approve of Tanya staying over at Eddie's when they weren't married or engaged yet but she had learned to bite her tongue. The young people of today did things differently. It wasn't like when she was young and people got married because they wanted to sleep with each other. Now everyone seemed to have sex and then afterwards thought about getting married to the person they were already copulating with. Things had changed a lot all right since she'd been young and she wasn't entirely sure they'd changed for the better.

Tanya looked anxiously at herself in the full-length mirror in the hallway. She thought she looked a bit tired. She was wearing a black pencil skirt, a low-cut black Ralph Lauren top and her new Fendi high heels. Around her neck was a simple string of pearls that her granny had given her for her twenty-first birthday. She hoped they didn't make her look too 'mumsy'. She wanted to look glamorous and sophisticated, but not old-fashioned. Her mother told her she looked as pretty as a picture. This worried rather than pleased Tanya. Her mother didn't exactly have great taste in art. That was evident in the huge painting of the headless chicken hanging in the 'good' room. It was so hideous that Tanya, when dining with the family on special occasions, always made sure she sat with her back to the offending painting.

The doorbell rang, making Tanya's heart leap. Oh God, Eddie was early. Then again he was always punctual so why was she surprised? Mrs Thomson made a move towards the hallway.

'No, Mum!' Tanya screeched. 'Not on your life! You can congratulate him again when it's all official.' She kissed her mother on the cheek, grabbed her bag and fled.

'You look stunning,' Eddie said appreciatively as he placed a protective arm around her shoulder.

'Thanks.' Tanya smiled back at him. She felt ridiculously nervous, as though they were going on a first date.

'Will I not go in and say hello to your folks before we head off? They might think it's rude if I don't.'

'Oh, no,' said Tanya, hurriedly moving towards his car. 'They won't be offended. They're in the middle of their dinner. I'll tell them you said hi later.'

Eddie followed her to his navy Beamer. He was wearing a dark charcoal-grey expensive-looking suit and looked fantastic. Tanya was so proud to be going out with him. It still hadn't really hit her that they were soon to be engaged. Her head was swimming with excitement. She wondered if Eddie felt the same way.

They found a parking space on Stephen's Green and walked from there to Town and Grill. Unfortunately it had just started to rain lightly so Eddie opened his big brolly which easily sheltered them both. Tanya slipped her arm around his waist and snuggled into him as they walked. Good old Eddie, he always thought of everything.

At the restaurant, they handed in their coats and were escorted to a quiet, cosy table in the corner. Alice wondered if Eddie had deliberately requested such a private table in advance. Still, it was good to be away from prying eyes and cocked ears. This was going to be their night and nobody else mattered.

After they sat down and were handed their menus, Eddie took Tanya's hand and squeezed it tightly. She felt her heart do an impromptu double flip. He wasn't going to propose now, was he? Oh God, she definitely needed a generous glass of wine first. He opened his mouth as if to say something but was interrupted by the handsome waiter offering menus. When asked if he wanted a look at the wine menu, Eddie simply said it wasn't necessary and ordered champagne. Tanya gave him an appreciative smile. He really was going all out to impress her tonight. How sweet! She felt like leaning across the table and hugging him.

'Will you go for a starter?' Eddie asked.

'Sure. There are so many tempting things on the menu,

I don't know where to start. I have to say none of this is looking very good for my figure though.'

'Never mind the weight watching,' Eddie reassured her. 'Tonight is special.'

They ordered their starters and tucked in fifteen minutes later when they arrived at the table.

The chilled champagne was already going down a treat and last night's hangover was now well and truly forgotten.

Eddie seemed to be in a kind of dream tonight, she noticed. Not his usual talkative self. She hoped he wasn't having doubts about his proposal. Maybe he was feeling jittery. Certainly Tanya knew how he felt. Her nerves were getting to her so much she could barely chew her food. She secretly hoped he wouldn't get down on one knee and propose in front of strangers or anything like that. Tanya didn't want a scene to be made here in the restaurant where the other diners would probably break into polite applause. Then again, Eddie was far too conservative a person to want to put them under the spotlight like that. She wondered whether he had, in fact, already bought a ring and whether he'd hidden it in the breast pocket of his jacket. Hopefully not. Men weren't great about buying things like that on their own. In a way she just wished he'd propose and get it over and done with. That way they could both relax and enjoy the rest of their evening as future man and wife. The nervous tension that hung in the air between them was almost unbearable. Eddie seemed particularly fidgety this evening, toying with his serviette and glancing around the room, occasionally waving to people he vaguely knew. By the time their main courses were served up Tanya could feel a large knot beginning to form in her stomach. Her mind was racing. Should she act totally amazed when he eventually popped the question? Or should she simply say yes straight away and not leave him in suspense? Should she let on that she had known of his intentions all along? She tucked into her fish with relish and started to gobble up. She figured that the quicker she finished her meal, the quicker he would propose. Eddie also ate quickly so that ten minutes later they were both finished.

'Dessert?' he suggested.

Tanya was stuffed and didn't honestly know how she'd find the room for dessert. But if she refused to have any and suggested leaving, then Eddie might panic and not pop the question at all. She reckoned he was still biding his time. Their champagne now well and truly finished, Tanya said she wouldn't mind a coffee along with her cheesecake.

The coffees and cheesecake with two spoons (they'd decided to share) were duly served. Then came the bill and still there was no sign of a proposal. Tanya could hardly hide her disappointment.

'Eddie,' she said, looking him directly in the eye when she could no longer bear the suspense, 'you said there was something important you wanted to ask me this evening?'

She watched her boyfriend swallow uncomfortably, pull at his tie and then open the top button of his shirt. He averted his gaze away from her. Clearing his throat he began to speak.

'Yes, Tanya, there is something I want to ask you and I've been trying all evening to bring up the subject but, I dunno, I guess I'm nervous about asking you.'

He ran a hand through his black hair and bit his lower lip. He looked like a lost, vulnerable, but totally adorable schoolboy and she wanted to reach out and hug him and assure him that anything he asked her to do, she would. But instead she kept quiet. He had to do this on his own without her help. If she cajoled him along it might hurt his pride.

'I'm intrigued,' she said, dipping into the cheesecake with her spoon and noticing that he hadn't touched it yet.

'Well, the thing is . . . oh God, I think I need another drink before I ask you. I wish I hadn't brought the car into town now.'

'How about we finish up here and get back to your apartment? We can have a drink there if it helps you relax. Come on, Babes, the night is young.'

Eddie looked suitably relieved. 'Are you sure?'

'Of course I am. I fancy a nightcap anyway.'

Eddie couldn't pay the bill fast enough. He left a hefty tip and then they walked back to the car, arm in arm in silence. Thankfully it had stopped raining now but it was still cold. Noticing her shiver, Eddie wrapped his black cashmere coat around Tanya's shoulders. Soon they were in the car and Eddie put the boot down so fast Tanya was concerned for their safety. Who knew that getting engaged could be such a stressful, emotional experience? They drove in relative silence out to Eddie's place in Sandyford listening to Amy Winehouse. Amy's voice sounded particularly tortured tonight. Although there was no traffic on the roads at this time of the night, the journey seemed endless, with every minute feeling like an hour. Finally they were in the lift heading for Eddie's fifth-floor apartment. Once inside, Eddie turned the heating up high and the lighting down low.

'Put on some lively music,' Tanya insisted, slipping off her high heels and pottering around his small sitting room with its smooth wooden floors in her stockinged feet. She wanted to make herself as comfortable as possible given the situation.

While Eddie struggled to uncork a bottle of expensive red wine which he retrieved from a hamper that a satisfied client had recently given him, Tanya took it upon herself to light a few vanilla-scented candles around the room. They'd been a Valentine's present from her to him. If that didn't help the romantic atmosphere then nothing would. Then she settled into the comfy cream cushions on the black leather sofa, and waited for Eddie to join her.

'Tanya . . .' he began, looking cuter than she'd ever seen him look before. He took a deep breath. 'Okay, here goes . . .'

She waited in anticipation, reaching out to touch his hand in a gesture of affection. She saw that it was shaking.

'Ye . . . es?'

'I've been thinking a lot. You see, I've lived in this apartment for three years now but I'm kind of tired of living in a box.'

She nodded emphatically. It was true. Eddie's apartment was very cute and cosy and very modern but far too small.

He went on. 'I'd like to upgrade to something bigger, a house with a garden maybe. I was thinking along the lines of a three-bedroom house in a nice suburban area.'

Three bedrooms? Tanya took it all in quickly. Why

would he want so many bedrooms unless he was thinking of starting a family? That was rushing it a bit maybe. She wanted to enjoy a couple of years of married life with him at least before she got pregnant.

'I understand.' She nodded, although she didn't really.

'I've done my maths and I think I can just about afford it. I'd like to spend the next month or so looking at suitable, affordable properties and I'd like you to help me choose a dream home.'

Tanya remained silent as his hand escaped hers and he rose to his feet. She felt her heart lurch. Oh God, this was it, wasn't it? This was the moment.

'Eddie, would you ever sit down? You're making me feel nervous.'

'Not half as nervous as I feel.' He crouched down on the floor beside her. 'I've been thinking of asking you for ages but was just trying to find the right moment. Even tonight at dinner it was hard trying to find the right words . . .'

Oh Jesus, Eddie, would you ever just spit it out? she thought exasperatedly.

'Tanya, I want you to move into my new house with me.'

She stared at him, confused, and then waited for him to elaborate. There had to be more, hadn't there? What about the ring? The wedding? What about her parents and their illustrious plans for the big family day out?

'You don't have to answer straight away,' he gabbled.

Answer what? He hadn't even asked the damn question. Had she heard the words 'Will you marry me?' yet? Eh, no.

'I know it's a huge decision,' he added, 'and I know you like living at home, but it really would mean the world to me if you came and lived with me. I want to wake up in your arms every morning, and for me not to start missing you every time I drop you home. Will you give it some thought, Tanya, and not take for ever to make up your mind?'

She looked at him, stunned. So that was it, was it? No proposal? No commitment? No trip to the altar? Tanya had never felt more humiliated in her life. And the worst thing of all was that Eddie had no idea just how much he had insulted her. How in God's name was she going to go back to her parents and explain that the wedding that never was, was now all off? Tanya felt so upset it took her all the will in the world not to burst into tears.

6

It was another overcast, warm sticky morning in LA and the smog hung low in the air. Alice stared out the window and wondered how she could kill another day without going out of her mind with boredom. She had been living in the City of Angels for three months now and the novelty of it all was beginning to wear off.

At first it had all been a bit of a fairy tale. Herself and Bill had been emailing each other non-stop for a month after their initial encounter in Dublin and had managed to fall in love online. Then he had sent her a first-class one-way ticket to LA. She had jumped at the opportunity to escape Dublin. But now she was beginning to feel a little lonely. The first few weeks here Alice had been in awe of the place. She'd loved the weather, loved the laid-back pace of life and had even enjoyed spotting random celebrities. Herself and Bill had acted like love-struck teenagers and the sex had been out of this world. Now something was missing, though. The novelty of living near Hollywood was beginning to wear off. In fact, when Bill had actually taken her to see the town of Hollywood itself, she'd felt very let down. The place was tatty and about as unglamorous as you could get. The amount of homeless people on the streets was also disturbing. Surely this wasn't 'the dream', was it?

Alice missed not having any company during the day when Bill was working. Even a little dog to bring for a walk would have been nice, but the strict no-pets rule of the complex of Bill's luxury ground-floor condo prevented that. It was such a pity Bill worked the crazy hours that he did. When he'd invited her out to come and live with him she'd imagined that they'd spend lazy afternoons together strolling Venice Beach arm in arm, later watching the sun set, followed by glamorous evenings sipping cocktails in Château Montmartre trying to see if they could spot Lindsey Lohan or Britney Spears but it was nothing like that at all. Bill was always so busy in his LA downtown office and even when he wasn't there his mobile phone never seemed to stop hopping. Of course Bill thrived on hard work and loved to be busy. He'd rise at cockshout every morning to get an hour or two in the gym before work and skipped breakfast preferring to grab himself a wheatgrass shake around 11 a.m. in his office instead.

There were times when Alice wondered whether she was his girlfriend any more. She spent more time on Facebook and Bebo wondering what everyone was doing back home than she did living it up in the city of dreams. LA was so massive that you had to drive everywhere and since Alice didn't own a car, she was pretty much stuck at home with a laptop for company and crappy American soaps on the television. Of course to the people at home back in Ireland she kept up the façade that everything was just hunky dory and that she regularly rubbed shoulders with the likes of Leonardo DiCaprio and Penelope Cruz at

Hollywood's hotspots but these exciting wild nights out were mostly in her head. The reality could not be more different.

Although people in LA were always terribly friendly and always wished you a nice day, they weren't the easiest people to make genuine friends with. So many people here were obsessed with themselves and with getting ahead in the world of showbiz. Alice had been signed to a model agency as soon as she'd arrived thanks to a friend of Bill's, but at castings the girls would just talk about the gym, or vacations, or their boyfriends or themselves. They never wanted to know about Alice. The first thing Alice had noticed about the LA models was that they all looked exactly the same. Everyone had breast implants, platinum-blond hair, chocolate tans and straight white teeth. Alice with her dark hair and relatively pale skin stood out as being different. But there wasn't a huge amount of work for fashion models in LA, and the jobs she got booked for were usually some film producer's party at his home where she'd stand at the front door holding trays of champagne that nobody wanted to drink because everybody seemed to drink water here and leave parties before 10 p.m.

Alice was beginning to miss life back in Dublin. In Dublin she had been somebody. Her name had meant something. She'd been high up on every guest list in town. Out here she was a nobody. People weren't interested in talking to her. Models were ten a penny and they all wanted to be famous actors or to date them. And they weren't very bright either. Very few of them even knew where Ireland was and seemed to think it was some kind of extension of England. One model at a casting had even told her that her English was pretty good.

'Oh, thank you,' Alice had laughed, thinking it was some kind of a joke. But, no, the doe-eyed blonde with the Dolly Parton-sized breasts had simply stared blankly at her and said, 'But if you really want to perfect your English, you should stay in the States a bit longer.'

You couldn't make it up!

Alice decided to treat herself to a manicure at the mall. That would kill an hour or so and then she'd have to decide how to while away the rest of the day. She pulled on a pair of shorts, a bright pink T-shirt and her trainers, grabbed her keys and her iPod and set off for the salon. She didn't have an appointment and when she arrived at the salon the therapist asked her if she wouldn't mind coming back in half an hour. Alice wondered what she could do to amuse herself. As she didn't have much money these days, going shopping wasn't an option. Of course Bill was always very generous but she wouldn't degrade herself by asking him for money for clothes. She'd done a few small modelling jobs in the past few weeks but the agency was notoriously slow at paying. She decided to buy herself a fancy new shower cream at Bath and Bodyworks and then purchased a copy of American *Vogue* and brought it with her to a nearby café where she ordered a cappuccino.

She sat at the window so she could people watch once she'd stopped flicking through her glossy magazine. The mall was thronged with shoppers and she sipped her cappuccino and observed the passers-by with interest. Then suddenly she felt her stomach lurch. Her heart started racing and she felt herself break into a cold sweat. It couldn't be, could it? But it was! It was Bill. In front of her very eyes. Walking past. And he was not alone. No. He was strolling along with his arm around a very slight blonde with long tumbling locks of hair. She seemed to be laughing at something he had said and they looked like they were very much a couple. Panicking, she crouched slightly beneath her magazine, trying to hide her face. He hadn't seen her but she sure as hell had seen him. And now she was in shock. Alice could feel herself trembling. How could this be happening to her? What was going on? Should she run out after them and confront them? She took a deep breath. She knew she needed to calm down. When she looked up again seconds later, they were gone. It took Alice a while to regain her composure. She didn't want to make a public scene. But what the hell was that all about? Was Bill cheating on her? How long had this been going on? Did that explain why he'd seemed distant the last couple of weeks and claimed to be working all the time? Was there really another woman in his life? Distraught, she picked up her magazine, and paid the bill. She needed to get outside and get some fresh air. She left the coffee shop and looked around to see where Bill and his blonde companion had gone. But they were nowhere to be seen. It was as if they had simply vanished.

Alice could feel a headache coming on. In a daze, she walked off to her manicure appointment. The nail technician was very annoying and wanted to chat. She kept asking her questions about Ireland and Alice silently wished she'd shut up and leave her alone with her thoughts.

'Is it an island?'

'Yes.'

'Can you drive to Ireland from England?'

'No.'

'Have you met Colin Farrell?'

'Yes.'

'Is he a friend of yours?'

'No.'

'Have you got a boyfriend here?'

'I don't know.'

That was the truth. Had she a boyfriend or had it all just been one long lie?

'Did you come to LA to act?'

'No.'

'Why did you come?'

Alice just stared at her. Now, there was a question. Why had she come indeed? What was she doing here? She didn't know anybody here. Bill didn't talk to her any more. And he was probably cheating on her. What other explanation was there? She wasn't getting much work. She was bored of the sun. If she stayed here any longer, then everybody in Ireland would soon forget about her. In a couple of years she'd be too old to model and then what would she do for money? Alice hadn't put anything by for a rainy day and house prices in Dublin were ridiculously high. Suddenly she had a horrible vision of spending her thirties in a bedsit with just a cat for company. She had no qualifications and wouldn't be able to get a job. She was too old to go back to college but she was wasting her time here in LA. Sure, it had been fun at the start but now she felt like an outsider. It was so empty. She had no friends and she just didn't belong here.

'Are you okay?' the concerned nail technician asked as she added a final coat of polish to Alice's long talons.

'Yes, sorry, I was in a world of my own there.'

'You're very pretty, do you know that? Did anyone ever tell you that you should think about becoming a model?'

'Eh, yes; yes, they did.'

But here she was in LA not working and not really modelling. If she was still back in Ireland she'd be cleaning up. She had lost weight since coming to LA. Well, it was almost impossible not to. Even if you wanted to buy calorie-laden food here it was pretty difficult. Now that her face was thinner, her features were more defined and she had never looked better. Her skin was nicely tanned also, and her hair was in great condition. If she went home now, worked like hell and saved every cent, then she'd have a deposit for an apartment in a year's time. But before she made any decisions, she'd have to go home and confront Bill.

R ose was already in the salon putting on her make-up when Tanya let herself in. Upon seeing her work colleague she jumped up and enveloped Tanya in a bear hug squealing, 'Oh my God, Tanya, congratulations! I couldn't be more thrilled for you! You will be the most perfect bride ever.'

Tanya froze. 'Listen, Rose, I'm not getting married. Why would you think that?'

Rose prised herself away, a look of confusion masking her face. 'But your mother . . .' she trailed off.

Tanya almost exploded. 'What? My mother rang you? I'm going to kill her, I really am. There's no wedding, Rose. Eddie has asked me to move in with him, that's all.'

'Oh,' said Rose hesitantly. 'Well, that's a start anyway, isn't it? I mean it shows that he's willing to make a commitment. That's more than can be said for my Martin who loves nothing more than to tell everyone who'll listen that he's a confirmed bachelor. Even after we had Johnny, there was still no sign of him wanting to live with us.'

Tanya immediately felt contrite. She took off her coat, hung it up and offered to make Rose a cup of tea. She supposed that Eddie's offer to move in with her wasn't the worst thing that could have happened. Poor Rose would be jumping for joy if she was in her shoes. That Martin of hers was a complete waster and if rumours were to be believed, he had more than just Rose on the go. When Rose had become pregnant a couple of years ago he should have got his act together and proposed but he was too selfish to give up his freedom and Rose's much longed-for ring had never been produced. She slaved in the salon to pay the rent on the little flat she shared with her son. Tanya, with her stable solicitor boyfriend, was a lot luckier than Rose and a lot luckier than most women out there if she really thought about it. Eddie was generous and cute and he didn't have a wandering eye. Maybe in time he would propose. After all, lots of couples lived together these days before getting married. It wasn't such a big deal. Maybe Tanya should see their cohabiting as a step to getting married. If only her mother hadn't got herself so excited about the wedding though. She was dreading telling her that she wouldn't have to buy a mother-of-the-bride outfit any time soon. Mrs Thomson had been away on a golfing trip with the girls so Tanya hadn't had a chance to tell her the bad news yet.

'I suppose,' Tanya muttered, still not entirely convinced. 'What did my mum say to you, by the way?'

'She said you were to ring her back because she wants to make an appointment with a few bridal shops for next week. I guess she'll be pretty disappointed then?'

'Hmm, that's the understatement of the year. So how busy are we today? Have we many appointments?'

Rose took out her hard-covered notebook. 'Let me see.

Mrs Dobson is your first. She's in for her mum-to-be massage.'

'Oh good, she's nice,' said Tanya. Mrs Dobson was eight months' pregnant and came in for a twice-weekly massage. Tanya actually enjoyed doing the mum-to-be massages, especially if the bump was very big and you could feel the baby move. Also Mrs Dobson was a nice, quiet woman who didn't yap away all through the treatment like some women tended to. It was very off-putting when the clients insisted on talking because it was harder to concentrate.

'And then you have Mrs White in for a pedicure.'

Tanya groaned. Mrs White was a dreadful snob who looked down on everybody although she had very little reason to. She didn't work and seemed to have more time on her hands than she knew what to do with. Her husband was a builder and had made a fortune in recent years with the property boom. Mrs White seemed to love nothing more than spending her husband's money in the salon which she visited at least three times a week. She wore a constant scowl on her face and never seemed happy. Tanya was not looking forward to clipping her toenails as the woman would undoubtedly boast throughout the entire procedure about her new car and where she was going off next on her holidays.

'Then after that you have a Mr Henry Duffy in for a back wax. Rather you than me,' Rose giggled.

'Yuck,' said Tanya. Back waxing was far from her favourite job. And middle-aged men were always so intolerant of pain. 'I just can't wait for today to be over. I didn't sleep a wink last night.'

'What kept you up?' asked Rose, gratefully accepting the cup of tea that Tanya offered her.

Tanya sighed. 'I was wondering if I should accept Eddie's offer to move in with him. Part of me wants to but another part of me wants to keep my independence too. I mean, he might get sick of me if we're living under the same roof and he sees me every day.'

'Nonsense. It'll be great. Anyway, living at home isn't exactly being independent, is it? Have you told him you'll move in with him?'

'No; I said I needed time to think about it. It's a big decision, you know?'

'I wouldn't have to think twice about it,' said Rose, nibbling on a chocolate biscuit. 'He's a fine thing, your Eddie is. If you don't move in with him somebody else might.'

Tanya raised an eyebrow.

'Don't you look so surprised, Missus,' Rose teased. 'Don't you know how rare it is to find a good man these days? If you don't want him, any another woman would snap him up as quickly as you'd blink. There are so many women out there desperate to find themselves a good catch. Look at the amount of them who come in here to get their nails and fake tan done for a night out. They're not doing it for their own sakes, you know. If there were no men in the world there'd be a lot more hairy white women about the place with chipped nails.'

Tanya burst out laughing. Rose could be hilarious sometimes. But there was some truth in her words of wisdom. Men like Eddie were a rare breed. There were plenty of idiots out there and she didn't want to settle for any of them. God, she honestly wouldn't know what to do if Eddie and herself broke up. The thought of going out there man hunting again was enough to terrify her.

Rose looked at her watch. 'It's nearly nine, love. We'd better put the OPEN sign on the door and start looking happy for our customers.'

'Yup,' said Tanya, standing up and clearing away the mugs. 'Another day, another dollar.'

At eleven o'clock, after Mrs Dobson's belly had been massaged, snooty Mrs White's toenails had been painted and Henry Duffy's gorilla-like back had been made to look as smooth as a baby's bottom, Tanya finally got a breather. She decided to ring her mother to warn her not to be ringing around the bridal shops and making fools out of both of them.

'Darling!' Mrs Thomson could barely keep the excitement out of her voice when she realised her eldest daughter was at the other end of the phone. 'I'm so glad you rang. I'll have to fill you in on the golfing trip. Do you know that Mary's daughter has just got engaged to a doctor from Cork? Apparently her ring is the size of the rock of Gibraltar! Did Eddie produce a ring? What's it like? How much did he spend?'

Tanya took a deep breath. 'Mum, Eddie didn't propose and there isn't going to be a wedding. Well, not in the near future anyway.'

The silence at the other end of the line was deafening. Tanya felt herself squirming. She was so annoyed with Eddie for putting herself and her mother through this. Her mother's whole world would crumble at this unfortunate piece of news.

'Mum, are you still there?'

'Yes, but I don't understand, love.' Mrs Thomson sounded completely shell-shocked.

'I got it all wrong, Mum. I already feel like a complete idiot so please don't make it any worse. When Eddie said he had something important to ask me I just jumped the gun and thought he was going to propose.'

'Of course you did, darling. Any girl would. I'm just stunned, so I am. The cheek of him leading you up the garden path like that.'

'Well, it would seem that marriage is the furthest thing from his mind,' said Tanya with a strangled little laugh. 'He's asked me to move in with him.'

'Well, I hope you told him where to go,' said Mrs Thomson. 'I mean really, who does he think he is? Does he expect you to move in and start cooking and cleaning for him without you getting anything in return for it?'

'I haven't given him an answer yet. I said I needed to think about it very carefully. I'm so confused right now but I don't really want to discuss it either, Mum. It's got to be my decision without any interference from you and Dad.'

'Your father won't be a bit pleased to hear about this. He was really excited about the wedding.'

'I don't think he was, to be honest.' Tanya sighed. 'He was probably just going along with you because you were so happy. I'm sorry that things aren't turning out the way we had hoped.'

'But what will we tell everybody?' asked Mrs Thomson, panicking suddenly.

'Mum, I warned you not to tell anybody in the first place so you just tell them whatever you like. It's nobody's business anyway. Listen, I'd better go. My next client is coming in at eleven-thirty and I haven't even had a chance to make a cup of tea. I'll talk to you later, Mum. Goodbye.'

With a heavy heart Tanya put down the phone. That hadn't been the easiest telephone call in the world to make. She hated disappointing her mother but none of this was her fault. If Eddie had proposed then everything would have been perfect but you couldn't force somebody to propose. Tanya sat down at the table in the tiny kitchen above the salon and, unable to wait till lunchtime, munched on a cheese sandwich she'd brought to work with her. She presumed Eddie would be waiting for an answer from her later on. He still thought everything was fine between them because she'd refused to let him see how hurt she'd been. Moving in together was such a big decision. Where would they even live? Eddie worked in town and she worked in Drumcondra. They'd have to choose somewhere to suit them both. It was bad enough commuting as it was. Would they take out a joint mortgage together? One that would bind them financially together for the next twenty-five years? Tanya didn't earn much as a beautician and didn't have much saved. Eddie had been left a bit of money a couple of years ago by a rich uncle so he'd probably use that as a deposit. Even thinking about such a big financial commitment was enough to give her a headache. You heard such horror stories sometimes. Dee, the owner of the salon, bought a house five years ago with her partner and then last year found out he'd been cheating on her. Neither wanted to sell the house so they continued to live together although they were barely on speaking terms. It sounded like a right old nightmare.

Rose popped her head around the door to let her know that her eleven-thirty appointment had arrived. It was to be a simple eyebrow pluck and eyelash tint. Nothing too stressful there. Tanya stood up, wiped the crumbs off her starched white uniform and went downstairs again. But nothing could have prepared her for the shock when her client looked up from her seat in the salon waiting room. Tanya stared at her, stunned. Talk about a blast from the past. It was Alice Adams.

'Can we go out for dinner tonight?'

Bill took off his jacket and threw it on the sofa. 'Honey, I can't. I'm entertaining clients tonight in the Ivy.'

Alice's eyes widened. The Ivy? Now that was a place she wouldn't mind going to. She'd read that Victoria Beckham often dined there along with A-list stars such as Jennifer Lopez and Tom Cruise and Katie Holmes. In fact anyone who was *anyone* in Hollywood ate there. It was *the* place to be seen.

'Oh, can I come too?'

Bill bent down and gave her a peck on the cheek. 'Another time, Babes. This is business. Just a load of guys in suits talking contracts. You'd be bored out of your pretty little head.'

Alice bit her lip to stop herself answering back. She was furious. Yet again Bill was going out without her. Was it really a business meeting? Maybe he was taking his other girlfriend out for dinner. She thought about telling him that she'd seen him earlier on in the mall but then decided against it. She wanted to pick her time carefully. She watched him disappear into the bedroom and soon she heard the shower being run in their ensuite bathroom.

He hadn't even bothered asking her how her day had gone. He probably didn't even care. As far as Bill was concerned the only person in their relationship of any importance seemed to be himself.

She wondered where the relationship had gone so wrong. How had he fallen out of love with her so quickly? Then again had he ever really been in love with her? He'd certainly told her often enough that he loved her when he'd been trying to persuade her to pack her bags and come and live with him in LA. He'd phoned constantly, sent flowers and endless text messages. He'd promised to look after her, yet since she'd got here he'd more or less ignored her. The only time he seemed to pay her any attention these days was when they were in bed. But even their sex life was practically non-existent now. By the time he arrived home in the evenings Alice was often asleep and he was gone every morning before she woke up. They were living two completely separate lives.

Bill emerged from the bedroom fifteen minutes later wearing a black suit and a crisp white shirt underneath which showed off his deep tan to perfection. He looked like a movie star and smelled great too. Was that new aftershave he was wearing?

'Don't wait up,' he said, kissing her on the top of her forehead.

'Will you be late home?'

'We might head to the Viper Rooms,' he said. 'These guys are from New York and are only in town for a couple of nights. We want to show them a good time.'

'So it's a big deal, right?' she said, trying to sound

enthusiastic but failing miserably to keep the disappointment from showing in her face.

'Very big deal. Like you wouldn't believe. Wish me luck, okay?'

And then he was gone. And she was left alone. But hey, what was new? She was kind of getting used to her own company at this stage.

She was bored, bored, bored, however. How was she going to while away another night without going totally crazy?

She stood up, stretched and yawned loudly before deciding that it was way too early for bed. Instead she thought she'd treat herself to a large Jameson and Coke. She'd bought the whiskey in Dublin Duty Free on her way over and it had sat on the kitchen counter in Bill's condo untouched since then. Now was as good a time as any to open it, she supposed. She poured herself a generous measure and then filled the glass with chilled Coke. She took a large gulp. Ah, that tasted so good. Then she took another one and then opened the window so she could have a cigarette. She never smoked when Bill was around. He couldn't stand the smell of smoke and she'd promised him she had kicked the habit for good. Of course she hadn't done any such thing. Cigarettes were her treat in her lonely existence here. She looked forward to them like nothing else. And besides, they helped suppress her appetite.

Alice stuck her head out the window and lit up. It was a calm night with no stars in the sky. It really was great the way you could open the windows here and not freeze to death like you would back home in Dublin. But the weather wasn't enough to keep her here. Sure it was cold in Ireland but at least she got a warm reception in most places. Alice was almost convinced that if she packed her suitcase and left for the airport without saying goodbye Bill probably wouldn't even notice that she was gone.

She suddenly heard the sound of loud female voices and tottering high heels on the pavement outside. She wondered whether she should stub out her cigarette and shut down the window before they spotted her. Too late. Two girls, who looked vaguely familiar and were linking arms and laughing, stopped at a halt outside her apartment. One of them was petite and skinny with Chinese features and pearly white teeth. The other was tall with white-blond hair and a diamond stud in her nose.

'Hey,' one of them pointed at her good-naturedly. 'You're smoking!'

'That's right.' Duh, Alice thought.

'Have you got any cigarettes left?' asked the blonde who must have been at least six foot tall.

'Sure.'

'Well, listen, we'll trade you, okay? You come over to ours. We just live in that condo there with the green door. We'll provide the shampoo.'

'Are you celebrating?' Alice was intrigued.

'Are we what?' said the Chinese girl, batting her oval brown eyes. 'Mindy here has just landed herself a speaking part in *Desperate Housewives*.'

'No way!'

'Way. So yeah, we're going to have a drink or two at ours and then head to Santa Monica for dinner. Would you and Bill like to . . .?'

'You know Bill?'

'Everyone knows Bill.'

'Well, he's out . . .'

'Come along by yourself then. Just don't forget the cigarettes. I'm Tyra by the way, although I promise you I wasn't called after Tyra "it's all about me" Banks.'

'Okay then, I'll be right over,' said Alice, feeling more upbeat than she had all day. A party was just what she needed to lift her spirits. She pulled on her skinny jeans, a pair of pink ballerina pumps, and a white cotton vest top that showed off her tan nicely. She threw her favourite lilac-coloured Swarovski studded handbag over her shoulder and left the condo which had lately seemed more like a prison to her. She rang the girls' doorbell and they immediately made her feel welcome.

Alice sat opposite Tyra and Mindy who looked more than comfortable sitting barefoot on their white leather sofa, their strappy sparkly sandals strewn on the floorboards in front of them. Tyra explained that although she was of Chinese origin she originally came from Boston, whereas Mindy was a true Californian.

Tyra was a fitness instructor and a bit model with a seemingly unhealthy obsession with watching *America's Next Top Model* while Mindy was an actress with an accounting degree. Her biggest claim to fame was that she'd snogged Leonardo DiCaprio when he was between girlfriends. She was now on a total high after bagging a small speaking role in *Desperate Housewives* and couldn't wait to meet Nicolette Sheridan and the rest of the cast.

'You're thin,' said Tyra, immediately offering Alice a glass of champagne. 'I'm guessing you're a model, right?'

'Yes, that's right.'

'Do you like it here in LA?'

'It's okay.' Alice shrugged. 'I've only been here three months. It takes a while to get used to living somewhere new.'

'At least you have Bill to show you around. I hope he's being a good friend.'

Alice pretended not to hear. She didn't really want to discuss Bill.

'He's cute, too,' said Mindy. 'If only I wasn't so in love with my agent.'

'Your *married* agent.' Tyra wagged a beautifully manicured finger at her.

Alice was glad she'd had her nails done professionally earlier. At home things like having perfect nails weren't as important as having perfect nails here. Every single building in LA seemed to house a manicurist. Having chipped dirty nails would be considered a crime. Almost as bad as having yellow teeth.

'Have you got a man back in Ireland, Alice? I'm sure you do.' Tyra topped up her champagne flute and flashed her visitor a pearly smile.

Alice stared back at her. She was completely stumped for words. What kind of a question was that? Didn't they know that Bill was her boyfriend?'

Tyra, noticing the look on Alice's face, started to backtrack immediately. 'Oh, um, of course you don't have to answer that. Tell me to butt out and mind my own business if you like. Me and Mindy are always talking about men. It's like our favourite subject at the moment, isn't it, Minds? I've got a date tomorrow with a hot

Hollywood producer. He's been divorced three times but I wouldn't say no to becoming wife number four. He lives in the hills in a twenty-five-bedroom mansion and has five swimming pools.'

Five swimming pools? Why would anybody need five swimming pools? Alice wondered. Wouldn't two, say, be enough? She wasn't quite sure what to make of these two girls. They seemed a bit silly and man mad. Of course, Alice didn't have very many girlfriends back home. She'd always tended to get on better with blokes. Still, the girls were a distraction at the moment. She didn't need to be home alone thinking about Bill right now.

'Well, I certainly hope Ty marries him and that he puts me, her best friend, in his new flick.' Mindy sighed with a toss of her mane. 'Hollywood is all about contacts. It's about who you know. Turning up for audition after audition can be such a drag sometimes. Even when they call you back for a second audition it's best not to get too excited 'cos it most often doesn't lead to anything.'

'Everyone in this town wants to act,' Tyra explained. 'Do you want to act too, Alice?'

'Funnily enough, no. I was never really any good at it. Even as a child in the annual Nativity play I was always one of the three wise men because of my height. The parts of the Virgin Mary and the Angel Gabriel always went to the other girls. Modelling's enough for me. Mind you, LA isn't the best place to pursue a career in modelling.'

'Maybe you should try New York?' Tyra offered hopefully.

'Yeah, maybe, but it's cold over there. I hate the cold. By the way, what age are you two girls?'

They honestly didn't look any older than college students.

'I'm twenty-four and Mindy's twenty-six,' Tyra revealed.

'But my acting age is between eighteen and thirty,' Mindy cut in quickly.

'I see,' said Alice. Goodness, these two girls were really making her feel rather old. They didn't ask her her age and maybe that was a bad thing. Maybe they didn't want to embarrass her. This worried her somewhat. Suppose she came home to Dublin and people felt that she was over the hill? That she was, God forbid, *past* it? It wasn't the nicest thing to think about. Suppose all she was offered were ads as a young mum? Commercials with two kids who weren't hers sitting around a table while she stood at the cooker pretending to stir a pot of stew? Could she really face going back to Dublin and turning up to castings with young sixteen- and seventeen-year-olds who were underdeveloped and thought she was ancient and well past her sell-by date?

'Another glass of champagne, honey?' Tyra offered, noticing her guest's empty glass.

'Sure,' Alice shrugged, 'why not?'

Wow! It was certainly unusual to come across girls who drank in LA. It was a pity she hadn't met them sooner. She held out her glass while Tyra refilled it and Mindy stuck some Michael Bolton on the CD player.

'So where do you want to go after this?' asked Tyra.

'I'm easy. I don't know Santa Monica all that well. Bill is always working. He never brings me anywhere.'

Tyra and Mindy looked suitably sympathetic.

'At least he's not under your feet all day,' said Mindy, sipping her champagne thoughtfully.

'Yeah, well, maybe that wouldn't be such a bad complaint.'

'Don't worry, we'll take you somewhere hot.' Mindy gave her arm a reassuring squeeze. 'I know a place where they do great cocktails.'

Alice smiled back at her. 'That would be nice.' She was starting to pick up a little bit. Maybe she'd become friends with these girls. It would probably make her less hung up on Bill if she had other people to pal around with. True, the girls weren't the brightest pennies in the pot, but they were kind of harmless.

'What's Ireland like?' Tyra joined them on the sofa and lit up a cigarette.

'It's different,' said Alice. 'It's cold for a start.'

'What are the men like?'

Both girls looked at her expectantly.

'They're different too,' said Alice with a wry grin.

'Cute?'

'Some are. Most aren't.'

'Are you fussy?'

'Yeah, I guess I am. That's probably part of the problem.'

She let her mind wander. Who were the cute guys back home? She could probably count them on one hand. Most of them were already spoken for. There weren't too many available ones floating around in their thirties anyway. And then she remembered Eddie Toner. He'd always been cute but he'd been a year younger than her so she'd never properly considered him. Alice had always gone for older, more sophisticated men. And besides, it would have been too much of a cliché to date the guy next door. So apart from the odd flirtation, she hadn't ever really given him much of a chance. Now she thought back to that night she had met Bill. What a coincidence that Eddie had walked by the car that same night. He'd looked divine. He'd recognised her too. In fact, he'd almost done a double take at the sight of her. She'd been looking her very best that night. At least that was something. There was no way he could have thought that she'd gone off or that the years hadn't been kind to her. She wondered if he was still single. Maybe he was married now to a nice sensible girl and had a couple of kids running around. She knew for a fact that he had moved out of home a few years ago. Her mother had told her with a sad face that he had gone travelling around the world with a couple of pals and that when he came back he hadn't come home to live with his parents. Alice always suspected that her parents would have been over the moon if their only child had ended up marrying Eddie. A retired dentist's son, he would have been a very respectable catch. That was enough reason, however, for Alice to completely dismiss Eddie as a potential boyfriend. She'd never wanted anybody whom her parents would be delighted to invite around for a cup of tea. And so she rebelled and started dating one misfit after another. The more baggage they had the more Alice seemed to be attracted to life's losers. She dated playboys and cokeheads and the more tattoos they sported the better. Her mother hated tattoos.

Alice had dated married men who always said they were on the verge of separating from their wives but never got around to it and she'd courted men who had different children by different women. She'd picked up famous men in celebrity haunts such as Lillies and Renards and had gone back to their hotels and shagged them. Even if they'd never followed up with a phone call, she'd convinced herself that it didn't matter. The big stars could have any eager young wannabe but they always chose Alice to bring back to their hotel penthouses for a nightcap. She knew how to seduce any man with a simple arch of her eyebrow. She'd learned all of that stuff from reading the racy books under her bed and by studying the old Hollywood films. So many women were so clueless when it came to getting men's attention but Alice always knew what to do.

For a start she never wore skirts up to her arse and low-cut slutty tops. No. There were so many women who went out dressed like that but they were obvious-looking. Far better to wear a tight polo neck, a high slit up your skirt and killer heels. Then you looked different, not too eager and a bit of a challenge. Men loved that. Men like Eddie would appreciate a classy girl. He was an intelligent guy. He was tall and handsome, well-dressed and still had a full head of dark hair which was more than could be said for so many of the men she had dated in her twenties. Maybe she just might look him up again next time she was home.

'Is Bill seeing anybody?'

Mindy's question came out of the blue, knocking Alice out of her short reverie.

'Excuse me?'

'I was just wondering if he had a girl, you know.'

Mindy shrugged. 'I'm not saying that *I'm* interested in him or anything. I was just wondering, that's all.'

Alice stared at her face for traces of irony but found none. Then she shot a look at Tyra who was looking straight back at her expectantly. Alice frowned. What was going on? Was that some kind of trick question? Did they think she was Bill's sister or something, or else were they playing some kind of cruel trick on her? Then again, they didn't seem in the slightest bit bitchy. Maybe they were just genuinely thick.

Alice decided to take it as a joke. 'Why? Do you think I'm Bill's housekeeper?' She gave a hollow laugh.

Now it was the two girls' turn to look confused. Alice noticed them exchange wary glances. What was going on? Surely neither of them had been with Bill, had they? Then again, anything was possible. Bill rarely confided in her and she knew next to nothing about his dating history.

'You mean you're dating Bill?' Mindy looked like she was trying to frown but was obviously finding it difficult due to a recent Botox injection.

'Of course I am. Why else would I be living here?'

The atmosphere had suddenly gone cold. Mindy examined her nails awkwardly while Tyra cleared her throat. 'We thought you guys were just buddies.'

'Really?' Alice frowned. She didn't like the direction this conversation was taking. 'Why would you think that? Did Bill say something?'

'Well, we invited you guys around a while ago for a barbecue but Bill said he was busy,' Mindy explained. 'Then we said to him that his girlfriend was more than welcome to come by herself if she wanted, but . . . oh, I don't think I should have said anything. Me and my big mouth, huh? It's always landing me in trouble.'

'No, go on,' Alice urged. 'Please.'

'He was like, "I don't have a girlfriend, Mindy" so uh, that's why I thought you were just friends. We thought he was just putting you up for a while till you found your own place.'

Alice was dumbfounded. She really was. Trying to steady her hand she pulled a cigarette from the box. 'Can you excuse me for a minute? I really need this.'

She stood leaning on the door of the apartment, staring at the oval swimming pool in the centre of the complex. None of this made any sense, or did it? Perhaps it made a lot of sense. Maybe Bill didn't really see her as his girl-friend at all. Sure he had sex with her whenever she was home, told her she was beautiful and bought her stuff, but he never actually seemed to want to be seen with her. He was never available, not emotionally anyway. He was like a closed book as far as she was concerned. Was it because he wanted to date other women? More than likely that was the reason. Alice bet that the woman she'd seen him with earlier in the mall didn't have a clue that he had another woman living at home with him. Why would she? Bill was obviously denying Alice's very existence. Was he ashamed of her? Did he not think she was good enough? Alice felt like crying. She'd never felt so low and worthless in her entire life. Had she really thrown away everything back home, together with her career, to come out here and be treated like a second-class citizen? She felt like such a fool now.

A hand on her bare arm made her jump. 'Do you mind

if I join you?' Mindy said softly, lighting up a cigarette of her own.

'No, of course not,' Alice said.

'I know what it's like to be with the wrong man,' she continued. 'It happens to me all the time. One minute they're saying they're madly in love with me and the next minute they're gone. I don't get it at all. You wouldn't believe the amount of money I've spent in therapy trying to get over my broken heart.'

'Bill never told me he was madly in love with me. He just asked me to come out here. I jumped to conclusions. I presumed he saw a future with me like I did with him.'

'Maybe it was lucky that you met me and Tyra tonight then. Maybe it was fate. Else this could have gone on and on and you would have truly ended up getting hurt.'

'Yeah.'

'You'll get over this too. You'll find somebody to cherish you. You deserve that.'

'Do I?'

'Sure,' Mindy squeezed her arm. 'In the meantime, us girls need to stick together.'

'Well, I guess I'd better be getting back to my apartment. Sorry, *Bill's* apartment,' Alice corrected herself before throwing her cigarette stub on the ground and stamping it out with the sole of her shoe.

'Why would you do that?'

'I don't know. To wait for him, I suppose. I need to talk to Bill.'

'Not tonight, though. You've been drinking. It's never good to have a serious conversation when liquor is involved.'

'What else would I do?' Alice felt helpless.

'Me and Tyra are going to hit Liquid Kitty. Tyra's just called for a cab. You should come with us. They play cool music there and serve even cooler Martinis. It'll be fun.'

'Yeah, okay, you're right. I need to get out. There's no point me going back home and hitting the Jameson bottle alone. Do you think I should ring Bill though?'

'Has he called you?' Mindy raised a knowing eyebrow.

'Well, no, but if he comes back and I'm not there he'll be wondering where I am.'

'Exactly.' Mindy nodded knowingly.

'Oh, okay. I get you now.'

Alice opened her eyes to an unfamiliar white ceiling. Her first thought was one of complete panic. Where the hell was she? What time was it? Why was she dressed in strange pink silk pyjamas and lying on a velvet couch surrounded by cushions with sparkly things on them? Why did her head hurt so much and her mouth feel as dry as an old flip-flop? And then she remembered. Oh God, yes. She'd gone out with those American chicks and ended up completely blottoed. She had vague flashbacks of going back to some guy's pool party in this LA mansion where they'd served copious amounts of champagne and where she'd fallen into the water. But how had she got home? Or wherever she was now. She sat up. She recognised the room now. It was the girls' place. Well, thank God for that anyway. At least she knew where she was. But the place was eerily quiet.

She tried to get up but her head hurt so much she had to flop back down into the mound of pillows again. It had been a long time since she'd let herself get that drunk and lose control. It had been an okay night considering her heart had been breaking. But the champagne had managed to obliterate her feelings of despair, albeit momentarily.

She lay on the sofa now considering her options. Not that there were very many left at this stage. Was she going to pack her bags and head for home or would Bill be able to come up with a plausible excuse for having his arm around that woman in the mall? Would he promise to change and start treating her like a real human being? Only then might she be persuaded to hang on a little longer. Somehow, though, she didn't fancy the chances of that happening. Eventually she mustered up the energy to get herself into a sitting position on the couch. Somebody had considerately left a glass of fresh orange juice on the coffee table beside her. There was also a note. Could it be from Bill? Had the girls told him where she had spent the night? Had he been out of his mind with worry?

But no. The note was from the girls.

Hey, girl! We've gone to our Pilates classes. Hope your head isn't too bad. There's lots of fresh food in the refrigerator you can use as soakage. Do you remember dancing on the tables? You Irish are such a blast!
Mindy & Tyra X

Alice cringed as she read the note. Her stomach was grumbling. All that booze on her empty stomach hadn't been a good thing. She hoped she hadn't disgraced the girls too much with her drunken antics. Certainly she hadn't remembered dancing on any tables but surely they wouldn't have made that part up. She vaguely remembered seeing Keanu Reeves at the party. In fact, she had a hazy memory of taking a photo of him, but maybe she had just dreamed it.

She noticed her handbag lying on the floor and scrambled to open it. Damn, her phone had run out of battery and was blank. She'd better get to Bill's. Her clothes were nowhere to be found. The girls must have tidied them away. Instead, she'd have to sneak across the complex in these flimsy pyjamas. How embarrassing! Hopefully she wouldn't bump into anybody on the way. She gratefully picked up the tall glass of juice and knocked it back all in one go. Ah, that was better. Then she put all the velvet cushions back on the sofa, rinsed the glass in the sink and stored it away. She opened the fridge after the girls' kind invitation to help herself but the sight of all those organic raw vegetables and strange-looking sauces was enough to make her feel sick. Had they never heard of a good old greasy fry-up in this part of the world?

A few minutes later she was back in Bill's apartment. She noticed the time. It was just coming up to noon. The place was as spick and span as ever and the bed had been made. No note, no nothing. No sign that he was big-time pissed off with her. Maybe he hadn't even noticed her absence. Or maybe at this stage she mattered so little to him that he no longer cared where she went or what she did. She plugged her mobile phone into the wall and as she waited for it to charge she stuck on the kettle. At this stage she was craving a hot mug of coffee. Minutes later she checked her phone and was flabbergasted to see that she had no less than seventeen missed calls from Bill. Crikey, that was a bit excessive, wasn't it? Then she checked her pictures and sure enough there was a picture of her with Keanu Reeves on her phone. Nice one. Sure her eyes looked a bit bloodshot but the photo pleased her endlessly. That would be one to put up on Facebook and maybe show the grandkids some day. At least she'd met one bona fide Hollywood star during her stint in this town.

She was almost afraid to listen to her messages from Bill. No doubt he'd be absolutely furious with her. She decided to go for a swim while the sun was still up. There was nothing to beat a hangover like a swim. And besides, the pool was always empty so she'd have it all to herself. The residents here never seemed to bother to use it. They were always at work, in the gym or at the beach doing press-ups. Even Mindy and Tyra had proved this morning that they wouldn't let anything as insignificant as a hangover get in the way of their determination to stay fit. What kind of a place was this anyway? Weren't people human here?

Alice stepped into her green-and-black-striped Roberto Cavalli bikini – a rare present from Bill which he'd bought her after mysteriously not coming home after a particularly important business dinner in Tinseltown – smothered herself in factor eight Ambre Solaire, retrieved a bottle of chilled fizzy water from the fridge, popped her Chanel sunglasses on her head, her iPod earplugs in her ears, and went out to relax on one of the cushioned sun loungers. Twenty minutes later, when the heat became too much, she slid into the gloriously warm pool and started doing gentle laps. Immediately she felt better.

On her fifth lap she was aware of somebody standing

very close to the pool. She stopped swimming, aware of a dark shadow over her. It was Bill. And he certainly wasn't smiling.

'Bill!' she called out with false gaiety. 'You gave me a fright! How long have you been standing there?'

'Long enough to make sure you were still alive,' he said grimly. Wearing an expensive-looking suit and dark sunglasses he looked very formidable indeed. Even a blind man could sense his fury.

'I was about to ring you,' she said, swimming towards the steps.

'When? When you'd finished in the pool? Don't you realise that I've been out of my mind with worry?'

Alice stepped out of the pool and wrapped herself in a fluffy white robe. It was hard to make eye contact with him while he was wearing his shades. 'I'm sorry, I was hungover. I ended up staying at Mindy and Tyra's place across the way. We went to some party, I don't remember where, but Keanu Reeves was there.'

Bill looked far from impressed. 'Were you drunk?'

Alice bided her time, shifting from one foot to the other, and shaking some of the damp from her hair.

'No, not drunk, I definitely wouldn't say that I was drunk,' she lied. 'But I was tipsy. The cocktails went to my head a bit.'

'And the whiskey,' he added. 'I noticed you opened the whiskey.'

Alice found herself getting annoyed. The sun was in her eyes, making her squint. Bill was accusing her of having a good time. What the fuck? This was ridiculous. Her eyes flashed angrily at him. He may have invited her over here. She may be living in his pad for free but she wasn't his bloody property.

'I am allowed to go out, you know, Bill. You have no right talking to me like this. You were gone and I got an invitation to go out so I went. Was that a crime? It's not like I had that many options last night as you sure as hell weren't prepared to take me anywhere.'

Bill seemed shocked by her response. It was the first time she'd ever spoken to him like this before. They stood staring at each other in hostility for a few moments. Then he reached out a hand but Alice was so wound up now she refused to back down.

'Don't you think I have any feelings at all?' she continued with her rant.

'I'm sorry, I've had a lot on my mind. I know I might have seemed selfish—'

'Might? You *might* have seemed selfish? My God, Bill, *you* were the one who persuaded me to come here. You got me to leave my friends and family behind in Ireland because you said you were crazy about me, and yesterday I happened to be in the mall and I saw you walk by with some strange woman.'

'Strange woman?' Bill frowned.

'Yes. Please explain to me what that was all about, Bill. You had your arm around her. How very romantic.' Alice then paused for breath.

'That was Debbie.'

'Who's Debbie?' she demanded, placing both hands on her hips.

'She's an old friend. We've known each other since High School. She's going through a tough divorce at the moment and phoned me for some advice. I felt sorry for her.'

Alice remained unconvinced. 'Really? And why did you tell Mindy and Tyra you didn't have a girlfriend?'

'I'm a private person,' he replied, 'especially concerning my love life.'

'Whatever you say, Bill, but I was taken by surprise as you can imagine. Listen, I don't want to be a burden around here. If you're tired of me just tell me. If you want me to leave, I'll do it,' she said eventually, 'but I don't want to wait around and watch you slowly falling out of love with me. It's just too painful.'

She headed back inside. Bill didn't follow as she'd half hoped he would, so she went into the bedroom, peeled off her wet bikini, hung it on the heated rail in their ensuite bathroom and dressed herself in jeans and a T-shirt. Then as calmly as she could, she went into the kitchen, got herself a stool, and dragged it back into the bedroom with her. As she stood on it, she heard Bill's voice speak to her. It was a lot mellower now.

'What are you doing, Alice?'

'What does it look like I'm doing?' she answered without looking at him before proceeding to lift the big empty suitcase down from the top of the large mirrored wardrobe. 'I'm packing my things and getting the first flight out of here. It's what you want, isn't it?'

'Leave the suitcase alone, Alice. Come on, less of the drama now. I'm sorry. I overreacted. I was just worried about you. I'm in love with you whether you believe me or not. You're different, Alice. I've never met anybody like you before and I'm sorry I haven't been giving you the attention you deserve. Let me make it up to you. Please?'

She looked down at him and her heart melted. He no longer looked cross, just a bit jaded. His sunglasses were now perched on his head and she could see dark shadows under his eyes. She almost felt sorry for him.

'Can we talk?' she said quietly.

'Sure. Come on into the kitchen. I'll make you a coffee.'

'Or maybe we could go out, Bill. I'm sick of sitting in that kitchen day after day. I feel like a prisoner here. I know you're out all the time so you probably don't feel like going out during your time off but sometimes I go crazy being confined within these walls with nobody for company.'

'Do you want to go into Santa Monica for a while? We could hang out in the Ritz Carlton or go somewhere more low-key for a beer or a soda?'

'I'd like to go to Rodeo Drive,' she suggested. 'I've never been and it's a dream of mine to go. Will you take me?'

'Sure. You put that suitcase back and get dressed. I'm taking the rest of the day off just to show you a good time.'

Alice stepped down from the stool, threw her arms around Bill's neck, and planted a kiss on his lips. She felt like a child that was being brought to Disneyland for the first time. An afternoon in Bill's company, cruising LA in his convertible, was just what she needed to banish her hangover blues. She couldn't believe how angry she had been with him just moments earlier. She was glad she had spoken out, though. It had worked. Threatening to leave had made him up his game and hopefully he'd now appreciate that she wasn't a doormat to be treated any old way. This was the new Alice. And from now on things were going to go her way.

Half an hour later Alice had changed into a chic pink and black Dolce & Gabbana dress. She'd brought it to LA with her and it had hung in the wardrobe ever since as she hadn't had an occasion to wear it. Now she teamed it up with dainty gold strappy sandals and a large Jimmy Choo bag of the same colour. She certainly looked the part of a Hollywood starlet, she decided, giving herself an appreciative glance in the full-length mirror before emerging from the bedroom. Bill had also made an effort, she noted, changing into off-white chinos and a navy Ralph Lauren cotton shirt. He'd also put on a rich-smelling aftershave that made her want to pounce on him. It was amazing how you could go from feeling so down to being completely euphoric in less than half an hour, she thought to herself as she slipped into the leather car seat beside her man and he started up the engine. It was amazing what one short outburst could do. Now that the air had been cleared, hopefully that would make all the difference.

It didn't take long to reach Beverly Hills and Alice enjoyed the ride, letting the wind rip through her hair and listening to Bill's CDs. If only every day was like this. Then she wouldn't have any urge to go home to Dublin. At every traffic lights Bill squeezed her thigh and gave her a peck on the cheek. They were acting like young lovers without a care in the world. Last night now seemed a million miles away.

'Do you know what I'd love, Bill? I'd love to do a

sightseeing trip of the stars' homes. Is it true you can really do that?'

'Yes, but it's so cheesy,' he teased her. 'That's a trip you're gonna have to take on your own sometime if you're hell-bent on doing it. I've a reputation to live up to. And besides, I've been in most of the homes anyway.'

It was true. As one of Hollywood's top entertainment lawyers Bill had dined out with Sly Stallone, taken brunch with Jennifer Aniston and attended parties in Steven Spielberg's home no less. He seemed so unfazed by it all. To him it was just part of the job and these people were just, well, people. It was one of the things that Alice admired most about Bill. He really didn't think anybody was particularly important and he oozed quiet confidence.

They soon arrived on Rodeo Drive. Alice was struck by how small it was. For some reason she had expected the world's most famous shopping street to be much bigger. All the big designer names such as Armani and Chanel were here and their shop fronts were achingly gorgeous. Alice was so glad she had made the effort to dress up. These shops didn't look like the type of places you could wander around in a tracksuit just having a browse. She didn't even have a bean in her purse but that didn't matter. She just wanted to buy something, anything, to say she'd bought it in Beverly Hills. Hopefully her credit card wouldn't max out on her. She hadn't checked the balance recently. She was almost afraid to.

'Where to first?' Bill slipped a protective arm around her waist. Alice felt like all her Christmases had come at once.

'I wouldn't even know where to start.'

'Come on, follow me.'

By the time they had finished, they had practically visited every boutique on the street. All the shop assistants looked like supermodels and some even offered champagne to the customers. Alice felt like a superstar. Bill had been unbelievably generous and now she was the proud owner of a Gucci leather jacket, a Chanel T-shirt and two Armani miniskirts. Bill hadn't even checked the price tags but had wordlessly handed over his American Express card at each till.

'I'm like Julia Roberts in *Pretty Woman*,' Alice giggled, laden down with all her bags.

'Well, let's not stop here, honey. If you really want the *Pretty Woman* experience, let's have afternoon tea in the Beverly Wilshire where the film was made.'

'Oh God, yes please, that would be amazing!' Alice's eyes widened in excitement. This was just the best day ever.

Minutes later, the pair traipsed through the marble lobby of the world-famous hotel. It was surreal actually being in the same hotel where Julia Roberts and Richard Gere had been filmed. The porter nodded to Bill, obviously recognising him from his frequent visits. Even the barman addressed him personally by name.

The afternoon tea was out of this world. Alice had a crick in her neck from looking around trying to spot random celebrities but alas, today, there were none to be seen. Still, the sandwiches and cakes were going down a treat and her hangover had long gone at this stage.

As the sun set, Bill and Alice finally left the luxurious surroundings of the plush hotel and headed back to Bill's convertible. They were soon back at Bill's complex and strolled hand in hand through the gates. They bumped into Mindy and Tyra on their way in.

'Hi, girls,' Alice said breezily. 'Thanks for looking after me last night. I hope I didn't make too much of a fool of myself.'

'Oh you were such fun!' squealed Tyra. 'We must do it all again soon. Hey, have you guys been shopping?'

'We hit Rodeo Drive,' said Alice, proudly holding up the labelled bags.

'Wow. You're so lucky. I'll drop in tomorrow and you can try them on for me. We're heading out for a walk on the pier and then a bite to eat in Bubba Gump. Do you fancy joining us?'

Alice looked at Bill but he shook his head. 'We had afternoon tea at the Wilshire so we'll probably just sit in and chill with a DVD and maybe a bottle of wine.'

Tyra gave him a friendly poke in the ribs. 'Ooh a romantic night in, I like it. Well, have fun. We'll catch you later.'

And then they were gone. And suddenly it struck Alice that Mindy hadn't said one single word.

How odd.

For days after their trip to Beverly Hills, Alice felt like she was floating on air. Bill was finally acting as if they were a real couple and acknowledging that she was his girlfriend instead of just some random lodger who happened to be kipping in his place. He brought home enormous bouquets of luxurious flowers which she lovingly placed around the apartment and called several times a day just to see how she was doing. Life was good again and Alice sincerely hoped it would continue as such. This is why she had come to LA, after all. For the good life. For a better life. To escape her mundane existence in Dublin. And to fall in love.

But sadly the fairy tale wasn't to last. After a couple of weeks Bill started becoming distant again and she felt she was losing him. He made all the excuses in the world for not making love to her and blamed his workload and the stress of being a top Hollywood lawyer. Alice wasn't buying it, however. If you wanted to make a relationship work, you bloody well *made* it work. And if one person didn't want to make the effort, there was sweet precious all the other person could do about it. She hated feeling that she was dependent on Bill. She loathed the way he could make her feel unloved by rejecting her amorous advances. She felt she was losing control fast.

But she wasn't quite as lonely as she had been at first. Tyra would sometimes pop over to keep her company. She would invite Alice to accompany her to Pilates classes or to go shopping or whatever. But funnily enough, Mindy never did. Alice had her suspicions about why the other girl was now keeping her distance and then one day when the two girls were having lunch at Café Crêpe she confronted Tyra about it.

'Ty, I wonder can you shed light on something for me?'

Tyra raised an eyebrow. 'Shoot, honey. What's on your mind?'

'I dunno. I get weird vibes off Mindy sometimes. As if she doesn't like me or something. Has she said anything to you about me?'

'Um, no. Not that I know of,' said Tyra, looking away.

'I know this might seem crazy and maybe I'm being totally paranoid but . . .'

Tyra turned to look at her again with a quizzical expression.

Alice took a deep breath. She might as well say what she was going to say and get it over with.

'Has Mindy ever been with Bill?'

Tyra didn't even try to deny it. 'Well, yes,' she said, biting her lower lip awkwardly. 'I didn't want to get involved but Mindy told me that Bill said you two had an open relationship, whatever that means.'

Alice felt as if she had been stabbed in the heart. The walls of the café felt as though they were closing in on her and she suddenly felt faint. However, she nodded sagely as Tyra emphatically explained that their liaison had taken place ages ago and that Mindy was well over Bill now.

Alice wasn't sure if she believed it. She toyed with her grilled Italian panini and thought back to the night she'd first met the girls and Mindy had pretended to be all sympathetic about herself and Bill, and had said something about girls needing to stick together and all that crap. Well, now Alice knew that she was being as fake as her implants. Mindy had probably wanted Alice to split up with him so that she could get it on with Bill herself. No wonder Mindy hadn't been a bit friendly since realising that her relationship with Bill was very much back on track again.

Tyra seemed to be getting uncomfortable with the way the conversation was moving. 'I don't really like talking about my friend behind her back,' she insisted. 'Mindy's been having a hard time with men recently and Bill didn't treat her so good. He used to flirt with her like crazy but once he'd got her into bed it was like he didn't want to know afterwards. Then she had to put up with seeing him bring back lots of different girls to the condo. It broke her heart.'

And it was breaking Alice's heart to hear all of this too. So Bill was a player after all. A love rat. Her instincts had been right. She just hadn't taken enough notice of them. How could she have fallen so hard for him? Why had she believed all his empty promises?

'Look,' said Tyra, sipping on her iced tea, 'I know it's not what you want to hear, but Bill's a good-looking guy. He's rich, successful, not married and not gay. He's a pretty unusual catch in this town. So many girls come to LA from all over the world thinking that their good looks can make them a star. In most cases that doesn't happen and they realise that they can either go home to the small towns that they came from and admit they didn't make it, or else they can hook up with a wealthy guy like Bill. You can't be surprised that he has his pick of hot chicks.'

Alice bit her lip. 'It's just a pity I didn't know any of this before I packed my suitcase and came over.'

'Maybe he's changed,' said Tyra, not sounding too convinced. 'I mean, guys do change once they meet the right woman.'

'Do they?'

'Sure, yeah, they can't keep partying for ever.'

'Yeah, well, I can't hang around. I don't know if Bill wants me in his future or I'm just the girl-of-the-moment. But I'm going to have it out with him. There's no point pretending everything is perfect when it's not.'

Tyra called for the bill. 'Show me a relationship that's perfect and I'll show you a big fat liar.'

Alice pondered Tyra's words later as she took a long hot shower after her afternoon swim in the pool. Of course, no relationship was perfect and you had to work at every relationship, but Alice knew time was against her if she wanted to get married. She didn't want to waste the next precious few years here in LA with a man who had no intention of committing and would inevitably eventually trade her in for a younger model. She knew Bill wouldn't be pleased, but when he came home this evening there would be some serious talking to be done.

*

'Honey, are you home?' Bill called as he walked into the sitting room, unfastened his tie and threw it on the table.

Alice was sitting curled up on the sofa with her feet tucked in under her. Her hair was wrapped in a big towel as she was giving it a conditioning treatment to make it shinier. The sun out here played havoc with your hair if you took chances, and as she considered it her crowning glory she made sure to treat it at least twice a week.

'Of course I'm here,' she muttered tetchily, not turning her attention away from the widescreen TV. 'Where else would I be?'

'Ooh, who got out of the wrong side of the bed this morning?' Bill joked as he bent down and kissed the top of her ear. 'Mmm, you smell really nice.'

'There's no food in the house,' Alice said when she eventually looked up at him, 'and I'm starving. Can we go out for dinner at the Cheesecake Factory? I haven't been there in ages.'

'Only if you promise not to eat all the cake yourself,' he teased.

He was in good form, Alice noted. He must have worked out some lucrative contracts today at the office.

He looked delicious this evening. If only she could put all her negative thoughts at the back of her head. If only she hadn't discovered about his sleeping around, even if it was before she moved to LA. A leopard never changed his spots, though, and Hollywood was full of temptation. She wasn't going to bury her head in the sand any longer. If Bill really loved her he'd have to prove it. Tonight the truth would out.

Bill sat in front of the TV, switching it to his sports channel. 'How long will it take you to get ready?'

'Not long,' she promised and went back to the shower to rinse the suds from her hair. After she'd dried it she put on a wine-coloured Missoni slip dress and flat, silver ballet pumps. Chic but not too over the top. Her hair was like something from a television ad. Even Bill looked impressed when she emerged from the bedroom.

Fifteen minutes later they were being escorted to an outdoor table at the Cheesecake Factory by an impossibly handsome waiter. Alice loved it here. The portions were enormous and the food was always great, as was the atmosphere.

Bill ordered steak and Alice opted for a big juicy salad that resembled a small garden when it arrived. Even after eating for fifteen minutes she seemed to have hardly put a dent in her generous-sized bowl. They both sipped on sparkling water and talked about anything and everything. But although their conversation was easy and casual, Alice kept wondering when it would be a good idea to bring up the topic of their future together. Then again that was a topic that most men would balk at so there was never going to be a right time.

'Do you want dessert?' Bill enquired when the waiter came back to take away their half-eaten meals. Alice was thankful she was wearing her Bridget Jones-style knickers as she could feel her belly expanding already. Still, the chocolate cake in this place was good enough to die for and if she said no, she'd just be dreaming about it during the night.

'I do,' she said impulsively.

'What about your diet?'

'What diet?' Alice said, feigning horror.

'You're always on some kind of diet,' Bill laughed. 'You and every other woman I know.'

'Well, tonight's my night off,' Alice insisted.

'You're in good form. Better than earlier on.'

'Yeah, well, I've been thinking about stuff. I feel a lot more positive now . . .'

Bill frowned. 'What kind of stuff?'

'Oh, you know . . . the future . . . where my life is going . . .'

Bill shifted uncomfortably in his seat. 'I think I might have some cake too.'

But Alice wasn't letting him get away that easily. She knew there was a good chance she was about to shoot herself in the foot but it was now or never. Better to know where she stood than trying to secure herself on quicksand for the next few years.

'Do you think you'll ever get married, Bill?'

The silence that followed was almost unbearable. Immediately Alice's fears were confirmed. Her handsome dining companion looked like she'd asked him whether he'd ever considered hanging himself or stabbing somebody just for kicks.

'Excuse me?' he eventually said, shattering the silence.

He looked as though he wasn't sure whether she was joking or not. Only Alice wasn't smiling. Or laughing. All she wanted now was a straight answer.

'You heard me,' she said in a dull tone of voice, her eyes betraying nothing.

'Well, no. No, I don't think I will.'

'I see.'

'No, wait, Alice, what are you getting at? Why would you ask me something like that out of the blue? Do *you* want to get married?'

'I think so.'

'But it's early days for us. To be honest I haven't even thought about it. Not where you and me are concerned anyway.'

The waiter came along and took their dessert orders. When he had disappeared off again, Alice resumed the conversation. 'So what am I? A ship passing in the night?'

'Who have you been talking to? Are Tyra and Mindy putting ideas in your head? I think you're spending too much time with Tyra, anyway, these days. She's a nice girl but she's an airhead. You need to meet more intelligent people.'

'And where would I meet them? It's not like you introduce me to anybody, Bill.'

Bill put his head in his hands and sighed with exasperation. 'God, would you give it a rest, Al? We went through this before. I thought we'd sorted all that shit out.'

Alice took a deep breath. She wasn't backing down. This was crunch time. 'Is it true that you slept with Mindy?'

The colour drained from Bill's normally tanned face. 'Did she tell you that?' he asked in a quiet whisper.

'No,' Alice replied truthfully.

'Who told you then?'

'Does it matter? Is it true?'

'Mindy had a thing for me a while back. We kind of had

a fling. It didn't mean anything. She's not my type.'

'I think she still likes you.'

'That's irrelevant. I'm with you now, Alice. What are you getting at? Aren't you happy? I really don't understand you sometimes.'

'I just want to know where I stand, Bill. If you say you're never going to get married then I find it hard to see a future for us.'

'I'd never say never, but my parents divorced when I was three and it really affected me. I saw my mom go through hell and I swore growing up that I'd never wittingly put a woman through what my mom went through as a result of her marriage breaking up.'

The waiter returned with their desserts. They remained untouched as Alice and Bill struggled on with their conversation.

'What about children, Bill? Don't you want kids?'

'Maybe some day but I don't want to be the type of dad who's never around to see his kids grow up. At the moment I'm kind of married to my job.'

'So I noticed,' Alice muttered wryly.

Eventually they left the restaurant, both feeling a little subdued, and both thinking that perhaps Alice shouldn't have come to LA to live with Bill on a whim. Back in the condo, Bill said he was sorry for not giving Alice the attention she so obviously craved and deserved. And Alice apologised for coming on too strong and for putting the proverbial gun to Bill's head in a bid for answers about their future together.

And Bill said that things would work out and everything would be different in the morning. But as they made intense love that night, Alice knew that things would indeed be different in the morning. And when Bill went to work, she packed her case, left him a note on the kitchen table, and took a taxi to LAX airport where she bought a one-way ticket back to Dublin.

Tanya's jaw nearly hit the floor when she saw her old arch enemy Alice Adams sitting in the waiting room. Her heart started racing and immediately the palms of her hands began to feel clammy.

'Hi, Alice,' Tanya said to the painfully thin girl sitting in the waiting area with dark circles under her eyes and a big suitcase at her feet.

The other girl looked up from her magazine and stared blankly. Immediately Tanya realised that Alice didn't recognise her. Although she looked tired and gaunt, Alice was sporting a nice tan and judging by her suitcase, she had obviously come back from a nice holiday somewhere hot.

'What can I do for you?' Tanya found herself asking brightly, trying to maintain professional composure.

'Just an eyebrow pluck and an eyelash tint. I haven't done my eyebrows in a while and I'm scared of developing a monobrow.'

Tanya gave an unnaturally sounding high-pitched laugh. 'Don't worry,' she said with forced gaiety. 'We'll have you fixed up in no time. Would you like a glass of water or anything before I start?'

'A water would be great.' Alice stood up, stretched her arms high in the air and yawned. 'Is it okay if I leave my case here? I've just come from the airport.'

'Sure. Were you anywhere nice?' Tanya enquired as Alice followed her into one of the cubicles and sat down on the bed.

'I was in LA.'

'Oh lovely. Just a little holiday, was it?'

'Not exactly.'

Alice had clearly no intention of elaborating and Tanya didn't like to probe. She went off to heat the wax for Alice's eyebrows. This was surreal, she thought to herself. How could Alice not recognise her after the appalling way she'd treated her in the past? Maybe she was pretending not to know her. Maybe she was ashamed of her behaviour. It was hard to tell. When Tanya came back into the cubicle, she found Alice staring at her oddly.

'Your face is awfully familiar,' she said. 'Have I met you somewhere before?'

'Yes,' Tanya told her. 'I worked with you a few years ago. I did your make-up for a magazine shoot.'

'Oh, yes, so you did. That's funny, I thought I recognised you at first but as you can appreciate I meet so many make-up artists in my line of work that it's impossible to keep track of everyone.'

Tanya took a deep breath. She was going to remain calm and not rise to the bait. She was a professional and she had a job to do. Of course, she still hadn't forgiven Alice for the cruel way in which she had treated her, but it made it even worse that Alice didn't seem to have the foggiest idea of what she had done. What a bitch! What made her think she could trample all over the 'little people' and get away with it? Tanya had never met anybody so selfish in her life. It was as if she thought her good looks and her little bit of fame in Ireland gave her the right to treat people like dirt.

Tanya had never forgotten that day she'd worked with Alice even though it was a long time ago now. She'd been so excited about getting to work on a shoot with one of Ireland's top models. Having just graduated from beauty college, Tanya had been determined to make a name for herself in the industry. All she'd needed was a bit of experience at the time to kick start her career so she'd signed up to an agency in an attempt to gain valuable exposure. Her new agent had phoned shortly after she'd signed up with an interesting proposal to put to her. Ireland's top model, Alice Adams, was going to be doing a six-page fashion shoot with a major glossy magazine for their special Christmas issue. It would be accompanied by a lengthy interview and it would also be the cover story for that issue. Of course there wouldn't be any payment involved because of low budgets but it would be invaluable experience for a novice like Tanya and she would be credited in the photo shoot as the make-up artist who'd worked her magic on Alice. Tanya had been over the moon after the surprise phone call. You just couldn't pay for that kind of exposure and goodness only knew what it might lead to. If she did a really good job then other people would notice and start booking her and, hopefully, Alice would be pleased and would recommend her to all her model friends.

She had arrived early at Alice's apartment as requested

and had spent a couple of hours making the Irish model look like a queen. At first she had given Alice a soothing facial using the most expensive products on the market followed by a make-over using Shiseido foundation and beautiful gold- and chocolate-coloured eye shadow that made her subject look like a screen goddess. Then she had used Lancôme powder to keep her whole look complete along with the best Estée Lauder lip pencil and deep red lipstick from Christian Dior. Alice had looked like a young Sophia Loren thanks to Tanya's expert skills with the make-up brush and she had looked amazing in the photo shoot, which had taken place in the sumptuous surroundings of the Ritz Carlton hotel in Powerscourt, Enniskerry.

Alice hadn't been particularly friendly before the shoot and when Tanya had asked for clean towels to work with, the model had simply shrugged and said there weren't any. In fact, Alice's apartment had been a bit of a tip. Underwear was flung on the carpets, dishes had been left unwashed in the sink, there was no loo roll in the upstairs bathroom and saucers full of cigarette butts and half-drunk tins of Diet Coke had been left in various unusual locations around the place. Tanya couldn't understand how a girl that beautiful did not seem to take any pride in where she lived. If only Tanya could have afforded such a luxury apartment. She would have looked after it so well with pretty vases of flowers in every room and bowls of fresh fruit on the tables. Alice didn't even seem to have any food in the house and when Tanya went to make herself a cup of tea she discovered the milk in the fridge was three days past its sell-by date.

Alice had spent most of her time yapping on her mobile phone as Tanya worked diligently on her face. At one stage she had even ordered Tanya to go out to the shop for her and buy her a packet of Marlboro Lights and an egg sandwich with strictly no mayo or butter. Oh yes, Tanya could remember the day like it was just last week whereas Alice, now lying on the salon bed waiting to have her eyebrows waxed, had obviously no recollection of it whatsoever.

'Don't take too much off,' Alice ordered. 'I don't want to look like an alien.'

'Don't worry,' Tanya promised through gritted teeth. 'I'll just do a tidy-up.'

Some things never changed. Tanya could see that now. Alice was still obviously used to giving orders. But that day, all those years ago, when Tanya had been treated as some kind of skivvy, she hadn't complained as she knew she'd have to act humbly in order to get the valuable experience and see her name in print in the magazine.

She had stuck around for the whole day and was there when the stylist arrived with expensive designer dresses for Alice to wear for her shoot. Alice had claimed to have fallen in love with all the six dresses but had nearly gagged when the stylist had told her how much they cost. Over a thousand euros each!

Alice had asked for a discount but the stylist had insisted that the dresses weren't for sale as they were one-off sample dresses.

At the end of the shoot, Tanya had come home and collapsed into bed that night with exhaustion. She woke the following day to find a missed call on her mobile phone. She rang the unknown number and was surprised to find herself speaking to the stylist from the shoot the day before.

'Hi. It's Sharon, the stylist from yesterday. Can I talk to you for a sec?'

'Sure,' said Tanya, rubbing her eyes. It was very early in the day to be chatting.

'I'm missing a dress from yesterday's shoot. You know the white one with the Swarovski jewels?'

'Of course I remember. It looked fabulous on Alice. How could it have gone missing though?'

'Alice says she doesn't have it. She said to ask you about it as she reckons you could have brought it home by mistake?'

Tanya was flabbergasted. How dare Alice make such an accusation! As if she had brought the dress home! It was an outrageous allegation. She'd rung her agent later to explain to him that she knew nothing about the dress. The agent had already heard the story. Apparently the stylist had phoned him too and made it very clear that the magazine would not be able to work with Tanya again

Her agent didn't blame her, however. 'This is off the record, Tanya,' he confided in hushed tones, 'but Alice Adams is well-known for being a bitch. Fair play to you for surviving the day with her. If you can tolerate divas like her, you're bound to go far in this industry. I know Alice probably stole the dress and is conveniently blaming it on you, but I believe in karma and one day that girl will get what's coming to her.'

Tanya was so relieved, but she was nonetheless

devastated that there was now a black mark hanging over her character.

'When will the magazine be out, do you know?' she enquired.

'They work a month in advance so you've got to be patient.'

It was agonising having to work that long but Tanya busied herself by putting an ad up in her local supermarket to do make-up for private weddings. She got a few jobs out of it and her customers were happy and recommended her to their friends, but the money was barely enough to survive on and she was spending too many days in front of the TV waiting for the phone to ring.

Eventually it was the day of the magazine publication. Tanya, when she woke up that morning, had thrown on a tracksuit and practically run down to the local Spar in order to see the shoot. Sure enough the magazine had just arrived and the shop assistant pointed it out to her. And there was Alice on the front cover. She looked absolutely stunning. Tanya picked up the magazine and frantically scanned the pages until she reached Alice's shoot. All six pages of it. The model looked like a goddess and the shoot was good enough for *Vogue*, Tanya thought proudly. On page six she checked the credits. The hotel was thanked, as was the photographer, the model and the hairdresser, but the make-up artist wasn't credited at all. Tanya felt her heart hit the floor. This could not be happening. There was no way. She turned over the page and anxiously skimmed through Alice's interview. Perhaps she had thanked Tanya in the interview. But no, nothing. The interview was all about Alice waffling on about how great she was. Tanya felt completely deflated. Never in her whole life had anybody used her so blatantly. Not only had she worked the whole day for free and hadn't been credited, but she had also been accused of thieving! The whole experience had wrecked her confidence. She'd been so eager about starting out on her own and had big dreams of working with the stars and maybe even ending up on a TV lifestyle show occasionally to give her beauty tips for the season. That had been the dream, anyway. All she'd needed was a foot in the door but Alice had slammed that door of opportunity in her face.

After that unpleasant experience she had taken down her little handwritten ad from the local supermarket and had started applying to beauty salons for a permanent job where she'd have a guaranteed wage every week with tips. Dee Tully had phoned her immediately after receiving her CV. She'd needed somebody straight away as she was about to go on study leave. The small but popular salon was based in Drumcondra and she would be working with just one other girl, Rose. Was Tanya interested? Was she what? Tanya didn't even have to think about it. She jumped at the opportunity. That was five years ago and she was still working in the same salon. She had put the whole Alice fiasco behind her and hadn't seen the girl since. Till now.

'Now, this will be quick,' said Tanya, applying the hot wax to Alice's brows.

'Good,' Alice said. 'Because I haven't got all day. I barely slept on the plane.'

The girl was still as charmless as ever, Tanya thought grimly. She had a good mind to wax off Alice's brows completely as revenge for what the other girl had done to her all those years ago. Immediately she berated herself for thinking such wicked, unprofessional thoughts. She was an upstanding beautician and would treat all her clients with respect. She stripped off the stray eyebrow hairs as Alice flinched and then she plucked a couple between her brows.

She gave Alice a little mirror to examine the results. Alice said nothing, her face set in a scowl. Tanya decided not to take any notice.

'You'll notice some redness for a while but that should die down and I wouldn't recommend putting on any eye make-up for a while.'

'Yeah, I know all that, I've had my eyebrows done before,' Alice snapped uncharitably. 'Can we do my eyelash tint now?' she added, glancing at her watch.

'Your eyelashes are quite dark anyway.'

'I know but I want them darker to save me putting on mascara every single day,' Alice said before lying back down on the bed again like Lady Muck.

It didn't take Tanya very long to dye Alice's long lashes and soon the model was ready to go.

'How much do I owe you?' Alice opened her handbag. Tanya noted that it was the latest Yves Saint Laurent design. Obviously Alice's career had gone from strength to strength and she was doing very well for herself.

'You can settle with Rose outside.' Tanya grinned plastically, relieved to be seeing the back of Alice.

'Okay, I will. What did you say your name was again?'

'I didn't, but it's Tanya. Tanya Thomson.'

'I'll try and remember that when I'm booking for my

next appointment then. You do spray tans here too, don't you?'

'We do.' Tanya nodded.

'Good, because this LA tan won't last for ever. Well, bye.'

And she was gone. Tanya felt a little light-headed and had to sit down for a minute. Meeting Alice unexpectedly like that had been her worst nightmare. Suddenly there was a knock on the cubicle door. Oh God, had Alice left something behind? Couldn't she just go?

'Come in,' she called weakly. But it wasn't Alice. It was Rose.

'Hold out your hand.' Her colleague smirked.

'Why?'

'Just do as you're told.'

Tanya held out the palm of her hand and Rose pressed something into it. Tanya looked down. It was a fifty-cent coin.

'A tip from Her Majesty, that last client of yours,' Rose giggled. 'Try not to spend it all at once.'

12

Tanya agreed to meet Eddie in Ron Blacks on Dawson Street for a post-work drink. Tanya hadn't seen him since he'd suggested moving in with her. She'd said she needed some time to make her decision. Now a week later she still hadn't quite made up her mind. She loved Eddie and didn't think she'd ever love anybody as much as him but she knew deep down that she would much prefer to be Eddie's wife than his live-in lover. Or partner. She hated that word. As if your other half was some sort of business colleague. But she didn't want to bring up the subject of marriage herself. Eddie was the man and it was only right for him to suggest it.

She sat just inside the large window of the busy Dawson Street pub and ordered a gin and tonic and flicked through the *Evening Herald*. She didn't have to wait too long as Eddie soon joined her. He looked dapper in a navy suit, crisp white shirt and wide silver tie. He removed his jacket and cashmere scarf and hung them over the seat.

'What's that you're having?' He nodded at Tanya's glass.

'A gin and tonic but I won't have another one. I'm

trying to be good.' She smiled up at her handsome boyfriend.

He went to the bar and came back minutes later with his drink. 'You look stunning, by the way.' He grinned, pinching her cheek tenderly.

'Thanks, I don't feel like it. A few crusty clients today. Sometimes I think nobody appreciates me.'

'Of course they do.'

'Anyway you seem to be in great form. Why is there a smile on your face, Eddie?'

'Well, meeting you for a start, stranger. I was beginning to forget what you looked like.'

'Haha.'

'So have you thought any more about us moving in together?' he asked, pulling at his fingers somewhat nervously.

'Yes, I have.'

'And?'

'I think it's a good idea.'

Eddie looked pleasantly surprised, and then leaned towards her and planted a tender kiss on her lips. 'Really? That's the best bit of news I've had all day. You don't know how happy you've just made me feel.'

She knew he wasn't joking. His face was the picture of happiness and his eyes sparkled. Tanya could hardly believe how much her decision had meant to him.

'But where will we live?' she wondered aloud. 'I mean, we'd better start looking at houses straight away. What do you have in mind?'

Eddie cleared his throat and then took a sip of his gin and tonic as Tanya waited patiently for his response.

'I have some good news for us,' he said enthusiastically, putting down his glass. 'Why do you think I was so keen to meet you this evening? My parents want us to move into their house in Stillorgan.'

Tanya nearly fell off the seat in surprise. Eddie had *got* to be joking. Did he honestly think she'd be willing to move in with his folks? Like what kind of a crazy idea was that? Personally she couldn't think of anything more daunting. Would she be expected to join the Toners for supper in the evenings? Would she be prepared to discuss recipes with his mother while Eddie and his dad watched the football in the room next door? Would his mother bring them breakfast in bed and the Sunday papers at the weekends? The whole idea simply filled her with horror. There was no way she'd agree to it. She was definitely going to put her foot down on this one.

'I'm sorry, Eddie, it's out of the question.'

She watched her boyfriend's face fall. She hated to have to disappoint him but really, the whole idea was just absurd.

'Don't shoot me down just yet, Tanya. Hear me out, okay?'

She nodded and toyed with her drink. He could say whatever he liked but she wasn't moving in with his family. That would be ten times worse than sharing with her own family. At least family members could disagree with each other and then make up later, but with strangers you couldn't do that. Tanya would have to be on her best behaviour all the time, talking about gardening with Eddie's dad and shopping with his mum. She gave an involuntary shudder at the mere thought of it.

'My parents wouldn't be there of course, silly. You didn't think that they would be, did you?' Tanya shook her head vigorously, afraid to speak. She let Eddie continue.

'You see, now that my dad has retired they've decided to move to Spain. Dad can play his golf there and Mum's planning on writing that romance book that she's always been threatening to write. It makes sense for them to go. They both love the sun and they already have friends living in the Costa del Sol. They've even said we don't have to pay them rent, just pay our bills and keep the house nice.'

Tanya couldn't believe what she was hearing. Eddie's parents' house in Stillorgan was a luxurious semi-detached house with a fine garden. It was very tastefully furnished with deep carpets and fabulous paintings hanging on the walls. There was so much room there that sometimes you wouldn't even know if there was anybody in the house. It was just so unbelievably generous of them to make such an offer. Mind you, Eddie's parents didn't exactly need the rent. They'd always worked. His dad had been a top dentist and his mother, a part-time florist, also owned a further two properties in Rathmines.

'They're going to leave Prince with us because they feel he might not like the heat over there. But I told them you love dogs and that we wouldn't mind taking him for regular walks.'

'You did?' Imagine! Eddie and his parents had clearly discussed this move in depth without even letting her know. They were obviously a lot more liberal than her own parents who still hadn't exactly come around to the idea that their eldest daughter was contemplating living with a man who wasn't her husband.

'Yeah, we can take him down to Sandymount Strand or UCD and let him run around. So what do you think? Isn't it a great idea?'

'Well, of course I don't mind looking after the dog, I love animals, but location-wise your folks' house is a long way from the salon . . .' Tanya said hesitantly. Much as she thought this was a dream offer, she had to carefully weigh up all the options.

'Okay, I get you, but we could think of some way around it. I'd love you to come and live in the house with me, Tanya. That way we could still manage to save enough money to buy our own house one day.'

That put a smile on Tanya's face. She was glad when Eddie brought up the future. And it was also a good sign that Eddie's parents wanted her and trusted her to move into their house. Maybe they saw her as a potential daughter-in-law.

'Can you give me till tomorrow to think about it?' she pleaded with Eddie.

'Sure. I know it's a big decision, and I've kind of just sprung it on to you. Now, do you want to stay for another or will I give you a lift home?'

'I'd like to go home now,' Tanya said putting on her coat. 'I've a lot of thinking to do.'

That night Tanya didn't sleep very well. She tossed and turned in the bed wondering what was the best thing to do. She couldn't very well turn down Eddie's parents' kind invitation to stay in their house, and she knew she'd be very happy living in the Stillorgan home. They could have barbecues out the back in the summer and share a chilled bottle of wine at the weekends. They could light fires and curl up on the enormous sofa just like a happily married couple. Only they wouldn't be married, she thought doubtfully. If Eddie really loved her wouldn't he have proposed instead of simply asking her to move in and share his bed? Also, she really didn't want to give up her job. She liked working with Rose and Dee was a great boss. You actually couldn't meet a better one. She had always encouraged Rose and herself to do extra training courses and had paid for them. And there were never any problems about taking holidays or time off when you really needed it.

It was now 2 a.m. and still Tanya couldn't sleep. It had been a very weird day altogether. Imagine seeing Alice, of all people, in the salon today. That girl had really knocked her confidence all those years ago. Then again should she really be blaming Alice for the way things had or indeed had not turned out for her? Maybe Tanya should have kept going regardless. Everyone in life got knocks but the trick was being able to deal with them. Had she quit too soon? Had she been too eager to take the easy way out and work for somebody else? She'd been working for Dee for five years now and although she enjoyed the job sometimes she'd watch *Ireland AM* on TV3 in the mornings before going to work and look on enviously as some beauty therapist with just the same qualifications as herself did make-overs on ordinary people and made them look extraordinary. I could do that, Tanya always thought wistfully as she prepared to leave the house for the long commute across town.

Tanya sat up in bed. She was wide awake now. Suddenly everything made sense. She could still make a go of it on her own. She wasn't even thirty yet. She had years ahead of her in which to make a name for herself. Maybe, just maybe, this was a sign that she should try freelancing again. There was nothing about the beauty trade that she didn't know and no treatment she couldn't handle. She could get some business cards professionally done instead of just sticking up an amateur-looking notice in the supermarket. She might even advertise in one of the glossy magazines. An investment like that was bound to pay dividends. Lots of busy women didn't have the time to be going to beauty salons so she could go to their houses. If the clients were pleased with her efforts then word of mouth would help her. She could apply to the film companies, ad agencies and fashion photographers to see if they needed a make-up artist. The more she thought about it the more excited she became. She wished it wasn't such a God-awful hour of the morning or else she'd be able to ring Eddie and discuss her plans with him. She was sure he'd be supportive. Eddie always encouraged her in whatever she wanted to do and she reckoned he'd be a help rather than a hindrance. She'd also contact some of the country's top model agencies to see if any of the models needed help doing their make-up for their portfolios. With a bit of luck it would only take a few months to get her name established. After much thought and deliberation, and a bit more tossing and turning, Tanya eventually drifted into a contented sleep dreaming of finally being a celebrated make-up artist to the stars.

Mrs Adams had nearly keeled over in shock when she saw her only daughter standing on the doorstep looking ill and drawn and obviously in much need of a good meal. She threw her arms around her and hugged her like she never wanted to let go.

'I'm so glad you're back, darling,' she whimpered, a lone tear escaping down her cheek.

'I'm glad I'm back too, Mum,' Alice said, delighted that her mother was being so welcoming.

She'd half expected her mother to be cross with her for arriving unannounced on the doorstep. She couldn't have been more wrong, however. Alice found herself being treated like the proverbial prodigal daughter. Even when her father had received a text message from his wife saying that Alice was back he'd rushed home early from work but not before stopping at a garage to buy flowers to welcome her home.

Her mother had immediately cooked them all a big plate of spaghetti Bolognese and Mr Adams had served fresh strawberries and cream for dessert.

'I should go away more often,' Alice beamed at them, 'if this is the kind of welcome I'm going to be getting each time I come home.'

'We've missed you,' said her father, squeezing her hand tenderly.

'Look at you, you're skin and bone.' Her mother frowned with concern.

'Am I really?' Alice brightened. 'Do you think I've lost weight? I wouldn't know because Bill didn't have weighing scales.'

She noticed her parents exchange wary glances at the mention of Bill's name. They'd made their disapproval pretty obvious when she'd announced out of the blue that she was moving to the US to live with a man she barely knew. They'd thought it was scandalous and had told her so. At least Mrs Adams had. Her father hadn't said much but the expression on his face had left Alice in no doubt how he felt about the whole thing.

'But he's a foreigner,' her mother had said repeatedly in a bid to make her stay at home and see sense. 'Could you not find yourself a nice sensible Irish man?'

'There are no decent Irish men,' Alice had answered gruffly. 'You've no idea what it's like in Dublin. It's incestuous. Everybody goes out with everybody else and there's never anybody new on the scene. And besides, Bill isn't a foreigner, he's American. He speaks English.'

Her father had shaken his head wearily. 'I don't understand it. There must be plenty of young, decent hard-working men out there but you won't find them in nightclubs, Alice. You're going to all the wrong places to try and meet somebody.'

Though at the time Alice had ignored their advice and their pleas not to go to America, she now had to admit to herself that they'd been right.

She looked from one to the other and was suddenly struck by how old they both looked. In their sixties now, they both had snow-white hair and although her dad still worked part-time at UCD as a history lecturer, her mother had long since given up her teaching job. They didn't do very much with their lives and had been married to each other for almost forty years. Suddenly it dawned on Alice that the reason they had been so protective of her all these years was because they had nothing else in their lives to focus on. She was their only daughter, their pride and joy. It was almost pathetic how pleased they were to see her, she thought to herself as she studiously sipped her wine. Of course her mother had written to her when she was in America, mostly boring letters about the neighbours and stories concerning the people in the bridge club. Alice hadn't written back because she wasn't much of a letter writer but she had phoned them a couple of times just to tell them she was having a great time and that she'd no intention of coming back to Ireland. Now she was home despite all her bravado. And she was at a huge advantage in that now they would probably be really nice to her in order to make sure she wouldn't leave again.

'Listen,' she said, draining her glass of sparkling water and immediately topping it up again, 'I just want to say how glad I am that I'm home. I missed you two a lot.'

Alice could see her parents' faces brighten and saw how easily they were pleased. She decided to continue humouring them.

'Oh I know', she continued sycophantically, 'that I haven't been the best daughter in the world and that I wasn't very good at keeping in touch, but you were in my thoughts every night and I always said a prayer for you at Mass.'

'You went to Mass over there?' Her mother looked too thrilled for words.

'Of course,' Alice lied. 'Bill wasn't a Catholic so being at the church was really the only chance I had to be by myself. I even met an Irish priest over there who said Mass and it was only after talking to him one day that I realised that my heart belonged in Ireland and that I wanted to come home to my family no matter what. I mean, there are only three of us so it's right that we should stick together.'

She thought her parents were about to explode with pride at this false revelation.

'So will you be staying here for a little while?' her father asked hopefully. 'You're always more than welcome here, you know that.'

'Oh I know. I'd love to stay here for a while. I gave up the lease on my apartment before I left for America but to be honest I don't want to live in town on my own any more. Anyway, it gets lonely being by yourself all the time.'

What Alice conveniently declined to tell her parents was that she was smashed broke and that even if she wanted to rent somewhere in Dublin there was no way in hell she'd be able to afford it. Living in LA meant that all her money had eventually dwindled and she now owed a small fortune on her credit card. Over the next few weeks she would have to work very hard and be extremely careful about spending money.

'Well, your old room is still here, Alice, and I slipped

upstairs earlier and turned on the heating in your room so that it'll be nice and cosy for you. You need to be careful not to catch a cold now since you've been used to the fine weather over in America.'

'Yes,' her father agreed, 'summer isn't quite here yet so make sure you wrap up well when you go outside.'

Alice smiled at them both. She'd forgotten how good it felt to have people fuss over you. Half the time with Bill he didn't even seem to notice she was there.

'So any other news?' she enquired politely. Of course they'd have no news that she'd be interested in. Her father never really talked about anything other than the plants in the garden and her mother's greatest concerns were always the goings-on of the neighbours. Her rambling letters to Alice had been full of useless information like the fact that the O'Briens' little old dog had to be put to sleep, and that the O'Donnells were getting their garage converted. She had even written to tell her that Harriet across the road had just got engaged at the ripe old age of forty and that her elderly mother Mairead was over the moon because they'd thought she'd be a spinster for ever. Like, so what? Not in a million years would Alice ever be able to figure out how her mother thought any of this trivia would be of interest to her. All these people were total nobodies and their mundane lives held no interest at all for Alice.

Mrs Adams rambled on and on about the trees that the council had planted on the road and the fact that the people who lived at number fourteen had applied for planning permission but had been turned down. She spoke about how the neighbourhood watch wasn't really working and that Mrs Durcan in the corner house had been burgled not once but twice in the last year.

'The police took over an hour and a half to arrive the last time,' Mr Adams added. 'The poor woman was terrified as she was in the house at the time. It was some foreign national and he still hasn't been caught.'

Alice's mother shook her head at the unfairness of it all. 'But at least she's seen sense now and has got a burglar alarm installed once and for all.'

Alice stifled a yawn. The jet lag was kicking in big time now and she didn't know if she could realistically stand another second of this conversation. She felt her eyes closing. Her warm bed was beckoning.

'. . . and Mrs Toner was showing me pictures of their new house in Spain which she printed off the Internet. They have their own pool and everything. Mind you, it's very small . . .'

Alice felt a sudden jolt at the name 'Toner'. What was all this about Spain? Were the Toners moving away? She remembered seeing Eddie outside the Shelbourne on the same night she had met Bill. Why on earth would he be going to Spain? What would he do out there?

She sat up straight in her chair. 'Are the Toners selling up?' she asked, wide-eyed.

'No, indeed, no,' Mrs Adams said. 'They were thinking about it but an estate agent friend of theirs advised them that this was a bad time to sell, what with house prices falling in the last ten months or so. He told them they'd be better hanging on for a while if they could afford to.'

'So they're going to Spain? Eddie too?'

'Ah no.' Her mother shook her head emphatically. 'Of

course Eddie's not going with them. His life is here. He's young and ambitious. Mind you, I'm sure he'll take advantage of the situation by visiting his parents out there and topping up his tan. They even invited me and your father over there for a week in May. Although, you know how your father hates flying . . .'

'But Eddie doesn't live next door any more, sure he doesn't?' Alice frowned. It had been a long time since she'd seen Eddie around here. When he'd been in college she'd often seen him cycling in and out of his front drive but God, that was years ago now.

'We met him at the Toners' summer party last year, didn't we, darling?' Mrs Adams glanced at her husband. 'I think he said he was living in Sandyford. Awfully handsome man really. I could never understand why you wouldn't have considered him, Alice. He was so much better than most of the yokes you used to entertain.'

Alice shrugged. 'Well, never say never. I might date him yet.'

'You might not get the chance.' Mrs Adams got to her feet and started making herself busy by putting away the dishes. 'He has a long-term girlfriend as far as I know. She was at the party too. Very pretty, polite young thing.'

But Alice didn't want to hear anything more about Eddie Toner's pretty young thing. Whoever she was, she wouldn't last too long now that Alice was back in town.

14

Mr Thomson thought it was a great idea that his daughter Tanya was thinking of going out on her own again.

'You're much more experienced now, love. If it's what you want to do, then do it. Nobody ever made any real money working for somebody else.'

'But it's not for the money I want to do this, Dad,' Tanya insisted. 'Lots of people would like to work for themselves but the fear of the unknown holds them back. But at least by being a freelance beauty therapist I don't have to take out a huge loan to buy a shop or anything. I just need a few trade things, a car which I have already, a phone which I have already and a few hundred decent business cards.'

Her father smiled at her. With that attitude he was sure that Tanya would go far with her venture. Eddie too was delighted with her plans to strike out on her own. The only person who was unsure about the whole thing was Mrs Thomson.

'But I thought you were happy working for Dee,' she sniffed. 'I mean, working for yourself could be dangerous. You could be called out to people's houses not knowing who they are or what to expect.'

'It'll be mostly through word of mouth,' Tanya insisted. 'I'm not going to be silly about this and put my own life at risk. I won't exactly be sticking my phone number in public phone boxes and hoping for the best, you know. I intend to have a chat beforehand with any new clients before I call out to them to make sure I get a good feeling about them. And I won't be doing men,' she added firmly.

'Well, that's something anyway,' her mother said, sounding relieved.

The more Tanya thought about it, the more she got excited about her new business venture. No more getting up in the dark and travelling across the city in the traffic. She could pick and choose her hours. Now that summer was nearly here, people would start thinking about booking holidays in the sun and they would want to get their fake tan done and their legs and underarms waxed so that they'd look nice on the beach. If the business went really well and she found herself being inundated with appointments then she could always rope in another beautician to share the workload. Now, all she had to do was give Dee her notice and tell Rose she was leaving. She wasn't looking forward to doing either.

Just as she had feared, Rose began to cry when Tanya broke the news to her before the salon opened for business that Friday. She sobbed into her tissue till there were no tears left.

Alarmed, Tanya had handed her another box of tissues.

'I'm not going for good, you know. Hopefully Dee will allow me to stay on for a couple of days a week.' She smiled kindly, wrapping her arms around Rose's bony frame.

'But it won't be the same without you working here every day,' said Rose.

'Nothing ever does stay the same in life,' Tanya said philosophically. 'But that doesn't mean we won't stay in touch. And you'll make friends with the new girl, I'm sure.'

'Have you told Dee?' asked the other girl, wiping her eyes so that her black mascara streaked her face.

Tanya shook her head. 'She said she'd be around after lunch to go through the accounts. I'll tell her then. I don't really want to leave but my circumstances have changed now. I really want to make a go of this.'

'I've often thought of leaving,' said Rose in a quiet voice before blowing her nose loudly.

'You have?'

Tanya was amazed. This was the first she'd heard anything about Rose wanting to leave.

Rose noticed the look of surprise on her colleague's face and gave a little smile. 'Oh, don't get me wrong, Tanya. I mean I do like working for Dee but I think deep down everyone dreams of doing their own thing and, you know, really making it and being somebody, but with Johnny it's not possible any more. When you've a kid you're limited to what you can do. All your dreams and ambitions kind of have to take a back seat, so you're right, Tanya. Seize the moment. Once you've kids everything will be different, believe me.'

'Everything happens for a reason and you're just the best mum in the world. I hope one day Johnny realises how lucky he is. Now, dry your eyes and let me put the kettle on. I think we both need a strong cup of tea before facing the general public.'

While Rose went off to the Ladies to dry her eyes and redo her make-up, Tanya popped a tea bag in each mug and listened to the kettle whistle. She really was touched by Rose's reaction to her leaving. It was nice to know that somebody you worked with cared that much about you. She pondered Rose's words carefully. She'd never thought of the other girl as having ambitions of her own as she'd always seemed to be so happy-go-lucky and never really talked about anything except Johnny or Johnny's father. This morning Tanya had seen a different side to her. Rose had dreams just like everybody else. Everybody was the star of a show called 'My Life' and Rose was no exception. Nobody wanted to be just another cog in the wheel. The problem, though, was that most people waited around for things to happen to them instead of getting out there and doing something about it. It was scary putting yourself out there because it made you insecure and everything could backfire. But that was a chance Tanya was prepared to take.

When Dee arrived at 2 p.m. and parked her sleek navy BMW outside the salon, Tanya's heart gave a little leap. Now that it was crunch time she could feel the butterflies forming in her stomach. What if she wasn't making the right decision after all? There might be no going back. She'd never actually resigned from a job before. She wasn't sure if she was supposed to write an actual letter of resignation and formally hand it in or not. Eventually she decided to tell her boss face to face. Dee was more like a friend to her. She couldn't imagine just wordlessly handing her a letter to say she was off.

Tanya took a deep breath and knocked on the door of Dee's tiny office.

Her boss was wearing her glasses and was deep in thought at the computer. Tanya hoped this wasn't a bad time for her.

'Do you mind if I have a word, Dee?'

'Not at all, Tanya, have a seat there. What can I do for you, pet?'

Tanya took a seat opposite her employer and clasped her hands together to prevent them from shaking. She'd had no idea that she'd be so nervous.

'I've been thinking a lot recently, Dee. As you know, Eddie and I are moving in together to his old family home in Stillorgan and—'

'So you're leaving us . . .' Dee interrupted with an air of resignation.

Tanya was stunned. How did she know?

'I always knew the time would come. In fact, to tell you the truth, Tanya, I know I'm lucky to have held on to you for so long. I knew the time would come when you'd inevitably want to spread your wings. You're a bright young girl with your whole future ahead of you.'

Tanya felt a wave of relief instantly wash over her. There was no trace of anger in Dee's open face. Just a hint of sadness, maybe, which made Tanya feel a bit guilty. She felt bad for letting people down.

'I'll stay till you find somebody else,' she promised. 'I wouldn't just walk out on you. You've been really good to me.'

'And you've been really good for the salon. The customers love you and I'm sure they'll miss you.'

'I can still work a bit part time?' Tanya suggested hopefully.

'That's very kind of you, and I appreciate it, but I'll probably have to find somebody who will work full time if she can.'

'Maybe even Saturdays?'

'Well, if you could work Saturdays for a while that would be fantastic, Tanya. Obviously Saturday, as you know, is our busiest day so we can always use a helping hand but you'll probably be so busy in your new job . . . of course I'll write you an excellent letter of reference . . .'

'I'm not leaving to go and work for anybody else, Dee. I want to break out on my own and see if I can make it.'

Dee smiled at her. She would miss Tanya enormously. She was such a diligent employee and had never given her a minute's trouble. 'I'm sure you'll do exceptionally well. I know you will. You deserve to. And I know exactly how you feel. I, too, worked for other people before I started up this place and I never once regretted going out on my own.'

Impulsively, Tanya leaned over and gave her boss a hug, something that she'd never dreamed of doing before. She felt a lone tear escape down her cheek. Good God, she hadn't expected this to be such an emotional day . . .

15

Alice woke up to the sound of the neighbour's dog barking next door. Good Jesus, would he ever put a sock in it? What an annoying creature. She wondered if he was a new addition to the Toner household. She never remembered them having a dog before. Maybe they'd got a mutt to replace Eddie when he moved out. She laughed privately at her own little joke and then eased herself up into a sitting position in the bed. What time of the day was it? The curtains were closed so it was hard to tell and she wasn't wearing a watch. That long flight home from LA had really knocked the stuffing out of her. She'd woken up three times already during the night and her body clock was all over the place now. Was it morning, afternoon or evening? She really didn't have the foggiest. She supposed she'd better get out of bed and find out. She stuck on a pair of her old fluffy pink slippers and a matching dressing gown and headed downstairs. The house was empty and the kitchen was spotless. Her parents had obviously finished their breakfast and had gone out for the day. The clock hanging on the wall told her it was almost noon. That meant it was still the middle of the night back in LA. She stuck on the kettle and searched in the kitchen cupboard for some coffee. Where was Bill now? she wondered fleetingly. Was he out entertaining clients or was he at home in bed? Maybe in bed with Mindy? Not that it mattered now to her anyway. She'd left him and had no regrets. At least that's what she kept telling herself. She refused to allow herself to miss him. Why would she waste time missing somebody who so obviously didn't miss her? He hadn't even sent her a text. Wasn't he worried that something might have happened to her? Did he really not give that much of a fuck?

She stepped outside, took her packet of cigarettes from her dressing-gown pocket and lit up. The sun was shining but there was a slight nip in the air. Mind you, after LA, no wonder it seemed cold here. She puffed away on her cigarette as she contemplated the shambles that her life was now. She was thirty, unemployed, unmarried and completely broke. Where had it all gone so wrong for her? Why hadn't she been able to make her relationship with Bill work? Maybe she hadn't put enough effort into it. Maybe she had come home too soon without giving LA life a proper go. That once-in-a-lifetime opportunity would never come her way again. That was for sure. Then again, she had to be realistic about Bill and not look back on their relationship through rose-tinted spectacles. If he had cheated on her with Mindy, God only knew who else he'd been cheating with. Maybe that woman she'd seen him with in the mall hadn't been an old friend after all. No, she was far better off without him. Good riddance to him and all that. Still, she couldn't help feeling quite insecure about what the future held for her now. After all, she'd once been described in all the papers as the next big thing. But that wasn't exactly today or yesterday. If only they could see her now, how they would laugh. Oh God, she really needed to get her act together and to stop wallowing in self-pity. That would get her nowhere. She couldn't just be lazing around here getting under her parents' feet and getting fat. She'd have to make things happen and start making them happen today.

She supposed she'd better start by ringing Danny, her old model agent. She wasn't looking forward to making that phone call one bit. He'd be more than surprised to hear from her all right. And she certainly wasn't expecting him to jump up and down in excitement now that she was home. He was a sarcastic prick at the best of times anyway and he'd surely want to know why she wasn't still living the high life over in America like she'd pretended to everybody she was doing. Oh well, she'd just have to swallow her pride, she thought wryly to herself as she stamped out her cigarette on the bird bath halfway down the garden. She'd better hide the stub in case her parents saw it. If there was one vice neither of them could stand it was smoking.

That blasted dog was still barking, she noticed. What was wrong with him? Something made her walk to the wall and have a peek over it. Dogs should be seen and not heard and she wanted to get a look at the culprit that was making all this noise. She stood on her tiptoes and craned her neck. Nothing could have prepared her for the shock of coming face to face with old Mr Toner. He had a pair of shears in his hand. He'd obviously been about to clip around the shed but just seeing him there with his shears up in the air like some kind of dangerous weapon almost made her scream out loud.

'Well, if it isn't young Alice!' He grinned at her as she waited for her heartbeat to return to normal. 'We thought you were off in America.'

'I was,' she replied, caught off guard. 'But I'm back now.' She smiled at him. She almost forgave him for giving her such a fright as he'd called her 'young Alice'.

'But don't you miss the sun?'

'I only got back yesterday so I haven't had time to miss it. Anyway, it gets boring waking up to the sun every day after a while. I don't mind a bit of rain now and then.'

'Well, myself and Mrs Toner have had more than enough rain here in this country to last us for a lifetime. We're going to live in Spain. Were your parents telling you?'

'Mum mentioned it all right,' Alice replied flippantly. She didn't want him to think they'd spent the night talking about the neighbours as if they had nothing going on in their own lives.

Mr Toner lowered his voice. 'My better half has arthritis, you know. The doctors have said that moving to Spain will do her the world of good.'

'Oh, I'm sorry to hear that, but yes, the climate in Spain will be great for you both, I'm sure. So what will you do with Mister Noisy there?' Alice suddenly spotted the Kerry Blue in the next-door garden. He'd now mysteriously shut up and was staring at her curiously with his head tilted to one side.

'That's Prince. We're going to have to leave him behind, I'm afraid.'

'But who will look after him?'

'Well, my son Eddie is going to come and live here so

we'll leave him in his capable hands. He's quite a handful as you can see. He's not even a year old so hopefully he'll calm down as he gets older. He needs quite a lot of exercise. My wife used to take him for long walks when he was a puppy but he's very strong now and she can't handle him on the lead any more. He goes crazy when he sees other dogs out and about.'

'I'll take him for a walk if you like,' Alice offered and then nearly bit her tongue off. What was she thinking? She didn't want to be responsible for a lunatic like that out and about on the streets of Dublin.

But Mr Toner suddenly brightened at the impromptu offer. 'That would be great.' He beamed. 'Are you sure you could handle him?'

'No better woman,' Alice replied, digging herself in deeper. 'I'm mad about animals. My mother would never let me get a dog when I was younger because she's allergic to dog hair.'

'Is that so?'

Alice nodded. What a random conversation this was. She should be making herself busy ringing the agency instead of offering to look after looney dogs that didn't even belong to her. Then again, it was so boring walking without a dog and she needed an excuse. She wanted to be as fit as a fiddle before turning up to castings again. She'd let herself go in LA and needed to get back on track ASAP. 'I'll take him this afternoon if you like,' she added before giving herself a chance to change her mind.

'I'll hold you to it,' said Mr Toner with a big grin, unable to hide his delight.

They shook hands on it over the wall and Mr Toner

went back to his gardening, thinking what a nice young woman Alice had turned out to be. And Alice went back inside the house, thinking that it was very clever of her to offer to do a bit of dog walking. Now she didn't need an excuse to drop into the Toner home any time she liked.

16

A fortnight after handing in her notice, Tanya found herself seated at the exclusive Chapter One restaurant in Parnell Street with Dee and Rose. It was her farewell party and it was so hard to believe it had come around so fast.

The three women laughed, raised their glasses and made a toast to the future. Dee insisted that there would be no more shop talk for the rest of the evening. They were here to enjoy themselves and that was that. Rose had even got a babysitter so she could stay out dancing. It had been ages since Tanya had had a proper night out. She'd been so busy getting her cards printed and contacting magazines about the price of putting in a small ad offering her services. Since telling her regular clients she was leaving, she'd had at least ten further enquiries about private-home bookings. People seemed more than willing for her to come to their houses to do beauty treatments and they promised to recommend her to all their friends. Tanya was feeling more and more confident about her situation and now that she'd made her decision it was also time to start thinking about her new home life with Eddie. His parents would be leaving the country for good in three weeks and

Eddie wanted them to settle in as quickly as possible once they were gone. They'd decided to sleep in Eddie's old room and his parents had said it was fine if they wanted to redecorate it. Tanya thought it was most generous of them and was already looking forward to going to places like Laura Ashley, Meadows & Byrne, and upstairs in Arnotts to look for ideas. It would be nice for her to put her own stamp on the place and it was exciting. As though herself and Eddie were a real married couple moving into their new home. Of course, it would be infinitely better if they *were* getting married but she wasn't going to allow herself to be negative. All that would come in good time; she just had to be patient.

'Are you ready to order?' The waiter appeared at their table, bringing Tanya straight back to reality. She shouldn't be thinking about Eddie or her new business venture tonight. Instead she would concentrate on having some girlie fun. She deserved it.

The women chatted about everything and anything. Dee told them that she'd booked a fortnight's holiday to Cyprus in June with her mother. She was terribly excited about it because she hadn't been on a sun holiday for two years.

'But who will manage the salon when you're gone?' Rose asked, looking alarmed.

'Well I trust that you'll manage it when I'm gone,' said her employer with an air of confidence. 'You could run the salon in your sleep at this stage, Rose. I couldn't think of anybody more capable.'

Rose couldn't hide her smile. She looked like she was about to burst with pride.

'Oh God, I won't let you down, Dee, I promise you. In fact, I was thinking of going away at the end of August myself. Maybe to Paris. I've always dreamed of visiting that city. I don't fancy going to a hotel in a sun resort with just me and Johnny and lots of other couples canoodling at the pool. I just want to go somewhere where we won't stand out.'

'Paris would be amazing.' Tanya nodded her encouragement. 'You deserve to go away and have some fun.'

'Are you going to take any holidays yourself, Tanya?'

'I'm not sure. I usually go off on a cheap last-minute package somewhere with Dianne, and Eddie heads off with the boys. But now that Eddie and I'll be living together it might be more appropriate to go somewhere by ourselves.'

'You still shouldn't rule out a holiday with Dianne though,' Dee advised. 'A break away never does anyone any harm. And besides, absence makes the heart grow fonder. Everybody knows that.'

Maybe she was right, Tanya thought, tucking into her delicious goat's cheese salad. Until she was married to Eddie and had his ring firmly on the ring finger of her left hand, she should at least try and hold on to her independence. Anyway, she wouldn't really be on for a mad girlie holiday where Dianne would be dragging her out to all the Irish pubs. A couple of years ago Dianne had insisted that the two of them go off to Playa del Ingles in Gran Canaria and the trip had been a bit of a nightmare if Tanya was being completely honest with herself. Dianne had wanted to party all night and sleep all day and Tanya had been so exhausted after the holiday that she'd come back feeling she needed another holiday to recover! If she was going away again this year she'd prefer to go somewhere quieter for some serious sun worshipping and lots of R and R.

After their starters the girls sipped on some fine Burgundy wine and waited for their main courses to be served.

'What are the plans for later, girls?' asked Dee. 'It's been a long time since I've hit the clubbing scene in Dublin. It's all probably changed now.'

'We might go to Krystle?' Tanya suggested. 'That's the new in place now. It's really nice and one of the managers knows Eddie so we can go up to the VIP area and relax. There's even a bed up there. It's a green leather bed. How cool can you get?'

'Oh, let's go there then,' said Rose excitedly. 'The only place I've gone to this year is Tamangos and even that's been a while. It's just so handy for me getting home as I live so far from town.'

'Well, you two Northsiders can get a taxi home together later,' Tanya laughed. 'I'll have to go home on my tod I suppose.'

'Unless you get lucky,' Rose teased, 'and then God knows where you'll end up.'

'Ah now, don't be saying that. I'm practically a married woman!'

Only she wasn't, she thought with a hint of disappointment. Living together wasn't the same. It just meant she was restricted because no fellow would be really interested in her if they knew she had a partner at home. Still, on the plus side no woman would be interested in

Eddie if they knew *she* was always waiting at home for him. She decided to push all these negative thoughts to the back of her head. Why couldn't she just be happy with the way things were? Plenty of girls out there would kill to be living with a handsome, caring guy like Eddie. So what if he wasn't putting a ring on her finger just at the moment. She could always buy her own ring. Hell, if her business venture really took off, she could buy a whole jeweller's shop. Their main courses arrived, much to the approval of the three women. The dishes were beautifully presented and smelled divine. Tanya tucked in gratefully, deciding not to even think of the calories involved. The evening passed by pleasantly with lots of fun and banter and after eating their mouth-watering desserts and fighting with Dee over the bill which she insisted on paying, they hailed a taxi outside to bring them into town. As they approached the bottom of Grafton Street, Tanya looked at her watch. Was it really only 11 p.m.? It seemed much later for some reason. Krystle might not even be open yet.

'Let's go to Samsara first,' she suggested.

'I'll go wherever you're going,' said Dee and Rose agreed.

Samsara was heaving, even for a Friday night. The place was thronged with people and there was no chance of getting a table as they were all occupied. Instead they stood at the bar and ordered cocktails. They could hardly hear each other speak over the loud music which was pumping. Tanya brightened considerably as the night wore on. She hadn't had this much fun in ages. Who knew that the other two girls could be so much fun? Wasn't it such a pity that in all the years she'd worked in the salon she'd never organised a night out with Dee and Rose? Apart from their annual Christmas lunches, which they always celebrated in Little Italy in Santry, they'd never socialised together. Maybe that had been a good thing though. Maybe that was why the three of them had always got along so well together. Sure didn't they say that it was a bad idea to mix business with pleasure?

'This was a good choice, Tanya, well done!' Dee shouted to be heard over the music. 'You obviously know all the hot spots in Dublin.'

'Oh, I don't know if that's a good thing though.' Tanya giggled and took a further sip of her Sex on the Beach. It was going down an absolute treat. 'I think I must have been single for far too long. This Dawson Street strip has been my second home for longer than I care to remember!'

'Nonsense, you're only young once.'

'I'm twenty-eight. Hardly a spring chicken.'

'Believe me, you're just a child.'

It suddenly occurred to Tanya that she didn't have a clue what age Dee was. At a random guess she was probably in her mid to late thirties and still looked great on it. With her glowing skin and shiny dark hair she always looked in the best of health and was an excellent advertisement for her own salon. It had paid her well through the years. Tanya vowed that she too would always look her best when meeting her own future clients. Women paid good money to be made gorgeous by their beauty therapists. If you turned up looking any old way, then how could you possibly inspire confidence in them and expect them to hand over their hard-earned cash to you? Her thoughts were interrupted by a tap on her shoulder. She turned around in surprise and was even more amazed when she found herself staring into the dark brown eyes of one of the most incredible-looking men she'd ever seen in her life. He must have been at least six foot three with a chiselled jaw, fair wavy hair and defined cheekbones. Tanya wondered if he was a male model or something.

'Excuse me,' he said in a deep sexy voice, 'I hope I'm not interrupting anything.'

As she had been caught completely unawares, Tanya couldn't think of anything to say. Instead Rose immediately answered for her. 'Of course you're not. I'm Rose, what's your name?' She stuck out her hand cheekily.

Tanya was gobsmacked. For a girl who never stopped talking about her son's father, Rose was well able to chat up a handsome stranger.

'I'm David,' he said, smiling back to reveal a nice straight set of teeth. He was almost too good-looking, Tanya thought. She didn't really trust men who were that good-looking as they were usually too full of themselves. 'Can I get you girls a drink?'

Tanya was decidedly unimpressed. Any fool could see that they were all holding full glasses.

'We're grand, thanks,' she said coolly.

He seemed to be unfazed by the fact that she was showing no particular interest in him.

'I seem to have lost my friends,' he said. 'This place is packed, isn't it? They could be anywhere.'

Tanya looked around. The place was indeed jammed

with punters jostling with each other at the bar trying to get served and people accidently dripping their full pints over other people's heads. 'Why don't you try phoning them?'

'I've tried but it's too loud in here. They probably can't hear their phones.'

'Ah sure, don't worry about it,' said Rose, her apparent eagerness more than making up for Tanya's aloofness. 'You're welcome to hang out with us till you find them.'

Dee seemed to find the whole scenario highly amusing. Tanya noticed a distinctive glint in her eye when she introduced herself. 'I'm Dee,' she said. 'And this is Tanya. So what brings you to Samsara, David?'

'I just came with some of the lads I work with. We usually go out after work on a Friday to unwind. You don't think I put on a suit especially to go to bars, do you?'

The women laughed. It wasn't that unusual to be wearing a suit in here as the place usually attracted a healthy after-work crowd anyway.

'Where do you work?' Rose wanted to know.

'Across the river at the IFSC. I work in banking.'

'Oh, so you'd be a handy person to know if I wanted to take out a loan, wouldn't you?'

Thankfully he seemed to get her sense of humour and laughed at her smart comment. Tanya could feel herself groaning inwardly though. She knew exactly where this conversation would lead. She rarely asked strangers how they earned a crust when she was out socialising because it always meant that they then asked you what you did.

And you ended up explaining your life away and talking about work which really was a pain in the arse.

'So how do you three know each other?' enquired the beautiful man. And yes, he really was quite beautiful, Tanya thought, taking him in. She couldn't believe he was single. How come nobody who looked like that had ever chatted her up when she had been available? It was sod's law, wasn't it? Then again, maybe he wasn't single. Maybe he was even married. It was hard to tell these days. Lots of men didn't wear wedding rings although you could usually tell by the thin white mark where their wedding ring should be. Mind you, this David fellow had a nice tan and no telltale tan marks on any of his fingers as far as she could see. She had checked of course, albeit very subtly.

'We work together,' Rose blurted out as Tanya felt herself wince.

'Really?' David seemed intrigued. Or maybe he was just being polite.

'And where do you all work?'

'At her beauty salon,' Rose said pointing to Dee.

'So you're the boss woman?' He grinned at Dee. 'If you're out with the boss do you have to be on your best behaviour at all times?'

'It's Tanya's going-away party tonight,' she explained, 'so we're allowed to let our hair down on this occasion.'

Tanya felt herself squirm now the attention was focussed on her once again.

'I'm going out on my own into the big bad world.'

'Really?' David said again.

It was hard to tell if he was genuinely being interested

or whether he was just making small talk while waiting for his friends to come back from wherever they'd disappeared to. Still, it was nice to have a bit of male company and he was charming as well as being exceptionally attractive. Not that Tanya would be at all tempted of course. Her heart belonged to Eddie and it wouldn't matter if Brad Pitt himself showed up here tonight. No man could compare to her Eddie.

By now the cocktails had been well and truly drunk and David insisted on buying a round which went down a treat with the three women. Then his mobile phone rang and as it was so loud he went outside to take the call.

Once he was out of earshot, it was time to dissect him, in a good way of course.

'What an absolute dish!' Rose exclaimed, pulling no punches.

'You're telling me,' Dee joined in with her praise. 'I didn't think they made men who looked like that any more.'

'Ah, yeah, but seriously, girls, do you not think he knows he's all that?' said Tanya.

Rose shrugged. 'Maybe so, but I still wouldn't say no, would you? I do admire confidence in a man.'

'Hmm, there's a fine line between confidence and cockiness though.'

He was back. 'My friends have gone to Temple Bar,' he said. 'I told them to get back up here but they've met some women apparently and are happy enough where they are.'

Rose laughed. 'I'm always amazed the way fellas act with each other. You wouldn't find women doing that.'

'Doing what?'

'Well, just leaving a place without saying goodbye to their friends and stuff. If a friend did that to me I'd never speak to her again.'

'Lads are different, I suppose,' he said. 'Oh well, I'm happy enough here,' he added, raising his cocktail glass.

Rose exchanged knowing glances with the girls. She obviously fancied her chances.

There weren't too many people in the VIP suite of Krystle when they got there.

'Don't worry,' Tanya said, slipping off her jacket and putting it on the back of a chair. 'The place will be jammers in half an hour. Just wait and see.'

She went to open her bag to pay for a round but David insisted he pay and got to the bar before her. Tanya pleaded with him to let her pay for the drinks but he wouldn't hear of it. She felt bad. She didn't want him to think she was leading him on. He'd been so generous already and had even paid for the taxi earlier. Rose had kind of made it clear that she fancied him, but Tanya had a suspicious feeling that her feelings weren't being reciprocated. She didn't want Rose to get hurt as she was a sensitive girl at the best of times.

Tanya went back to her seat. As soon as she sat down Rose leaned over to her. Her eyes were a little glassy now and Tanya feared that the drink had maybe gone to her head a bit.

'Do I look okay?' Rose asked.

'Yes, you look fine.'

'Do you think David finds me attractive?'

Tanya examined her nails awkwardly. 'I'm sure he does, but what about the father of your child?'

'What about him? He never shows me the slightest bit of attention these days. I think David's gorgeous.'

'Yeah, he's nice, but remember, it's always good to play hard to get. Men love a challenge. Do you fancy a water or something?'

'No, why? Do I look like I need one?' Rose seemed insulted.

'I wouldn't mind a water,' said Dee diplomatically, sensing where Tanya was coming from.

Tanya stood up. 'I think I'll ask David to get us all glasses of water. I don't know about the rest of you but those cocktails seemed very strong.'

She went up to David who was patiently waiting to be served. 'Would you mind getting us some water as well as the cocktails? I don't want any of us passing out at this early stage of the night,' she said, making a joke of it.

'Are you fading already?' He looked concerned.

'I'm just a bit worried about Rose, that's all.'

'Sure, go back to your seat. I'll take care of it.'

She did as she was told and David soon followed with the drinks. The first thing Tanya did was make sure Rose got the water into her. 'You'll feel better, honestly.'

'I feel fine,' said Rose indignantly. 'I'm well able to look after myself.'

Twenty minutes later the place had indeed filled up and was now heaving with the beautiful people. At this stage Dee glanced at her watch and said it was about time she got going. 'Do you want to take a taxi home with me, love?' she asked Rose.

But the younger girl was having none of it and seemed to be determined to stay on and party. Dee had made her mind up though, and she said her goodbyes and left the club.

'I'm in no rush to go home,' Rose said after Dee had gone home. 'It's not like my other half will even miss me as he's out himself.'

'You have another half?' David looked surprised.

'For what it's worth. He's my kid's father.'

'Do you have a man waiting at home for you?' David gently turned his attention towards Tanya.

'Yes, I do,' she admitted. There was no point lying about it. It had never been her intention to lead David on in the first place. Now that she had come clean about her relationship status she felt immensely better. Her male companion however looked ever so slightly disappointed.

'I should have guessed that somebody as beautiful as yourself would be taken.'

Tanya squirmed uncomfortably on the seat and shot a nervous look at Rose who thankfully didn't seem to have heard and was looking into space as well as tapping her foot in time to the music. 'Thanks,' she muttered, not knowing what else to say.

She expected David to make his excuses and leave. After all, he was a terribly handsome guy and could probably have his pick of any girl in the club. Tanya knew that if she was still single she'd definitely be interested. Since he didn't seem taken with Rose, he'd probably go to the bar any minute now and not come back. But to her surprise he stayed. And when Rose asked him to join her downstairs for a dance, he obliged.

Tanya waited upstairs minding the drinks as they went off to dance to Justin Timberlake. But she wasn't alone for long. Suddenly she felt a pair of arms around her and somebody screeching in her ear. 'What the hell are you doing here, Missus?'

It was Dianne and she looked well-oiled.

'Hey!' Tanya greeted her with a kiss. 'It's my leaving do tonight so I'm out with the girls from work.'

Dianne looked confused. 'So where are they?'

'Well, actually Dee has gone home and Rose has gone off to dance with some bloke we met earlier on.'

'Sounds like you're having a wild time then,' her friend laughed.

'Ah, would you stop being so sarcastic? We have had a really good night. We started pretty early though. Rose is fairly trolleyed. Who are you here with, by the way?'

'Natasha and Sarah. At least, I started the night out with them but Sarah has already scored and Natasha spent half the night in the loo getting sick so I've just put her in a taxi. I was going to go home myself but then I thought I'd come back up one more time and see if I could see anyone I knew. And here you are!'

'Just you and me, like two abandoned souls,' Tanya giggled. 'So where were you earlier?'

'Ah here and there,' said Dianne, slipping into the seat beside her. 'We were in the Shelbourne, actually, at one stage and bumped into your other half.'

Tanya's eyes nearly popped out of her head. 'Really?'

'Yeah. Did he not say he was going out?'

'No.' Tanya felt a bit miffed. He hadn't said a word.

'Who was he with? The lads from work?'

Dianne looked a bit uncomfortable. 'Um, he was there with two women but they could have been from his work.'

'Yeah, well, maybe they were,' Tanya said quickly. 'There are quite a few girls in his office. I think I'll give him a call though. Maybe he's still in town.'

'That's a good idea. Tell him to ditch the birds and come and join us in Krystle instead.'

Tanya shot her a look. 'That's not even funny, Dianne.'

'Oops. Sorry, I was just winding you up. Go on, ring him anyway.'

'I think I might step outside on to the balcony, though, as it's hard to hear in here.'

'Yeah, go on then. I'll mind the seat for you.'

The balcony looked over the outdoors part of the club and was full of smokers all talking in very loud voices. Tanya hoped she'd be able to hear Eddie when he eventually answered his phone. If he was out and about then she could meet up with him and they could get a taxi home together. She dialled his number and let it ring till it rang out. Well, that confirmed that he was still out because if he was at home he would have answered immediately. It was impossible to hear your phone ringing when you were in a busy pub or a nightclub. She decided to phone him one more time and if he didn't answer, well it couldn't be helped.

The phone answered this time on the third ring. 'Hello?'

It was a woman's shrill voice. Tanya nearly dropped her phone in shock. What was going on? Where was

Eddie? And who had his phone? She was too stunned to reply and quickly knocked off the call. Then, as if in a daze, she turned on her heel and walked back into the VIP area where Rose and David had now joined Dianne and the three of them were chatting like old friends.

'Well?' Dianne asked as Tanya sat down. 'Is Eddie going to join us?'

David looked up from his drink. 'Who's Eddie?'

Dianne seemed to think this was the funniest thing anybody had ever said and burst out laughing. 'They're a band from Dundalk. A brother and two sisters.'

David looked at her like she'd just grown a second head.

'He's my boyfriend,' Tanya said quietly. 'And no, he's not joining us.'

He wouldn't be joining them because he was obviously off enjoying himself with other women, Tanya thought angrily. Did he think it was funny getting some tart to answer his call? Gosh, this was a side to Eddie that she had never seen before. Why did he think that behaviour was acceptable? Was he miffed that she had planned a girls' night out without him? Was that it? Was this his idea of getting back at her? Some kind of silly revenge? How pathetic.

'Hey, look.' Dianne nudged her. 'Your mate has fallen asleep.'

Tanya glanced over at Rose who had her head resting on David's shoulder and indeed looked like she was out for the count. Good God, some people really couldn't hold their drink at all. Rose should have gone home with Dee when she'd had the chance.

'Wake up, Rose.' She leaned forward and poked the other girl. 'We'll get you home now as soon as we can, don't worry.'

'I'll be grand,' said Rose dozily. 'I'll just lie down here and get some rest.'

'She's in a bad way,' said Dianne, stating the obvious. 'Look, I'm going home now anyway so I'll see her home safely in the taxi.'

'Are you sure?' Tanya said gratefully. It would be a relief to know that Rose was going home. It was time she was in her own bed. Deep down she felt she should also be getting into the taxi too but she was so upset and confused after her phonecall to Eddie's phone that now she just wanted to stay here, drink some more and flirt shamelessly with David. The evening had started out so promisingly but had gone rapidly downhill in the last half an hour. Tanya stood up and helped Rose get to her feet.

David stood up too. 'I take it you've decided to leave?' he said, looking disappointed.

She looked him straight in the eye. 'I'm not leaving but my friends are. Please be an angel and get me a Jameson with ice. On second thoughts, make it a double.'

Luckily the girls were able to hail a taxi almost immediately. The driver wasn't too sure about letting Rose into the car. 'She's not going to be sick, is she?' he asked with the air of somebody who had experienced this more than he cared to.

'She'll be fine,' Tanya assured him. The taxi sped off and Tanya went back into the club where David and her double whiskey were waiting for her. She smiled at David, feeling a bit light-headed now. She took a gulp from her drink and then another. David patted her on the back and said he'd have to excuse himself for a moment to go to the bathroom. Tanya assured him she would wait and when he was out of sight she took out her phone again and punched in the digits of Eddie's number. He'd better have a bloody good excuse for his behaviour tonight. But she wasn't in luck. Eddie's phone was now switched off.

17

Prince had no manners, Alice decided. He really was the most badly behaved dog ever. She'd brought him all the way down to UCD so that he could run around the grounds but he'd made a show of her, barking at other dogs and even chasing a swan into the lake and she'd had to get down on her hands and knees to haul him out.

She was sure that people were laughing at her and she felt like turning around and snapping at them that he wasn't even her bloody dog.

Now he was soaking wet and undoubtedly smelly too, so she marched him back up Mount Anville hill and they walked all the way back to Stillorgan. Never again, she told herself. Dog walking was supposed to be a nice, pleasant, relaxing way of spending the afternoon but this was taking the biscuit. No wonder poor Mrs Toner couldn't handle him any more. You'd need the assistance of the army to control this lunatic. By the time she eventually reached the Toner home her thighs were killing her. Well, that wasn't such a bad complaint, she supposed. No pain, no gain and all that. She must be incredibly unfit. Well, the sooner she was back in shape the sooner she could get back on her agency's books and start making a decent living for herself again. She needed to buy a car for a start. It really wasn't the thing for somebody of her age to be getting the bus along with students and foreigners or OAPs. It would be enough to drive you senseless. When she reached the Toner home she rang the bell urgently. Honest to God, she couldn't bear a single second longer in the dog's company. Luckily the door was opened pretty much straight away by Mrs Toner. She looked thrilled to see Prince.

'How did you two get on?' she enquired, her face lighting up. 'Jack told me that you'd come home and I can't tell you how grateful we are for your kind offer. I've felt so guilty recently about not being able to take him out for a walk. Oh, he looks a bit wet. Did you take him swimming?'

Huh! As if! What kind of a weirdo did the woman take her for?

'Well, no, Mrs Toner. Prince decided to go swimming all by himself. He chased a swan in Belfield and the swan led him a merry dance right into the dirty lake.'

Mrs Toner seemed to find this hilarious. 'Oh God, he's not the brightest, is he?' she laughed.

Well, that would be the understatement of the year, Alice thought to herself.

'But he's so loveable,' the woman continued and then invited Alice in for a cup of tea.

Alice was about to make her excuses but then changed her mind and said she'd love to come in. Prince ran through the house and out to the back garden where he gratefully lapped up a bowl of water. Alice sat down in the sitting room while Mrs Toner went off to the kitchen to boil the kettle. The room was full of photos of Eddie. There were cute pictures of him as a baby and of him on holidays with his parents and, good God, there was even a photo of herself and Eddie taken the night of his debs. Alice winced when she spotted the dodgy photo on the mantelpiece. She was a good stone in weight heavier than she was now, and she was supporting a dreadful perm *à la* Gloria Estefan. Just beside that particularly awful photo was another more recent one of Eddie with his parents. It looked like they were on holidays somewhere hot and Eddie was wearing shorts and a vest top that really accentuated his masculine frame. He looked tanned, happy and healthy. God, he really had turned into the most gorgeous creature, Alice admitted to herself. How had she possibly not considered giving him a chance before? Hmm, well, once she was looking fit and gorgeous again she'd meet him and he'd fall for her all over again like he had the night of his debs. That night he'd told her that he'd loved her but she'd told him not to be silly, had got ridiculously drunk and had kissed one of his friends. He hadn't spoken to her for ages after that. But over the years they'd both matured and often stopped for little chats when they'd run into each other. Anyway, the debs was such a long time ago and everyone makes mistakes when they're young, Alice told herself.

Mrs Toner was back with the tea and a packet of Jaffa Cakes. Yum! Alice was starving. Then again, if she was going to be serious about getting her figure back then maybe she should lay off all chocolate treats.

'Biscuit?'

Well, one wouldn't kill her.

'Thanks, Mrs Toner. Just milk with the tea, no sugar.'

'So Alice, your mother was telling us you've been off in LA doing lots of modelling work. She's so proud of you.'

Was she indeed? So that's what her mother had told people. Well, obviously she wasn't going to tell the neighbours that Alice had run off to America with a man she barely knew to live in sin.

Alice plastered a big smile on her face. 'That's right. It was great out there. Fabulous weather but there's no place like home. I hear you and Mr Toner are off to Spain?'

'We are. Very shortly now,' she answered, looking very pleased with herself. 'We've got a lovely place down near Marbella. A stone's throw from the beach. It has everything you'd want.'

'Fantastic.'

'Yes. At first I was a bit nervous about going over but as Jack said, everyone speaks English over there and you can buy nearly everything that you'd get here. I'll just have to stock up on the tea bags before we go out. You can even buy the Irish papers over there.'

'Oh, sure I know.' Alice nodded. Hadn't she been out to Puerto Banus a couple of times on holidays herself? Although she couldn't remember drinking tea or reading the papers when she was there. In fact, she didn't remember very much about her weekends in Puerto Banus except that they were about as wild as you could get.

'And we'll play our golf. I find golf very relaxing. Jack is much better at it than I am and he plays a few times a week. We're going to join a club out there so it will be a good way of meeting people. Do you play a bit of golf yourself, Alice?'

'No, no, I don't actually.'

As if! Golf was just for boring old farts. Alice couldn't think of anything drearier. She didn't want to talk about golf or Spain any more. It was time to turn the conversation around to something more interesting. 'I'm sure Eddie will miss you when you're gone?' she ventured.

'Well, I'm sure he'll manage just fine,' said Mrs Toner softly. 'We don't really see much of him in Ireland as it is. He's always so busy working these days. I often say to Jack I think the young people of today don't have the same quality of life as we did when we were their age. Oh, sure, people have more money for everything and anything but the pace of life is so fast now and it's all so competitive.'

'Mmm. But you must be delighted that Eddie's doing so well.'

'Of course we're proud of him and of course as he's our only child we dote on him, just like your parents dote on you being their only child. I often thought it was lucky that you and Eddie were the same age and could play with each other as youngsters.'

'Yes, it was great. I was always terribly fond of Eddie.'

'You must come to our going-away party and meet up with him again.'

Alice's eyes opened wide. A going-away party?

'That sounds brilliant, Mrs Toner. I love parties. When is it on?'

'Friday week. Your parents and lots of the neighbours will be here so it'll be a great old knees up. I'm sure it'll go on till the early hours.'

'Well, I can't wait, Mrs Toner,' Alice said, standing up

and air-kissing the other woman's cheek. 'It has been so much fun catching up with you again. It really has. I had a real laugh out with Prince today and I look forward to many more enjoyable walks with him.'

'And you promise to come to the party then?'

'Oh, Mrs Toner, don't you worry about that. I'll be there.'

Tanya felt like somebody was hitting her head with a sharp stiletto heel. God, it was such an unpleasant feeling. Not only that but she was gasping for some water. If only she'd remembered to leave a pint of water beside the bed the night before. Then again by the time she'd staggered home this morning she wasn't fit to do much but stumble on to the bed, fully clothed. She hadn't taken off last night's make-up and she still had the stamp from Krystle nightclub stamped on her left wrist.

Thoughts of last night were coming to her in dribs and drabs. She remembered that David guy trying to kiss her at the end of the night. And she remembered declining his advances, thank God. He'd been a really attractive guy but if she'd done the dirt on her boyfriend she knew she'd never be able to live with the guilt.

The phone rang. For a brief moment Tanya thought it could be David phoning. She had some vague recollection of giving him her number just before she got into the taxi last night. He'd said he'd wanted it so that he could text her to make sure she got home safely. 'Hello?'

'It's me.'

Eddie sounded as hungover as she felt, Tanya thought.

'Eddie?'

'Mmm.'

'I tried calling you last night,' she said groggily.

'Yeah, sorry I didn't see your missed calls till I got home and by that stage it was too late to call you back. Was your leaving do fun?'

She couldn't believe how casual he was being about the whole thing. He really had a cheek. She took a deep breath, determined not to come across as being too overexcited. 'When I rang you some woman answered the phone,' she continued coolly.

'Some woman?' He sounded confused. 'Are you sure you rang the right number?'

'I'm absolutely sure.'

'That must have been Paula then. She must have answered the phone when I'd gone to the bathroom or something.'

'Who's Paula?'

'Paula from the office. You've met her plenty of times out with me before. She's married to Donal, one of the partners.'

'Oh,' said Tanya, feeling momentarily foolish.

'Well, you hardly thought I was out on some kind of secret date or something, did you?'

'Of course not,' she said, quickly backtracking. 'And was Donal out with you too?'

'Nah, he wasn't feeling great so he went home after one. Paula's sister joined us in town and we ended up in Lillies of all places. Bad move. My head's not the best today. So how was your night?'

Tanya told him all about the dinner in Chapter One

and then about having drinks in Samsara followed by Krystle. She decided not to tell him about meeting David, and the fact that he'd paid for all her drinks and that she had given her number to him.

'Sounds like a fun night all round,' he said. 'Oh listen, before I forget, Mum and Dad are having a party in the house on Friday week so you're to keep the date free, okay? It's important for you to be there.'

'Oh, oh right. Will it be a dressy affair, do you think?'

'Ah, no, just casual. It'll mostly be the neighbours and stuff but Mum's really looking forward to it. She's bringing in caterers and everything so we have to make an effort.'

'No problem.'

Tanya very much doubted that it would be a wild night but it would be extremely rude of her not to show up and make an effort, considering she would be living in the Toners' house very soon.

'So what are your plans for the day, Eddie? I'm thinking of going into town and looking around the shops for a bit. Do you fancy joining me?'

'Jesus, Tanya, I'm dying. You should see the head on me. The last thing I feel like doing is sitting in stuffy shops watching you trying on clothes.'

'Okay, there's no need to be so rude. Anyway, if you're in that kind of a mood it's probably better that we don't meet up.'

'I'm sorry,' he said, sounding genuinely contrite. 'I just overdid it on the champagne last night. It's all my own fault.'

Champagne? Eddie was drinking champagne? But he

rarely drank the stuff. He was a real beer man if ever there was one.

'Who was celebrating what?' she asked suspiciously.

'It was Paula's sister's thirtieth birthday so she insisted that we join her.'

Tanya wasn't sure if she liked the sound of that. Paula's sister was obviously unattached or else she wouldn't be spending her birthday with her sister and her sister's colleague. Maybe it was her who had answered the phone. Maybe she had been secretly planning on getting Eddie drunk and dragging him to Lillies with the intention of seducing him.

'I see.'

'Listen, don't be getting all moody on me now, Tanya. You didn't invite me out last night so what was I supposed to do on a Friday night? Go back to the empty apartment and watch *The Late Late Show* all by myself?'

'It was a work thing. It wouldn't have been appropriate for you to come along. The other girls didn't bring dates. Listen, I'd better go into town now before the crowds become unbearable. You go back to bed and hopefully when you wake up you'll feel better.'

'Yeah, sounds like a plan.'

'And maybe we could do something quiet tonight? Like go to the Merrion Inn for food?'

'Sure, why not?'

He didn't sound a bit enthusiastic.

'Okay, I'll see you later then,' she said abruptly, ending the call before he could manage to annoy her any further.

She decided to take a quick hot shower to make herself feel better and then head into town. Realistically she couldn't afford to be buying new clothes since she was now technically unemployed and facing an uncertain future financially but she might just treat herself to some fancy underwear or something to cheer herself up. Just as she'd finished in the shower she heard her phone ringing in the bedroom. She wrapped a bath sheet around herself and then tried to make a run for it. But too late. She'd missed the call. She picked up her phone. She didn't recognise the strange number at all so she listened to her message minder.

It was from David.

'Hi, Danny, it's me,' said Alice with a joviality she didn't feel.

She'd finally mustered up the courage to call her model agent and was determined to come across as bright and breezy and not let him know how desperate she was to start working again.

'Who?'

'Alice, I'm back from LA so I'm signing in again.'

'Well, well, well, there's a blast from the past,' he said. 'When did you get back?'

'Just the other day. So please keep me in mind if there's any work going.'

'It's quiet enough at the moment, but keep signing in and we'll put your card back up on the wall and your profile details on the website.'

'Okay, thanks, Danny.'

There now, that hadn't been too bad after all. At least she had made contact and hopefully there would soon be offers of work pouring in again. She went over to her father's computer and decided to look up the website for herself. She nearly died when she saw all the new faces that the agency had recently signed up. There seemed to be lots of skinny Eastern Europeans on board now. Alice reckoned they mustn't buy any food and send all their money back home to their families. Those foreign girls weren't like the Irish models who were often rich kids who did a bit of modelling just for something to do in between shopping sprees and celebrity parties. The Irish girls liked to drink champagne till the early hours in the VIP areas of the latest hip clubs and moaned when they were asked to stand scantily clad in Stephen's Green on a freezing winter's morning holding whatever product it was they were being paid to promote. The foreign girls never complained, however. They knew they could earn as much money in an hour here as they could in a month back home in Latvia or Poland or wherever they came from. Alice had seen the hunger in their eyes and the sheer determination to get on and make something of their lives. They weren't in the modelling business for the fame. Money was their motivation.

Alice's heart began to sink a little faster when she clicked on the various photos. God, you could even see their ribs in some of the shots. Alice had always been one of the agency's favourite swimwear and lingerie girls but comparing herself to these scrawny teenagers was depressing. She felt like a hippo.

She logged off. There was no point clicking on any more photos. She'd seen enough of the competition now. It was depressing, but it was just what she needed to get herself motivated again. She decided to put on her tracksuit and go for a jog. There was nothing like a good run to shift those extra pounds.

Just as she was tying her hair back in a ponytail to go

off for her marathon her phone rang. It was Danny. Jesus, that had been quick!

'Hey, darling. I've just got a call in. You're to go to the Factory at two p.m. sharp. They're casting for a coffee commercial so it'll be a lucrative job. Go on down and do your best. I'll be sending a few of you down because they want to see as many girls as possible this afternoon and they hope to make their final decision tomorrow. Wear something chic but casual.'

'Right on, Danny, I'll certainly do my best. Talk to you later.'

She looked at her watch. She only had two hours to get ready. She rang Peter Marks in Stillorgan and they said they could fit her in immediately so she called a taxi to bring her to the shopping centre. Wasn't that a stroke of luck now that she had called Danny this morning? If she got this casting she'd be well on her way. TV commercials paid big bucks so she might even be able to buy a car without taking out a loan.

Once she'd got her hair blow-dried nice and straight she got another taxi home. She decided on a charcoal-grey trouser suit, black patent ankle boots and a baby-pink cashmere jumper. It was certainly chic but casual, she thought, catching a fleeting glance of herself in the hall mirror before grabbing her keys and getting into yet another taxi. She'd better bloody well get this job, considering all the money she was spending on taxis.

When she got down to the Factory she was stunned to see how many girls had turned up. There must have been about forty girls waiting their turn, and all for just one job. Jesus, everyone in Dublin must be a model these days.

She scowled to herself and joined the rest of the girls who were all busy preening themselves by brushing their hair and touching up their make-up. Alice recognised a good few of them. They seemed amazed to see her there. And none too happy, she supposed. Everybody knew Alice was serious competition.

'Hey, you! We thought you'd gone and disappeared off the face of the earth,' said Sadie Joyce in a loud voice.

Hmm. You wish, thought Alice privately. She'd never really liked Sadie. They were both the same height and colouring and so had often been up for the same jobs. Alice had usually ended up getting them which made Sadie resentful.

'Well, I'm back, Sadie, thank God.'

'Didn't you like LA? I heard you were modelling over there. We all thought you'd end up on the cover of American *Vogue*,' the other girl said with a smirk.

'Oh, you know, I was enjoying myself over there way too much to be working. My life was like one big holiday but of course I missed Ireland and catching up with all the girls I work with here.'

Sadie opened her mouth as if she was about to say something smart but they were interrupted by the voice of a small, stout, efficient-looking woman with a pen and clipboard.

'Alice Adams?' she barked.

'Yes, that's me,' said Alice brightly, almost jumping for joy at the excuse to get away from that little Rottweiler, Sadie.

'You're up first.'

'Oh good.'

She practically ran into the audition hall.

*

'Oh dear, we were kind of looking for somebody taller.'

'I can do taller,' Alice pleaded, standing on her tiptoes and trying to stretch her neck. 'In high heels, I can be at least four inches taller.'

'Well, we're kind of looking for somebody older. Y'know, a Yummy Mummy type.'

'I'm thirty.'

'You don't look it.'

Normally Alice would have taken this comment as a compliment but not now.

'I look way older when I'm wearing more make-up, I promise. Honestly. Everybody says so. And I'm great with kids. I've worked with children on commercials before.'

Alice cringed as she spoke but she really was desperate to get booked at the end of this casting. If she lost out on the job it would mean she wouldn't be able to buy the new car she dreamed of owning. The thought of spending the next few weeks on smelly buses or paying exorbitant taxi fares was too dreadful to even contemplate. She'd forgotten just how shitty castings could be. Being judged solely on your looks wasn't something you ever got used to. Danny had always told her not to take rejections personally but it was hard not to. It certainly always felt personal. And humiliating to say the least. There were obviously far too many beautiful women in Dublin city and not half enough work to go around. Alice took her willowy frame to the centre of the floor and walked up and down three times before the panel of three as requested. Then she gave a half-hearted twirl, flicked her long mane of dark hair over her shoulder, and flashed her trademark bright smile.

The two scowling women and the bored-looking young man with the funny red glasses seemed less than impressed.

'You're not what we're looking for. Next!'

Alice sighed. Jesus, you just couldn't win in this game, she decided. It was the absolute pits! You were always either too short or too tall, too blonde or too dark, too thin or too curvy. They wanted somebody with red hair, spiky hair or no hair. Or else they wanted a girl who would be willing to stand on Grafton Street in a bikini in the middle of winter with a bowl of fruit on her head to promote some holiday brochure.

Alice grinned through gritted teeth and thanked the panel politely, although what she was thanking them for, was anybody's guess. Still, the circles in this industry were so small, you basically had to lick arse everywhere.

'Will you tell the next girl to come in?' the older woman said, almost yawning as she spoke.

Alice fled the draughty hall, her cheeks burning with embarrassment. How dare those gobshites treat her like a piece of rubbish? Didn't they even know who she was? She was a name in this town. A somebody. At least she had been before she'd fecked off to LA on a whim, she thought with a frown. Out of sight, out of mind, and all that. Had people already forgotten about her? Once safely outside she took a deep breath to calm her nerves, and then sat on the cold stone steps of the building and lit up a cigarette. What a complete waste of time and money today had been.

She was soon joined by Louisa, a tall sexy blonde who was also one of the agency's top girls.

'Hey, Alice, it's good to see you back. That's some tan you've got there,' she said generously.

'Thanks,' Alice muttered and offered the other girl one of her cigarettes.

'God, I think I will. That wasn't the most pleasant casting ever, was it?'

'Oh, you know, you win some, you lose some. I'm actually not that bothered,' Alice said untruthfully.

'Yeah, well, it's the third casting I haven't got this week. I'm beginning to feel so unloved.' Louisa gave a mock sigh which made Alice laugh. 'Hey, do you need a lift home? I'm going to see my mum in Foxrock so there's no problem dropping you off in Stillorgan on the way if you like.'

Alice brightened. Yes, that would be great. She'd actually just been thinking she'd rather walk home rather than face another journey with some ignorant cabbie forcing his unasked-for opinions on her. Wasn't it such a shame that all the people who knew how to run the country were too busy driving cabs to be able to do it, huh?

'Thanks, Louisa. I'd really appreciate it, if it's not too much trouble.'

'No trouble at all. But I've also promised Sadie a lift too so do you mind if we just wait for her? Hopefully she won't be too long.'

Alice's heart sank. That's all she needed. A ride home with Sadie telling them how fabulous she was. Brilliant.

They waited and waited as a steady stream of girls

emerged sporadically from the building, each looking more dejected than the other. Anybody who thought the business of modelling was glamorous was seriously deluded, Alice thought to herself. You needed nerves of steel to be able to survive in this game. And then suddenly, walking on air, with the triumph of somebody who had just won an election, or even the lottery, Sadie emerged, blinking into the sunlight. The grin she had plastered on her face was enough to make you sick.

'Girls, have you been waiting for me? I'm so, so sorry for keeping you.'

'No worries,' said Louisa. 'We were just having a cigarette anyway. So are we ready to rock and roll then?'

'Oh no, I'm afraid I'll have to let you girls go on without me. You see, they've asked me to hold on for a while in here.'

'That sounds good,' said Louisa.

'Oh, it's more than good, it's great. They've only asked three people to stay behind and I'm one of them but thanks so much for waiting, it's so good of you. Bye.'

She gave the two girls a little wave and skipped back into the building.

Alice stared after her in disgust. What an obnoxious pain in the arse. She hoped to God that Sadie wouldn't get the final audition.

But she did. And they paid her eight thousand euros, as she made a point of telling Alice the next time she met her.

Tanya had been surprised that David had taken the trouble to phone her. So many men expected women to run after them and do all the chasing these days. But she didn't want to lead him on either. It would be a dangerous game to play. Herself and Eddie had been getting on really well over the last couple of days and she'd got over her annoyance over last Friday night.

'Listen, if you're ever around the IFSC . . .'

'I won't be, David,' she said firmly. Sometimes it was necessary to be cruel to be kind.

But he didn't even seem fazed. 'Well, you have my number on your phone now so . . . you never know.'

She had to laugh at his brazenness. He'd go very far in life with that attitude, she reckoned.

One day some woman would be very lucky to get him, but that woman definitely would not be her.

As soon as she got off the phone it rang again. For a slip of a second she thought it might be David again. If it *was* him, he was now beginning to show serious signs of being a stalker. But it wasn't. Instead it was a woman enquiring about a private hot-stone therapy treatment. Tanya was so pleased she nearly did a little dance on the spot. Her first client! Hurrah.

The appointment was a huge success. Mrs Doyle had said afterwards that the hot-stone massage was the best ever and was just what she'd been looking for and before she let Tanya out the door, she'd booked her again for another massage in a fortnight's time. Tanya was thrilled that everything had gone so well. She now felt quite upbeat about the future. As Dundrum wasn't too far from Sandyford she decided she may as well call out to Eddie's apartment. He wouldn't be home from work yet but as she had her own key to his place she might as well let herself in and wait for him to come home. She might even make him a nice dinner as a treat. He'd appreciate that.

First of all she popped into Tesco in Dundrum Town Centre to get some ingredients for the dinner and once she'd done that she set out for Eddie's apartment. It would be a nice surprise for him to find her waiting for him.

Eddie's apartment was cold and dark when she arrived so immediately she turned the heating up high and switched on all the lamps and put on some classical music. There, that was much better. The place looked lived in and homely now. Then she took out all the vegetables that she had bought in Tesco and placed them on a chopping board. She was going to make some delicious ratatouille for Eddie as she knew it was his favourite meal. She also took a bottle of Chianti from the fridge, and poured herself a generous glass. She could share the rest of the bottle with Eddie when he came in from work. No doubt he'd be tired from his busy day at the office and would appreciate her efforts enormously. She chopped up a clove of garlic and then dropped the pieces into the frying pan along with some olive oil. While they were sizzling she chopped the onions and the green and yellow peppers. She loved cooking. And thankfully Eddie liked eating. Staying at home and cooking for Eddie was what made her happy. Nightclubs weren't really her scene at all, and although she had enjoyed the other night out with the girls she'd never been so relieved when the taxi had finally brought her back to the safety of her own home. As Tanya was putting all the ingredients into a large saucepan along with a can of plum tomatoes, she heard the key in the apartment front door and immediately she brightened.

'Hey, this is a nice surprise,' said Eddie, his face lighting up at the sight of his girlfriend. He threw his briefcase on the sofa, undid his tie and wrapped his arms around Tanya's slim waist. 'Mmm. Smells nice.'

'Sit yourself down there and don't be bothering the cook,' Tanya laughed. 'Do you fancy a nice chilled glass of Chianti while you're waiting?'

'How can you always read my mind?'

She poured him a glass and brought it over to him. He looked tired after his busy day in the office. Tired but still his usual gorgeous self. She went back to the cooker to stir the ratatouille, and then added some salt and pepper to the bubbling mixture. It shouldn't take too long, she reckoned.

Over a relaxing dinner she told him all about her appointment with Mrs Doyle earlier. Eddie seemed genuinely delighted for her.

'I know you'll do really well, hun. The clients will love you and you'll be a huge success.'

Tanya beamed at him across the table. 'Thanks. Not all boyfriends would be as supportive as you, you know.'

'I know,' he teased. 'Oh, by the way, in case I forget to mention it, my mother was on the phone to me earlier and she suggested that your parents might like to come along to the party on Friday night?'

'My parents?' Tanya's eyes widened. Now, that was a positive sign. If the Toners wanted to meet her parents that must mean they considered her relationship with Eddie to be fairly serious.

'I'm sure they'd love to come,' she said appreciatively. 'It's very nice of your mum to invite them.'

'Well, considering we'll be living together as from next week, it would be a bit strange if our parents hadn't met each other.'

'I suppose. Well, I'll tell them to be on their best behaviour.'

'Likewise.'

'You can bring that mad sister of yours along too, if you like.'

'Elaine?' Tanya laughed out loud and took a long sip of her wine. 'Elaine wouldn't dream of showing up to a family get together like that on a Friday night. She'll be out with her grungy college pals no doubt discussing how they're going to change the world.'

'You should ask her anyway, you never know.'

'I know my sister only too well. She wouldn't want to go along to a party where there are no young people.'

'You and I will be there. We're young.'

'Not to Elaine, we're not. She probably thinks we're ancient.'

'Not everybody there will be of retirement age though,' Eddie insisted. 'The Adams family will be there.'

'The Adams family?' Tanya giggled, feeling the wine going to her head already. 'That's hilarious. Do the Adams family really live next door?'

'Yeah and they're as odd as their TV namesakes but they get along well with my folks. They have gardening and golf in common. So, anyway, they're coming along with their daughter, Alice.'

Tanya felt the colour drain from her face.

'Alice Adams?' she said in a loud nervous whisper as she felt her heart hammer in her chest.

'Yeah, she's a model and has been for years. I haven't seen her in ages. She only moved back with her parents the other week apparently.'

'She's your next-door neighbour?' Tanya was aghast.

'Yep! And from next week she'll be yours too, hahaha.'

Tanya failed to see anything funny about it.

21

At last Alice had finally got herself a job. She had been booked for the early morning fashion slot on TV3's *Ireland AM* and couldn't wait for it. It would be good to get back on television for the exposure. However, when she arrived at the television station she was absolutely horrified to learn that she would be modelling a particularly hideous-looking maternity range. Not only that but the stylist told her she would have to put a fake bump up her dress in order to look pregnant. Alice was sorely tempted to walk out in protest. Why the hell hadn't Danny warned her that this was a pregnancy slot instead of high fashion?

She stood outside the studios in the freezing cold wind and lit a cigarette in order to calm down. Okay, she was annoyed and they should have told her what the slot was, but she felt she had no choice but to act professionally in this instance and simply swallow her pride. If she were to walk out of this job, Danny would be very slow to put any more work her way and she badly needed all the work she could get at the moment to help try and clear her credit-card debt.

She stubbed out her cigarette, went back inside the

building and made her way to the make-up room to get her hair and face done. The two dresses that she was given to wear were horrendous. She wouldn't wish them on her worst enemy. And the fake pregnancy bump that she was forced to wear was the itchiest, most uncomfortable thing ever. Hopefully this would be the first and last time she would ever be asked to model something so humiliating. She took comfort in the fact that it was so early in the morning and that everyone she knew would be at work and not at home watching television.

She smiled inanely at the cameras when she was required to stand in one of the awful dresses as the presenter and Alan Hughes chatted to each other about the importance of pregnancy wear.

'This dress would be perfect for a wedding or a christening,' she heard the stylist chirp in an annoying sing-song voice and Alice struggled not to laugh. A wedding or a christening? For God's sake! The only place this dress was fit for was the garbage bin. She was thrilled when the slot was over and the hired taxi arrived to take her back home to Stillorgan where she discovered to her horror that her mother had gone and taped the show.

'It'll be nice one day to show the grandkids,' Mrs Adams insisted before offering to make her daughter a nice cup of strong tea.

Show the grandkids? She must be joking! Hell would freeze over before she ever showed that embarrassing clip to anybody, Alice thought privately.

Nevertheless she gratefully accepted her mother's offer of a cup of tea and a couple of pieces of toast. She was feeling tired now and wanted to get back into her warm bed for a few hours' kip before resurfacing again. She wanted to look bright and relaxed for the Toners' party tonight. It was imperative that she looked her best. She wanted Eddie Toner's eyes to pop out of their sockets at the sight of her and realise that he was still hopelessly attracted to her. She couldn't wait for the moment to arrive.

She'd spent the last few days on a fruitless mission trying to bump into Eddie by calling around to take that useless mutt out for his daily walk. But the one time he'd called over, she'd been out with the dog. Mrs Toner said it was a pity that she'd missed Eddie and she couldn't agree more. Indeed, she missed him in more ways than one and had probably missed out big time by turning him down all those years ago. Still, tonight she'd get another chance to knock him dead again. And she could hardly wait.

Even though everybody had said that it wouldn't be a dressy affair, Alice had decided she was going to make a huge big effort and wear the drop-dead gorgeous D & G dress that Bill had bought for her out in LA. She'd wear it with the highest of heels and make sure to dazzle all the guests. She didn't think she'd have much competition at the party anyway. It would be full of boring old sods talking about bridge or whatever. And no doubt Eddie's frumpy girlfriend, whoever she was, would just show up in boring old jeans so she would certainly have no trouble wiping the floor with her. She had it all planned. A grand entrance would be made and all eyes would be on Alice, the girl Eddie had once been in love with, and she was going to relish every moment of it.

She put down her empty tea cup and headed for bed, dreaming of the party ahead and the fun she was going to have at it.

She woke with a start hours later at the sound of her mother hoovering outside her bedroom. Jesus, the woman could be so bloody inconsiderate at times. But then a quick glimpse at her watch told her that it was nearly lunchtime, so she supposed it was time to get up.

She looked out the window and saw a white van outside the Toners' house. They must be the caterers. She was half tempted to pop around and offer to help but then thought better of it. They might suggest that she bring their mad dog for another walk. Instead she would go about putting on her fake tan. She still had quite a good colour from LA but she wanted to look like a bona fide Hollywood star who had just flown in from California. Alice wasn't going to do anything by halves when it came to preparing for this party.

Her parents thought she was quite mad for dressing up so much and when she waltzed into the kitchen later that evening and gave a little twirl her father's jaw fell open in obvious shock.

'Where's the bottom half of your dress, Missy?'

'This *is* my dress,' she insisted. 'And don't be lecturing me. This dress happened to cost a fortune and I'll let you know that it always gets lots of attention.'

'I'm not surprised,' Mrs Adams muttered with an air of distinct disapproval as she checked her hair in the kitchen mirror and asked her husband for a hand fastening her pearls around her neck.

At eight o'clock, Mr Adams anxiously looked at his

watch and said it was about time they got going. His wife agreed. It would be considered the height of rudeness to arrive late. But Alice nearly died. 'We can't be the first to arrive,' she pleaded with them. 'It would be so mortifying. Can't we wait at least fifteen minutes?'

They grudgingly agreed to wait a while. Alice cheekily decided to help herself to a gin and tonic from the drinks cabinet which was really only there in case visitors called.

She saw her parents exchange worried glances as she poured a generous measure and then threw a couple of ice cubes in for good measure, but she didn't care. They never gave out to her these days in case she ran away again for good. That meant she could pretty much do what she wanted at home, which suited her fine. She was the boss and the game would be played her way. Anyway, imagine arriving at the party dead sober with her parents and them being the first to arrive? Sure they'd be a laughing stock. But at twenty past eight Mr Adams was running out of patience.

'We're going now,' he said. 'They'll be wondering why we're not there yet. After all, we live next door so we can't blame the traffic for being late.'

Alice felt her heart somersault. Oh God, this was it. She was finally going to come face to face with Eddie again after all these years. How would he behave towards her? Would he embrace her like a long-lost friend or would he ignore her? No, he wouldn't ignore her, she decided. Eddie was far too well brought up to do something like that. She took a deep breath and stood up. It was crunch time.

'I actually can't believe you're making me come along to this yoke,' Elaine grumbled as she got into the family car with her sister and her parents. 'Honest to God, you'd think I was fourteen again. Do you not think I'd have better things to be doing on a Friday night?'

'But you didn't have any plans. So you said earlier,' Mrs Thomson pointed out. 'Anyway, it's good for you to get out of the house and enjoy yourself now and again, Elaine.'

'But I won't be enjoying myself, that's the point,' Elaine grumbled. 'It'll be like an annual old folks' home Christmas party.'

'Listen, if she doesn't want to come, don't make her come,' Mr Thomson said to his wife. 'I'm not going to listen to her complaining all evening.'

'He's right,' Tanya told her sister. 'If it's going to be that much of an ordeal for you, then don't bother. I would have liked you to have come along for the support but since you're determined to ruin the evening for all of us, then you'd be better off staying here.'

That certainly stunned the youngest Thomson daughter into silence. She folded her arms in the back seat and looked out the window in a sulk. She didn't want to be ejected from the car and have to spend the night at home by herself while the rest of her family went out. Sure, it wasn't going to be the most exciting night of her life but it was just one night. How bad could it possibly be? There'd be lots of free food and drink at it and she couldn't face another night studying like a loser.

'I'm sorry,' she muttered eventually. 'I'll go.'

With that Mr Thomson turned on the engine and they set out for Stillorgan. Tanya couldn't stop fretting all the way to the party. She hoped Elaine wouldn't disgrace herself and insult anybody. And she hoped her parents would get on with the Toners. This was a big step in her and Eddie's relationship. If their families got on well, that was a very positive sign for the future. Still, she couldn't help being anxious about the night. Especially since she'd found out that Alice Adams was going to be there. She would have thought that Alice was too up herself to go to the Toners' party. But then Eddie had admitted that the families had always been close and that he'd even brought Alice to his debs. This bit of information had displeased Tanya no end. If he'd brought the girl to his debs, he must have fancied her. He must not have seen her for the bitch that she was. Alice was a stunning-looking girl and men were blinded by good looks. She'd asked him straight out whether anything had ever happened between himself and Alice and he'd been quick to say no.

'But did you fancy her?' she pressed him, despite the fact that she was dreading his answer.

'Ah, stop it, Tanya,' he'd said wearily as if speaking to a spoilt child. 'That was all so long ago.'

But he hadn't said he hadn't fancied her. That was the

thing. He hadn't even bothered to deny it and Tanya's worst fears had therefore been confirmed.

There were quite a few people already at the party when the Thomsons arrived. Mrs Toner herself answered the door, shook hands all round, took their coats and then went straight off to find her husband. Then Mr Toner appeared on the scene, made everyone feel very welcome and got everybody a drink. Tanya could feel herself relax now. It had been a good idea to bring her family after all. It was less awkward than, say, getting both couples together in a restaurant. This way the initial introductions were a lot less formal and took any pressure off. She found Eddie in the kitchen talking to the Smyths from across the road. When they heard she was moving in with Eddie, they immediately welcomed Tanya to the neighbourhood. She wondered if the Adamses would be just as welcoming. From what she had found out, the Adamses were a conservative, polite, fairly old-fashioned couple and they'd had Alice fairly late in life.

Tanya was just about to accept a top up of wine from Eddie when she noticed the expression on his face visibly change. He was looking over her shoulder and immediately she felt her heart sink. She didn't even have to turn around to know that Alice must have just arrived. And Eddie looked like a love-struck teenager.

23

Alice was more than happy with the way the evening had turned out so far. She'd made her grand entrance into the party and everybody had turned around to stare at her as she walked in. She felt about ten feet high. So far it had been fun catching up with all the neighbours, most of whom acknowledged that they'd often seen her in the papers and wasn't it great to have a real life celebrity living on the road?

All the compliments pleased her no end. She was really glad she'd made a huge effort with her appearance tonight and she glided around the house like a peacock, amazed at the courage that gin and tonic seemed to have given her. It was only when Mrs Smyth said in a loud voice that she thought that she had seen her on television earlier that morning, that her preening smile momentarily disappeared.

She allowed Mr Toner to open up a bottle of champagne for her even though nobody else seemed to be drinking it, and was secretly delighted when Prince snuck into the house without anybody noticing and went wild with joy at the sight of Alice. The stupid dog obviously thought she was taking him for a walk but the rest of the guests weren't to know that. He jumped up and down excitedly and started barking so loudly that nobody could hear themselves.

'My goodness, even the dog is bowled over by your beauty,' one man said jokingly to her, and she simply smiled graciously back at him, thrilled to be the centre of attention.

But Eddie Toner's reaction to seeing her was the icing on the cake. He'd literally looked stunned to see her when she'd caught his eye across the room. She'd given him a demure smile and a little wave, and he'd made his way over to her as if in a trance.

'Hi, Alice,' he said softly.

'Hi, Eddie.'

'Thanks for coming. It really means a lot to my parents to have all the neighbours here to wish them well. We're delighted with the turnout this evening. We weren't expecting this amount of people to show up.'

'Well, you're obviously a popular family around here,' she laughed, batting her long dark lashes flirtatiously at him. She studied his handsome face. The years had definitely been kind to Eddie and he'd matured into such a good-looking man. While some men of his age lost their hair along with their youthful looks and gained an ungainly beer belly, Eddie was toned and slim and she bet he possessed a rippling six-pack under that crisp, white shirt he was wearing. Truly he looked good enough to eat. She could see he was impressed by her too. He couldn't take his eyes off her. No doubt his attraction for her still hadn't waned and this pleased her no end. It meant she still hadn't lost it. She, Alice

Adams, was still capable of seducing men with a single glance.

'Can I get you a top-up?' he offered, noticing her empty glass. That was Eddie. Always the gentleman. Even when they'd hung around together as teenagers he'd always held the door open for her or offered up his chair if she'd had nowhere to sit down. His manners had always been impeccable.

But her confidence took a bit of a hammering when he suddenly said to her, 'Oh, Alice, I'd also really like you to meet my girlfriend, Tanya. She'll be moving in with me so maybe the two of you will become friends.'

Alice felt like she'd received a sharp slap across her face. Although she forced herself to keep smiling, deep inside she was seething as Eddie topped up her glass with champagne. So he was moving in with his girlfriend, was he? Well, that was bad news. It obviously meant they were very serious about each other. Suddenly a blonde woman was at Eddie's side. Alice scrutinised her as she shook her hand limply.

'I'm Alice,' she said, giving the other woman a watery smile.

'I know. I'm Tanya. I met you the other day in the salon, remember?'

Suddenly the penny dropped. So that's why she had recognised her! Of course, she was that beautician. And Eddie's girlfriend, soon to be live-in lover. Oh, what a small world it was, Alice thought. Far too small for her liking.

'Oh yes, indeed. I remember you now. How are you?'

'I'm fine,' Tanya answered crisply and reached for Eddie's hand.

She doesn't like me, Alice decided. She doesn't like me at all. No surprises there. Alice reckoned most women didn't like her because they felt threatened by her beauty. Not that Alice was terribly bothered. She didn't have very many female friends anyway as she usually got on much better with blokes. Still, she was going to be the bigger woman here and kill her love rival with kindness.

'I love your dress,' she cooed, taking Tanya by surprise.

'Oh thanks, I just picked it up in Top Shop.'

'Your own dress is fabulous,' said Eddie appreciatively, giving Alice the once over as Tanya visibly flinched.

'Your father was looking for you.' Tanya started to pull her boyfriend away. 'We'll catch you later, Alice. Good to see you again.'

She whisked a bewildered-looking Eddie away. Alice smirked to herself. She had just won round one. Tanya had made the cardinal mistake of immediately coming across as possessive and jealous whereas Alice had kept her cool and had simply oozed charm.

She watched the couple disappear into a small crowd of people. Although Tanya was undeniably pretty with her cute dimples, blond curls and a tiny waist, she was more of a cute girly girl whereas Alice knew she was all woman with her dark sultry looks; the type men would kill for. Tanya could try and hide Eddie away all she liked but, as their new next-door neighbour, Alice would always be able to find him. And she would find him too. Alice hadn't fancied him in the past but she'd always been secretly flattered that he'd been so obsessed by her. And by the looks of things he still fancied the pants off her. He would be her brand-new challenge. Why should this Tanya one get to live in this big house with him while she, Alice, had to put up with living with her parents next door as though she was still a schoolgirl? The injustice of it all! She had met Eddie first. Finders keepers and all that! They had known each other since they'd been in nappies and had grown up together. He had written little love poems for her and had often given her a lift to the shops on his bike. He had put an anonymous Valentine's card through her letterbox every February until he reached the age of seventeen although he'd never admitted it. He'd looked at her longingly with puppy-dog eyes although she'd never actively encouraged him in any way. Yes, Eddie Toner had been madly in love with her all those years and she wasn't going to let him go now without a fight. Huh! As if Alice was going to take a back seat now while some little blow-in took her place in Eddie's affections!

Alice wondered who she could go and talk to next. She didn't want to be roped into some boring conversation about plants with one of the Toners' neighbours, but she felt decidedly conspicuous standing here alone in the middle of the room. Suddenly a tall, dark, interesting-looking girl caught her eye. She was standing idly in the corner drinking Heineken straight from a can and was wearing jeans, trainers and a black T-shirt. Alice decided she may as well go over and introduce herself as the other girl looked like she could possibly be the most interesting person in the room.

'Hi, I'm Alice,' she said to the girl who seemed to be staring into space.

'Oh hi, I'm Elaine,' the other girl said disinterestedly, looking at her as though Alice was some kind of salesperson wanting to sell her an encyclopaedia.

'Are you a friend of the Toners?'

'No, I've never met them before in my life. Why? Are you?'

'I live next door. I've known them all my life. I've always been especially close to Eddie, the son.'

'Good for you,' an unsmiling Elaine said and continued to drink her Heineken.

Alice was baffled by the girl's surly nature. If she didn't know the Toners then why was she here? She was hardly part of the catering staff that had been hired in as she wasn't wearing a uniform. And besides, she was drinking so she couldn't be here to help out.

'So what's your connection?' she asked Elaine straight out.

'Should I be wearing some kind of ID?'

Alice laughed. Now this girl really was funny.

'I was just wondering, that's all.'

'I'm Tanya's sister. She's Eddie's girlfriend.'

Alice was startled. Tanya's sister? She didn't look a bit like her. Maybe they were adopted but she thought better than to ask.

'Oh yes, I've met Tanya. In fact, I met her by sheer coincidence. I'd just come in from LA and popped off at the salon to get my eyebrows done.'

'I see.'

'Are you in the beauty business yourself?'

'No, are you?'

'I'm a model,' said Alice, now beginning to think that this Elaine girl was quite the rudest person she'd spoken to in a long time.

'What does that entail?'

Ah seriously, was the girl having her on? Alice wondered. Did she never watch Fashion MTV or *America's Next Top Model*? Good God, what planet was the girl living on? And didn't she ever buy fashion magazines?

'Well, you know, you do fashion shows sometimes and other times you get booked for a press call to promote a product. They might get you to stand in a street in a mini holding lottery scratch cards or something.'

'I really don't know why anybody intelligent would do something like that,' Elaine said. 'I mean, I know a couple of the girls in Trinity with me do that kind of thing but I just think it's degrading to women.'

Alice couldn't believe the sheer audacity of what she was saying. Did she even realise she was being insulting? For some reason Alice didn't think she was. The girl just seemed to speak her opinion and cared less whether people agreed with her or not. Alice's instincts told her that this girl was not being particularly malicious. She was just tactless, that was all.

'Hey, do you have a cigarette?' Elaine asked suddenly.

'Marlboro Lights?'

'That'll do fine. But I need to go down the garden to have one 'cos my parents don't know I smoke.'

'Neither do mine.'

Elaine looked at her oddly. 'What age are you?'

'Thirty,' said Alice, feeling a little foolish. Yes, she was a bit old to be hiding away from her parents at her ripe old age. 'Come on then, let's go down the garden.'

Safely behind a bush Alice lit her own cigarette before lighting Elaine's and took a long drag.

'People say I should be a model,' said Elaine. 'But I'm not into wearing loads of make-up and dresses and high heels and stuff. I'm too much of a tomboy.'

'You'd make a good model though,' said Alice and she genuinely meant it. Not only was Elaine tall and thin but she also had flawless skin and huge blue eyes.

'I just don't think I'd be into it.'

'The money's great, though, especially if you're a student.'

'Is it? How much are we talking about?' Elaine enquired nonchalantly, blowing rings of smoke up into the sky.

'A hundred and fifty an hour for a press call. You'd get at least that.'

'No way. Is that what you get?'

'Actually I get twice that because I've been modelling a while and I've built up a name for myself.'

At least that had been true until a few months ago when she'd abandoned ship altogether. It would take a while to crawl back on to the scene again. Before she'd left for LA she could sometimes have made between four and five hundred euros an hour. Granted it wasn't the ten thousand pounds a day that Linda Evangelista once apparently claimed she wouldn't get out of bed for, but it wasn't too bad for just prancing around for a bit in front of the cameras.

Elaine was all agog. 'I seriously didn't think models were that well paid,' she said. 'I mean I get nine quid an hour working part time at a shoe shop in town where I'm expected to run around like a fecking eejit looking for sizes while simultaneously trying not to get sick from the pong of people's smelly feet. It's the pits.'

'Well, then, why don't you give it a shot?'

Elaine frowned. 'But would it cost me money, like? Would I have to get professional photos taken and buy a whole new wardrobe of clothes?'

'Not at all,' said Alice, shaking her head. 'Just ring my agency and ask for Danny. Tell him I told you to call and he'll see you. When you go along to the agency make sure you don't wear much make-up and bring along a headshot and a full-length photo. That's all you'll need.'

'Jesus, it sounds like an easy way to make a quick buck,' said Elaine, brightening. 'Maybe I should have started before now.'

'Well, it's not too late,' said Alice, stubbing her cigarette out into an empty cup. Just as long as you don't think you'll take any jobs from under my nose, princess, she thought, following the younger girl back inside the house and catching Eddie staring at her from the distance. Nice one. He'll have seen her chatting to Elaine and think that she was a really nice person being so kind to Tanya's younger sister. So far so good.

Tanya decided this party was anything but fun. Alice had turned up dressed to the nines, obviously determined to steal her thunder and everybody else's while she was at it. Swanning about in her ridiculously short dress, she was acting as if she practically owned the place. Tanya had caught her batting her eyelids at Eddie several times during the evening but when she'd blatantly pulled him on to the makeshift dance floor in front of everybody, Tanya had really seen red. 'What a lovely couple they make,' one elderly dear had observed loudly much to Tanya's annoyance.

She couldn't wait to take off her new high heels which were digging into the back of her feet. She should never have worn them without breaking them in first. She just wanted to go home now. She was convinced without a shadow of a doubt that Alice had now set her sights firmly on her man. This was supposed to have been a fun, relaxing evening. All her family were here and this was the house she and Eddie planned to live in together. So why, oh why, was Alice Adams of all the people in the world, the person who happened to be living next door? Life was so unfair.

Of course she couldn't say anything to Eddie about it because he would probably say she was being childish and paranoid. Maybe she was but she just couldn't help it. Alice looked every inch the supermodel tonight. Nobody could deny her that much. She was a far cry from the girl who had walked into the salon the other week tired and drawn-looking with dark circles under her eyes. Tonight she looked like a completely different woman and had gone all out to impress. It had worked. Even the most committed man in the room couldn't have failed to notice how stunning she was.

Tanya unhappily topped up her glass of vodka and Diet Coke. How much longer would she have to stay here tonight? Her parents really seemed to be enjoying themselves, and were mingling well with the other guests. They didn't seem to be showing any signs of wanting to leave. Even her notoriously unsociable little sister, Elaine, was beginning to let her hair down and was knocking back the tins of Heineken. In fact, at one stage, to Tanya's absolute amazement, she'd seen her disappear down the garden with Alice herself. What the hell had that been all about?

'Hey, how are you keeping up?' Suddenly Eddie was by her side, sliding a protective arm around her waist.

'Oh, I'm having a great time,' she lied, smiling up at him. 'Your parents really have gone to so much trouble. The food is fantastic and there's so much drink there's no fear of anybody going thirsty.'

'Well, they really wanted to do this,' he said. 'And so many people have turned up that it's a credit to them. The DJ is great, isn't he?'

'Yeah,' Tanya muttered unenthusiastically.

'Dad has given him strict instructions to play all the golden oldies, you know, like the Eagles and the Beatles and all that.'

'God help us all.' Tanya managed a laugh. But her smile soon vanished again when Alice brazenly took Eddie by the hand ten minutes later and dragged him off to dance to Abba's *Waterloo*. Alice was wriggling her hips and tossing her long hair over her shoulders. Tanya thought it was a bit inappropriate. The next thing she knew she was dragging Elaine up to dance, and Elaine, who was always very particular about her music, was rocking around the place to Abba. Who would have thought it?

Eventually, when Tanya thought she could not bear the party any longer, she was relieved to see her father putting on his coat.

'Are you thinking of leaving, Dad?' she asked hopefully.

Thankfully he had decided to call it a night and Tanya breathed a sigh of relief and rounded up the rest of her clan to go home.

After they'd all said their goodbyes and were bundling into Mr Thomson's car, Tanya turned to her little sister. 'Well, did you have fun after all?'

'Funnily enough I did enjoy it,' she admitted. 'Much and all as I didn't think I would.'

'I saw you were talking to that Alice girl for ages.'

'Yeah, she's a bit of an odd fish. At first she was quizzing me like there was no tomorrow. So much so that I thought I was at a bloody interview. But as it turned out she was very helpful.'

Tanya was intrigued. 'In what way?'

'Well, she's persuaded me to become a model.'

'What?'

'Hey, it might not be such a bad thing. I'm sick to the teeth of being a penniless student and Alice said if I joined her agency I could clean up and I'd be driving my own car within a couple of months. That certainly gave me something to think about.'

And it also gave Tanya plenty to think about. What on earth did Alice Adams think she was playing at? She wouldn't help anybody if her life depended on it. Tanya would never forget the way she'd blatantly used her a few years ago and left her without a shred of confidence. Something was clearly amiss. That girl was up to no good. Tanya was convinced of it. First of all Alice had spent the night coming on to her man and now she was trying to be her kid sister's new best friend and bloody mentor. Suddenly the film *Single White Female* sprang to mind, and Tanya felt very uneasy indeed.

'H i, Danny, it's me, Alice. Just checking into the agency. Is anything up?'

'Well, speak of the devil, darling, I was just about to phone you.'

Alice's heart leapt with excitement. What? Another job already? Well, things were certainly picking up now, thank God. Suddenly her future in modelling didn't look quite so gloomy any more.

'What is it?'

'It's a fashion show in the Hodson Bay Hotel in Athlone on Wednesday evening. There's a minibus leaving the agency at two p.m. sharp so make sure you're on time.'

'I will be. Thanks for the booking, Danny.'

'Oh, by the way, just to warn you, this is a maternity show so you'll have to wear some kind of fake bump. I don't know if you've worn one before . . .'

Alice could feel her blood pressure soar. 'I had one before the other morning on TV3. People will begin to think I'm pregnant!'

She felt like sobbing. How could this be happening to her?

'Well, the owner of the maternity shop was most insistent that you open the show for her. Come to think of it, she actually said she saw you on TV3 and was very impressed.'

'So I might be in the running for Ireland's top maternity model even though I'm not even preggers?'

'At least you're getting work, Alice,' he replied in a humourless voice. 'Your regular clients don't even know you're home yet so be patient. So we'll see you on Wednesday then.'

Yeah, I can't bloody wait, thought Alice, putting down the phone. God Almighty, were there no other shops looking for models apart from maternity shops? She pondered Danny's words carefully. He was right. The clients didn't know she was back. Well, she'd have to sort that out herself now, wouldn't she? She couldn't expect Danny to be doing it on her behalf. There were forty-five models on his books so he couldn't be looking after all their best interests at the same time. There was only one thing for it: she'd need to get on to the clients personally herself.

The first person she called after her conversation with Danny was a woman called Phyllis who owned a chic boutique in Sandymount. She had always asked especially for Alice when booking a model for a press call.

Phyllis sounded delighted to hear from her and promised to put any future work her way. 'We just had a press call last week to announce our new spring/summer wear,' she informed Alice. 'But I hadn't realised you were back so we booked another girl, Inga, instead.'

'Oh,' said Alice, feeling disappointed.

'But now you're back we'll be sure to keep you in mind,' she added enthusiastically.

'Thanks.'

Then she phoned O'Reilly PR and asked to speak to Fiona, the boss.

'Alice, it's good to hear from you again,' the woman said. 'We didn't realise you were back in action.'

'Well, I've just come home from LA.'

'It's a pity I didn't know because we were launching National Vegetable Week last week and we booked a new girl called Inga, but we'll be sure to put more work your way. Keep in touch, darling.'

Alice put the phone down once again. Hmm. Bloody hell. Who was this Inga anyway and which rock had she crawled out from underneath? She was probably from some foreign undeveloped country and weighed about six stone.

She gave a deep sigh and then mustered up the courage to phone another agency. The name 'Inga' came up again. Alice felt like throwing her mobile at the wall in disgust. These PR people were so fickle. One minute you were their flavour of the month and the next they got a taste for something or somebody else. Alice had always been their number one choice and now some eejit called Inga was grabbing all her work. Well, she'd soon put a stop to that.

The next person she called was Michael Ryan of O'Grady's department store. At this stage she was almost beginning to lose her nerve.

'Hey, Alice, there's a name we haven't heard in a long time. Welcome home, kiddo. I thought you were living it up in Hollywood or I would have booked you for our new ad campaign. We've just given the job to another girl.'

'Inga, I suppose,' said Alice wryly.

'Inga? No, we did consider her but she's all over the place these days. We wanted somebody a bit more exclusive so we went for Sadie this time.'

Sadie? Oh God, that was even worse. Why hadn't she been more sensible and come home much earlier instead of holding out and hoping that things would improve between herself and Bill? She couldn't believe she had wasted so much of her precious time with him. And now it would seem that he had cost her a hell of a lot of money, too. It would take her for ever to crawl back on to the scene again. Models in this town were so easily replaced. That was the problem. They were ten a penny and the next big thing always seemed to be much younger, hungrier and eager to work for less money. She said goodbye to Michael and wondered who to call next. This whole morning was turning out to be very demoralising indeed.

She went through her contact book wondering whether she should get in another couple of phone calls before lunch. Maybe, just maybe with one of the agencies she would strike it lucky. But just as she was about to lift the phone again, she heard a car pull into the next-door driveway. Maybe Eddie was visiting his parents one last time before they headed off. As far as she knew they were leaving tomorrow.

She twitched the curtains just a little so as not to make it obvious she was spying, and she spotted a red Nissan Micra parked next door and a blond head in the driver's seat. It must be Tanya. She stepped quickly back from the window, terrified that the other girl might spot her. Then a few seconds later she took another look and could see that Tanya was struggling, trying to remove a big awkward-looking suitcase from the boot of the car. Alice felt more depressed than ever. So this was it. Madame was finally moving in.

Alice sat down on her bed and lit a cigarette. Normally she never smoked in the house but this was desperate altogether. Eddie, who had always adored her, no longer did. Somebody else had replaced her now in his affections. He had moved on or at least moved his new girlfriend in and she, Alice, was still living at home, penniless. It was as if all those years had just come to nothing. She hadn't a thing to show for any of her hard work. And now none of her old clients wanted to know because they had found Ingrid or Inga or whatever the hell her name was. Alice took a deep, dramatic drag. Life didn't get much shittier than this. She was about to kick off her shoes and climb into bed and snuggle up under the duvet to try and ward off her depression when suddenly her phone rang. She jumped up eagerly. Hopefully it would be one of her old clients with a bit of good news. But the number flashing was one she didn't recognise. She frowned as she took the call.

'Hello?'

'Hi, Alice, it's Elaine Thomson here. Remember you met me the other night?'

Alice sighed. Elaine was the last person she wanted to hear from. It was bad enough that her sister was at this moment parked outside ready to take over what really should have been her life.

'Oh hi, Elaine,' she said fairly unenthusiastically.

'Listen, I've been thinking of all the advice you gave me the other night and I've decided to take you up on it and give the old modelling thing a bash. You said you'd help me . . .'

'Oh yes.' Alice groaned inwardly. Why had she agreed to help the other girl at all? That must have been the drink talking or she wouldn't have bothered. It wasn't like she was in a good position to help anybody right now. What with Inga, and Sadie, and all those other girls already taking up offers of work that should be rightfully hers. Did she really need any more competition in the already oversaturated modelling world? Eh, that would clearly be a no. Then again, Eddie would think she was very considerate and selfless in helping Elaine's career. It would earn her a few brownie points. She'd already reluctantly agreed to walk the Toners' dog for them when they were away and Mrs Toner had been so grateful she'd called over with a huge bouquet of flowers, a box of Milk Tray, a two-hundred-euro voucher for Brown Thomas, and best of all a set of keys to the house. Alice had immediately given the chocolates to her mother as from now on she wasn't going to let a sweet or a piece of chocolate pass her lips. However, she had been enormously pleased that the Toners had trusted her with the keys to their home. Now she could let herself in and out of the house as much as she pleased and there wasn't a damn thing Little Miss Tanyakins could do about it.

'Yes, of course, Elaine,' she said, trying to inject some enthusiasm into her voice. 'Of course I'll help you in any way I can. I think modelling would be great for you. Now, have you got a pen on you? The first thing you need to do is take down Danny's phone number.'

Now that Tanya had settled comfortably into her new home with Eddie she began to realise that it had been the best decision she'd ever made. They'd grown much closer since moving in together a month ago and they hadn't even had the slightest argument between them. She enjoyed pottering around the large house in her spare time and she tended lovingly to Mr Toner's plants which were his pride and joy. The garden would be the one thing he would really miss when he was in Spain, he'd confided in her, and she had promised him she would look after it like it was her very own. It was so nice to be at home every evening when Eddie came in from work, to wrap her arms around him, ask him about his day, and share dinner together and a nice bottle of wine in front of the telly and then make love and fall asleep in his strong arms without having to worry about getting home. She no longer felt like a visitor in somebody else's home because she'd put her own touch on the place by buying in nicer, more modern furniture and having the entire house completely repainted. Everything was going swimmingly except for one little problem: Alice.

Alice was like a constant thorn in her side. And

although Eddie said she must be imagining it, she was sure that the other girl was keeping a constant watch out for her. In fact, she had seen Alice peep out her bedroom window at her on more than a couple of occasions. She was sure of it. But to make things worse, Eddie seemed to think Alice was bloody brilliant. She was always dropping around with fresh scones she claimed to have baked although Tanya had her suspicions that Mrs Adams had baked them instead. And it galled Tanya no end that she had a set of keys to their home.

She couldn't put her finger on the reason why, but she really didn't trust Alice. For all herself and Eddie knew, she could be snooping around their house when they were out without her even knowing. Prince adored Alice and practically ignored Tanya even though she often brought him home tasty treats from the butcher's. It wasn't her fault that she didn't have time to exercise him. In the last few weeks her business had really taken off and her phone was hopping with requests. She could hardly keep up with the demand.

But nothing had prepared her for the sheer joy she'd felt when a big American production company had requested she go down to Kerry and work on location over three days' filming. She'd almost screamed when she'd got the call. This was the stuff of dreams. One of those pivotal moments where all your hard work seemed to eventually pay off.

Not only would there be a very healthy fee involved but this was also the kind of interesting work she'd always dreamed of getting. Sure, she didn't mind giving massages and the like at people's homes and doing make-up for weddings was particularly lucrative, but working on an actual set with real actors and to one day be able to see the results of her work on celluloid would truly be the stuff of dreams.

Eddie was equally enthusiastic when she shared her good news with him.

'You really deserve this, hun,' he said, wrapping her in a bear hug. 'This is just the break that you've been waiting for.'

'Okay, but you're not supposed to sound *that* eager,' she joked. 'Won't you miss me when I'm gone?'

'Sure, but it's only for three days. How did I manage to look after myself before you came into my life?'

'God only knows,' Tanya laughed, placing a plate of piping-hot spaghetti carbonara down in front of him.

'This smells good.'

'Let's hope it tastes even better.'

She joined him at the table. For the past few days she hadn't been able to keep the smile off her face at the excitement of being able to work on the faces of real Hollywood stars who would soon be flying into Ireland to film the blockbuster movie. She hoped they wouldn't mind getting their picture taken with her so she could put them up on her Bebo site.

'Yum. Did anybody ever tell you that you're a wonderful cook?'

'Well, yes, all my ex-boyfriends have commented . . .'

'Stop that!' He waved his fork playfully. 'I don't want to know about your exes.'

'Speaking of exes,' she said, aware that she might be stepping on dangerous territory. 'Alice has invited my sister Elaine around to her house tomorrow to give her some tips on modelling. What do you make of that?'

Eddie's expression seemed to change. He cleared his throat somewhat deliberately. 'First of all,' he stated clearly, 'Alice is not my ex and second of all, I think it's pretty nice of her to help Elaine. Not everybody would do that.'

Tanya was now sorry she'd brought up the subject. The last thing she needed to hear was how great Eddie thought she was. Only the other day, Alice had called around with a new collar and a medal for Prince and Eddie had been touched by her generosity.

'It's nothing,' Alice had insisted, standing in their hall wearing a simple white T-shirt and navy jogging pants with her hair tied simply back and still managing to look amazing. 'I'm always thinking about poor Prince. He must really miss your mum and dad, Eddie.'

Eddie, to Tanya's horror, had spontaneously thrown his arms around Alice and thanked her for being so thoughtful. Tanya had just watched the scene unfold before her eyes in disbelief. Was Eddie really that gullible? She had a good mind to tell him exactly what Alice had done to her all those years ago. But something prevented her from coming out with it. She was worried about coming across as spiteful and unforgiving. She just didn't know how to bring it up. Besides, Alice was always so sweet to Eddie. Tanya noticed how sulky she was when he wasn't around. She was always frosty with Tanya and never bothered asking her anything about her day. Couldn't Eddie see she was a complete fake?

'But why would Alice want to help Elaine? I mean, she doesn't even know her.'

Eddie put down his knife and fork deliberately and wiped his mouth with his napkin. 'Not everybody does stuff just so that they can get something in return, Tanya.'

Tanya lowered her eyes and began picking at her food. She felt slightly ashamed and cursed herself again for bringing up Alice's name. As far as her boyfriend was concerned the girl just couldn't do anything wrong. It was as if she had some kind of magic spell over him. Did Eddie still have feelings for her? Tanya couldn't shake off the niggling feelings that warned her that he possibly still did. After all, didn't they say that you never really forgot your first love? And Alice had once been Eddie's dream girl. He'd even admitted it one night when they'd both been a bit drunk. Tanya had felt sick at the revelation. Did he still harbour those same feelings now? Had Alice been the one girl who'd got away? The girl on the pedestal whom he could never have yet would always fantasise about? Well, maybe she was. She'd disappeared when Eddie was madly in love with her but she was certainly back now, Tanya thought unhappily to herself. She was back now and was showing no signs of moving away.

27

Alice glanced at her watch. Elaine Thomson had just phoned to say that something had come up and that she'd be a couple of hours late. Alice wondered what on earth had possibly come up. Huh! What on earth could be so important? She obviously wasn't taking this modelling lark at all seriously. Alice didn't have all day to hang around and coach some brat about the pros and cons of modelling. Still, she'd bumped into Eddie just the other day and he'd thanked her profusely for looking out for young Elaine. Alice had simply shrugged and said it was no problem at all. Sure, what was the point of being at the top of your game if you couldn't pass on a bit of goodwill to up-and-coming girls?

'And when she's a supermodel I'll take all the credit for it,' she said, flashing her brilliant smile at him.

Eddie blushed like a schoolboy. 'And how's the modelling going for yourself?' he enquired over the hedge as they'd both been in their respective gardens at the time.

'It's all going great,' she said. 'I'm doing a shoot for Irish *Tatler* next week and then I'm doing a press call for a new airline that's starting up next week out of Dublin airport. It's a low-budget airline to rival Ryanair and I'm going to be the face of it.'

'Good for you,' he said, looking genuinely impressed. 'Not, of course, that there's anything low-budget-looking about you,' he added swiftly with his cute trademark smile.

'Oh, stop flattering me, Eddie. You've always had a habit of flattering me, tut tut.'

Alice couldn't help the big smile spreading all over her face. She was loving this. Eddie still fancied her. She could tell. Thankfully it was another nice sunny day so that she had the opportunity to wear a vest top and a tight pair of denim shorts to show off her tan and figure to perfection. What a stroke of luck that Eddie just happened to be checking on the plants at the same time as she was topping up her tan on her mother's old deckchair!

Prince started to bark excitedly at the sound of Alice's voice.

'You've certainly got a fan there,' Eddie laughed good-naturedly. 'Will you be bringing him for a walk later on?'

'Of course,' Alice ventured. 'I know how much his walks mean to him.'

And of course she knew what Prince meant to her too. He was her one connection to Eddie Toner's world. He was the reason she had free access to the Toner home any time she liked and she made sure to make use of that golden opportunity any time she could. The Toner home was always spotless whenever she called in. There was never a cobweb to be spied or a speck of dust in sight. That one Tanya must do nothing but polish and clean at this stage. She was obviously trying to be such a perfect wifey type that Eddie would never let her go. Hmm. Alice was beginning to think that she should up her game a bit. Eddie and Tanya were getting to be too cosy for comfort.

She waited until Eddie and Tanya had gone out for the day before she popped around to their house. Prince nearly went berserk at the sight of her. No wonder some people adored their dogs, Alice thought, struggling to keep him still so that she could fasten the lead on to his collar. They were the only creatures on earth to look at you like they were totally besotted with you no matter what you looked like. And they were so grateful for any little attention you threw their way.

She took him for a brisk two-kilometre walk during which he insisted on trying to stop at every lamppost to cock his leg and claim his territory.

When she came back, to her annoyance she found Tanya's car parked in the drive. How irritating! If only Eddie could be home alone instead. She rang the doorbell defiantly. Even she realised it would be too ignorant just to let herself in when somebody was already in the house.

On the third ring, and just as she was about to give up, the door opened. It was Tanya, looking a bit worn out, her hair scraped back off her face and wearing not a screed of make-up.

'I'm just dropping Prince home,' said Alice cheerfully.

'Oh thanks, Alice,' Tanya said politely. 'Sorry, I almost didn't hear the bell. I was down in the garden tending to Mr Toner's plants.'

Alice thought the least Tanya could do was invite her in for a cup of tea. But no such invitation was forthcoming. So Alice went back to her own house next door. Her father was sitting at the kitchen table reading the newspaper. He looked up brightly at the sight of his only daughter. 'Well, you'll never guess who's in the paper today,' he said, opening it up on page fourteen where there was a huge smiling picture of Alice sitting on a motorbike where she'd been promoting some festival.

'Oh, thanks for showing me, Dad. Don't throw it out, sure you won't? I'll cut it out and keep it in my scrapbook.'

'It's good to see you getting more work now and getting your confidence back,' her father said knowingly.

'Um, what do you mean?' she asked, pouring herself a tall glass of water at the sink.

'Well, I couldn't help noticing you were a little dejected for a few days after you came home from America. Myself and your mother didn't like to interfere as you've always been so independent, but you seem like you're back to the old Alice we know and love now.'

Alice smiled at him. 'Thanks, Dad, I appreciate it.'

That was some speech for her father, she thought, clearing away her glass and making her way upstairs again. But, she frowned, she hoped they didn't think she was making too much money. They had no idea how much debt she was still in and she couldn't afford to be contributing to the household bills or paying rent or anything like that just yet.

She looked out her window and saw Tanya getting into her car. A few seconds later she drove off. Alice stared out as her car disappeared around the corner. Tanya had never shown any signs of wanting to be on friendly terms with Alice. In fact, sometimes Alice felt the girl could be downright hostile. Maybe she thought Alice was a threat. And she'd be right there too. It infuriated Alice the way

Tanya acted like she was Eddie's wife and that the Toners' house was hers. And Alice had been so friendly and welcoming to the little bitch. Well, she thought, all fired up now after Tanya's earlier snub, things are about to get nasty now. The games are about to get a lot tougher. All's fair in love and war. But there can only be one winner, bitch!

Alice set about vigorously tidying her room and sorting out her drawers with gusto. Although she never offered to help with the general household chores, her room was something she had to look after herself. Her mother refused to tidy Alice's room. Still, she thought, as she set about putting her odd socks in pairs in the top drawer, she wouldn't be here for much longer hopefully. As soon as she moved out she would hire a Filipina maid to come in and look after the housework. Better still, if she could get that Tanya one with all her airs and graces to move out of the house next door, then Alice could simply move in. The whole thing was so frustrating. Why couldn't Eddie just accept that he was still in love with Alice and that they were clearly meant to be together? Why was he fighting it? Both he and she knew that the chemistry between them was irresistible. Even Tanya could see it. Even her own mother could see it for God's sake.

'Are you not a bit chilly?' she'd asked Alice after she'd noticed her chatting to Eddie over the wall. 'You're practically falling out of that skimpy little top,' she'd added with a note of disapproval.

Good, thought Alice. That's exactly why she had worn it when she'd headed out to the garden earlier with a watering can on the pretence of doing some work. And it had worked. She'd noticed that Eddie could hardly keep his eyes off her and was obviously clearly distracted by her.

She sat down on the bed, already sick of tidying her bedroom. She just wasn't cut out for housework at all. Why was she picking up bits of fluff off the floor when she should be concentrating on how to win Eddie back?

And then she had an absolute brainwave. She put her head in her hands to try and concentrate properly. Tanya wasn't half as attractive as she was, or particularly successful, or funny, but something must be drawing Eddie to her or else he wouldn't have asked her to move in with him. Okay, she was supposedly this great cook, but Alice could easily buy a few cookbooks and learn how to make some nice dishes. But more than that, Tanya was steady and reliable. She wasn't the type to go off the rails so that was probably what Eddie liked about her. She was comforting and safe. She never put a foot wrong. So now Alice had this idea. Okay, her plan was maybe a tiny bit underhand, and she might even get caught out, but desperate times called for desperate measures.

She grabbed her set of keys for the Toners' house and skipped outside with the lead. She met her mother coming up the drive laden down with bags of groceries. 'Would you ever help me bring these inside, love? My arms have practically been torn from their sockets with the weight of them.'

'I can't, sorry.' Alice skipped on by in a hurry. 'I've got to go in next door and feed Prince.'

Mrs Adams shook her head ruefully. For one who was never fond of animals as a child and in fact was terrified any time any came within half a mile of her, she certainly had taken to the Kerry Blue next door in a big way. They'd become practically inseparable.

Minutes later Alice was back in her room with Prince who seemed baffled by the whole change of plan. He obviously thought that he was going for another walk, the thick eejit.

'Now, Mister,' she said to him, giving him some chocolate to calm him down. 'You're to be nice and quiet for me or else there will be no more—' She stopped herself just in time from saying the word 'walk'. The very mention of that word would be enough for him to bark the house down. Then her parents would really think she'd lost the plot for smuggling Prince into her bedroom. She'd even put a blanket on her bed in case he decided to jump up on it and go to sleep. Hopefully he wasn't riddled with fleas.

Then with Prince carefully imprisoned in her bedroom and the door tightly locked, she made her way downstairs, past her mother who was busy unloading the grocery bags in the kitchen, and out into the garden. She went down to the very end where she'd be safely out of earshot. Only then did she ring Eddie's mobile number.

'Hello?' He answered immediately.

'Oh, Eddie, hi, is that you?' she cried dramatically. 'I am so, so sorry to be ringing you at work but something dreadful has happened.'

'What is it? Please calm down, Alice. You're scaring me.'

'Oh God, sorry Eddie, but it's, well, it's Prince.'

'Where is he?' Eddie sounded alarmed.

'That's the thing,' she said, trying to make her voice sound as frantic as possible. 'I don't know where he is. I just called around to give him some tasty treats and I discovered the side gate was open. Somebody must have forgotten to shut it after them. And so I started calling for the dog but there's no sign of him.'

'Oh, God.'

'Now listen, don't panic. I'm sure he'll be found.'

'I'll leave the office right away. I've got to find him. He's my mother's pride and joy. She'd die if anything happened to him. Is Tanya there?'

'No, she must have gone out.'

'She must have left the side door open. Jesus, how could she have been so careless?'

'I don't know,' said Alice, thrilled that Eddie was blaming Tanya without her even pointing the finger. 'But don't rush home yet. I'm going to pound the streets looking for him and if I have no luck within the next hour I'll phone the guards and the nearest dogs' home to see if anybody has left him in.'

She could hear Eddie sigh dramatically at the other end of the phone. Good. Everything was going to plan.

'Okay,' he said wearily, 'but you'll keep me informed, won't you? I won't rest easy till I know he's safe.'

'You just leave it to me,' she purred and ended the call.

She decided to wait a half-hour or so before calling back. She was worried that Elaine might call around sooner rather than later and then her game would be up. That wouldn't do at all.

'Eddie, is that you?' she said when she called him back a while later.

'Yes!' he said breathlessly. 'Any news? I'm out of my mind with worry.'

'Well, you needn't worry any more,' she cooed. 'I've found him!'

'What? Where was he? Is he okay?'

'He's fine. I have him here with me now. He seems a little confused but, apart from that, he's in good form.'

'Where did you find him?'

'He was wandering about on the road about a mile from here.'

'Oh God, he could have been stolen. Or even killed. Thank God you found him. How can I thank you?'

'Oh, there's no need for that. I'm just so relieved he's home safe and sound. You know I adore Prince.'

'Well, I insist you call around later for a drink at least.'

'Oh, actually that would be nice. Are you sure you don't mind?'

'Of course not, you've just saved my life. I don't know what I would have done if I'd had to ring Mum and Dad in Spain to let them know that something had happened to Prince.'

'You can relax now. He's safe and sound. But just remember to be careful in future about locking the side door. You know how adventurous Prince is.'

'I'll have to tell Tanya. It must have been her who left the door open. I don't know how she did it.'

'Well, let's not go around blaming anybody. I'm sure she didn't mean it. She's probably just got a lot on her mind with her business taking off and everything . . .' she trailed off.

'Yeah, but still, that's no excuse,' he said, sounding annoyed.

Alice was glad he couldn't see the satisfied smile spreading across her face.

'I'll see you later then? Does nine suit? Do you want to check it with Tanya first to see if she doesn't mind?'

'If she doesn't mind?' Eddie sounded baffled. 'Of course she doesn't mind. Anyway, I don't have to go and check everything with Tanya first. It's my house.'

When Alice ended the call she almost exploded with joy. She couldn't hide her delight. Eddie had made it perfectly clear where Tanya stood with him. *It's my house.* Well, that said it all, didn't it? He didn't refer to it as *their* house. No, he'd made it very clear. He was the one who wore the trousers. Theirs didn't sound like much of an equal partnership to Alice. With a bit more patience and careful planning on Alice's part Tanya would soon be packing her bags and driving off into the distance, leaving the coast clear for Alice. Alice could have hugged herself with delight. Just then the doorbell rang, abruptly bringing Alice's ecstatic mood to an end. Shit, that must be Elaine already.

28

Elaine was standing at the door as predicted, fresh-faced and smiling, looking even younger than her years. It was a pity she didn't smile more often, thought Alice; she was much prettier when she did. Prince jumped up at her enthusiastically.

'Well, you caused quite a bit of drama this morning,' said Elaine, patting the excitable dog on the head.

'Oh, so you heard already?' Alice asked, ushering her into the kitchen.

'Of course. Tanya rang me in a panic earlier. Apparently Eddie had been on to her giving out yards. Sorry I'm late, by the way. I had a deadline for a college assignment. I had to get it in or else I'd be dead meat.'

'Tea or coffee?' Alice offered, afraid to look at Elaine, in case she saw the delight creeping into her face. So Tanya was already in the bad books? Alice couldn't be happier.

'Have you anything else?'

'Like a soft drink?'

'Have you not got anything stronger? I've had a rough day trying to finish my assignment in time. I need a stiff drink.'

Alice was taken by surprise. This Elaine one was a bit

cheeky, wasn't she? Alice didn't know if she'd been so forward when she was her age. Nevertheless she went to open her parents' drinks cabinet in order to oblige. Anything to keep Tanya's little sis happy. Anyway, a drink might loosen her tongue and get her to spill the beans on her sister's relationship with Eddie.

'How about a vodka and orange juice?'

'That'll do nicely,' said Elaine, immediately sitting down at the kitchen table and making herself at home by kicking off her shoes.

Alice thought she might as well pour one for herself. It was a nice sunny afternoon and they could sit out in the back garden and catch some of the last rays before the sun went in.

Alice poured two generous measures of vodka, filled the glasses with fresh orange juice and added a handful of ice cubes.

'Ah, bliss. Thanks, you're a star,' said Elaine, taking her glass from Alice. 'Have you any crisps or peanuts to go with this?'

Alice shook her head resolutely. 'You need to start watching what you eat, Missus. Cut out the junk food. When I was your age I could eat what I liked, too, but it'll catch up with you eventually. You have to make sacrifices if you're serious about modelling.'

Elaine groaned. 'If you think I'll start changing my diet to lettuce leaves and celery sticks, you can forget it. I like my food too much.'

'Have it your own way,' said Alice, taking a seat opposite her. 'But there's nothing for nothing, you know. As a professional model you can't afford to have any wobbly bits on you. Jelly bellies don't entice the clients, nor do thunder thighs.'

Elaine laughed. 'All right, I get you. It's just that when I'm studying I tend to stuff my face and I get these crazy cravings for McDonald's. But I'll try to be good from now on.'

'Nothing tastes as good as being thin.'

'Haha, I'll keep that in mind next time I reach for a Kit Kat in the college sweet shop!'

'Joking aside, there are far more models than there are jobs going so you have to keep ahead of the competition.'

'Okay, enough said,' said Elaine, beginning to sound bored now. 'So anyway, I rang your man Danny and he sounded nice enough on the phone.'

'Don't be fooled. He's only nice to people if he thinks he'll make money out of them. This business is all about bringing the bucks in. So when are you seeing him?'

'Next week,' Elaine replied, taking another gulp of her drink.

'Maybe you should get some professional shots done before you go and see him. I could give you names of a couple of photographers I've worked closely enough with to call friends. There are so many gangsters out there working as photographers who make their living out of wannabe models. You need to be careful.'

'Thanks for the tip off.'

'And you could get Tanya to do your make-up for free.'

'That's a good idea, yeah. I'm sure she wouldn't mind if she has the time. She's the best there is and I'm not just being biased because she's my sister.'

'I believe you.'

'I'd need to catch her though before she goes away.

Herself and Eddie are planning a romantic break somewhere after she's finished down in Kerry.'

'Oh?' Alice could feel her face fall. So the happy couple were looking at holiday brochures together now, were they? Alice could just imagine them canoodling over cocktails by the pool somewhere exotic and it was enough to take all the good out of her afternoon.

'Yeah, the lucky bitch. I wish it was me jetting off to sit on a nice sunny beach. Not that I could even afford a day-trip to Lucan at the moment, the way my finances are looking.'

'What's she doing in Kerry?' Alice enquired, trying to sound upbeat but failing miserably.

'Oh, she's got some big job working down there on a film set with Hollywood stars no less. Some people have the life.'

Indeed, they did, thought Alice glumly. Still, on the bright side of things, at least Tanya would be out of town for a bit leaving Eddie to his own devices. Maybe he'd invite her around for another drink without Madame there glued to him as usual. She had to remain positive.

When Elaine was finished her drink she asked for another one. Really she had the cheek of Reilly, Alice thought. Still, you had to admire her for her chutzpah. She'd probably go far in the modelling world with that thick skin of hers.

Alice duly poured her another large one but refrained from helping herself. She had to watch it and not be calling around next door later drunk as a skunk or Tanya and Eddie would think she had a secret drink problem. She hoped her parents wouldn't come home any time soon or they would no doubt wonder what Elaine was doing here polishing off their Christmas drinks. But they were off looking at garden furniture somewhere and probably wouldn't be home for a while yet.

If Alice thought that by plying the youngster with alcohol she'd get some interesting titbits about Eddie and Tanya's relationship she was sorely mistaken. Elaine seemed to have no interest in the couple and looked decidedly bored every time Alice tried to steer the conversation in their direction. Eventually she looked at her watch. 'Well, I suppose I'd better get a move along,' she said, standing up. 'Listen, thanks for all the advice. I appreciate it.'

'No worries,' said Alice, accompanying her to the front door with Prince trotting along beside them. 'And give some thought to getting those professional shots done, won't you?'

'I will do. It's just . . .'

'What?' Alice questioned.

Elaine faltered. 'Well, I mostly live in jeans. I don't have very many fancy clothes to dress up in.'

'Hmm. Well, you could always borrow my stuff. Or maybe Tanya would let you raid her wardrobe. We could go around and see what she has.'

'That's a great idea.'

You bet, thought Alice, grinning slyly.

'You what?' Tanya spluttered.

She could hardly believe her ears. What was Eddie thinking of? How could he possibly have invited Alice in for a cosy drink without even letting her know first?

'It was the least I could do,' he defended himself, loosening his tie and then removing it altogether and throwing it on the bed. 'The girl went out of her way to save our asses earlier on after *you* left the side door open and nearly got the dog killed.'

Tanya could feel an anger rise inside her that she wouldn't have thought was possible. How many times did she need to tell him that it wasn't her fault the dog got out before it would register in his thick skull?

'For the hundredth time, I didn't leave the side door open,' she insisted. 'But if you want to entertain Alice this evening, you can do it by yourself. I neither like nor trust the girl and I won't be a hypocrite and sit there laughing and chatting to her like she's some long-lost friend.'

Eddie turned around and looked at his girlfriend in disbelief. 'I don't know what you have against Alice. She's never been anything but friendly to us but you always insist on being so hostile. Your behaviour is pretty childish. Even you must realise that, Tanya.'

Tanya plonked herself down on the edge of their double bed and folded her arms in protest.

'I've had a hard day at work, Eddie, and I'm just not in the mood for light chit-chat with somebody I don't even particularly like. If you want to play the host, then you go on ahead. I'm going to have a long hot bubble bath and then I'm going to get into this bed and read my book. If you don't want to join me, then that's up to you.'

'Would you ever just listen to yourself? You're being ridiculous. Alice won't stay long, I'm sure, but she'll think you're some weirdo if you insist on staying up here out of her way, but if that's what you want to do then suit yourself.'

He wasn't backing down. Tanya watched on in despair as he wordlessly changed out of his work suit and into a pair of jeans and a shirt. Really he could just be so stubborn sometimes!

'Oh, all right then,' she eventually relented. 'I'll join yourself and Alice for a drink just this once. But don't for a minute think I'm happy about it.'

'No, don't come down, Tanya,' he answered sulkily. 'You're not bothered, so fine. I'll go down and be sociable. I'll just tell Alice you've got a headache or something. I'm sure she won't mind.'

That was the problem though. Alice wouldn't mind at all. Tanya was sure of it. In fact, she'd probably be immensely relieved if Tanya didn't show her face and then she could have Eddie all to herself. Just like old times' sake. How cosy. Well, Tanya thought, hell would freeze over before she would allow that to happen under her nose. She got up defiantly from the bed and went into the bathroom to run herself a hot shower. She needed to freshen up and make herself look decent. Knowing her luck Alice would show up looking like the bee's knees even though it was supposed to be just a casual drink between neighbours. Huh! As if that was the case!

And she was right. After Eddie answered the doorbell forty-five minutes later Alice flounced into the sitting room as though she were opening a Versace fashion show. To make things even worse, Prince ran around in circles barking hysterically with joy after setting his eyes on his new 'mistress'.

'You look fabulous, Tanya,' she said, air-kissing her arch rival. She didn't seem to notice the other girl visibly flinch. 'It's really kind of Eddie and yourself to invite me round.'

Tanya glowered. She wasn't buying Alice's niceness for a second. 'Well, we have to thank you for finding Prince safe and well,' said Tanya grudgingly. Although she smelled a rat where Alice was concerned, she was nevertheless determined to be polite so as not to give Eddie an excuse to argue with her later on.

'It was no problem. I mean, I love Prince as much as you do. He's like a family member at this stage. I'd die if anything happened to him.'

She was wearing a low-cut red cotton dress that clung to her every curve, Tanya noted with some dissatisfaction. Personally she thought her attire was way over the top for just a friendly chat with the neighbours. Tanya herself was wearing a simple denim miniskirt and a navy tank top. What did Alice think this was? Some kind of cocktail party?

'Would you like a glass of red or white wine?' Eddie offered, all smiles.

'A glass of red would be great,' said Alice, flicking her dark hair over her shoulder in a deliberately flirtatious manner. 'But please don't open a bottle on my behalf. I'll have whatever you two are having.'

'I prefer white,' Tanya said, immediately ignoring the glance that Eddie shot at her.

'Okay, white will do me fine. Red wine just makes my teeth red anyway,' she added with a girly giggle. 'Isn't the weather just fabulous for this time of year? Your sister Elaine was over at mine earlier. Did she tell you? I'm giving her some advice about trying to break into the modelling business and as it was such a nice day we decided to sit out in the back garden with some vodka and orange.'

'You were drinking?' Tanya was astounded. 'During the day?'

She nearly bit off her tongue for sounding so shocked and prissy, especially when Alice just laughed off her question.

'Ah sure, sometimes you just have to live for the moment,' she said gaily, crossing her impossibly long legs on the leather couch and glancing at Eddie for support.

He smiled back at her fondly. 'Exactly. That's what I always say. Life's far too short to be taking things seriously.'

Tanya could feel herself bristle. Alice was making her out to be some kind of fussy old nun or something. She wasn't so shocked about people drinking during the day. Sure she often did it herself when she was on holidays or when she was out having a boozy lunch in the Unicorn with the girls as a treat. But she really didn't think her younger sister Elaine should be knocking back vodkas in the middle of the afternoon when she had important exams coming up shortly. Why would she spend an afternoon getting wasted with her new buddy Alice?

'So how's the new business taking off?' Alice gave Tanya a saccharine smile.

'Oh, you know, all good. The phone never stops hopping which is a good sign. Soon I won't be able to keep up with all the demand.'

'Ah, good complaint.' Alice nodded. 'And what about yourself, Legal Eagle?' She grinned at Eddie.

'Couldn't be better.'

'Listen, Elaine's told me that Tanya's off hobnobbing with the stars down in Kerry for a few days so if you're stuck for anything you know I'm only a hop over the wall . . .'

Eddie and Alice both laughed, but Tanya was outraged. What did Alice exactly mean by that? Stuck for anything? Why would he be stuck for anything? He had a car and was well able to get around. Maybe Alice was insinuating that if Eddie was stuck for a bit of hanky panky then she'd readily oblige . . . she wanted to reach out and slap the brazen smile off Alice's face. The house phone rang suddenly in the hall.

'I'll get that,' said Tanya, jumping straight up. She was shaking now. She hadn't felt this angry in a long, long time.

'Hey, Tanya! It's Dianne. How's everything? I haven't seen you in yonks. Where the Dickens have you been hiding? We need to go for a few bevvies soon, do you hear? Tanya? Tanya, are you still there?'

'Yes, I'm still here,' Tanya hissed, holding the phone very close to her ear. 'Listen, you're not going to believe this but Eddie's ex, Ms Malice, is here in our house as we speak, flirting with my boyfriend and wearing a skirt up to her arse. I'm not joking, Dianne. You'd have to see it to believe it! I can't speak too loudly. Sorry.'

Dianne was intrigued. 'What the hell's *she* doing there?'

'I don't know. I've been asking myself the same question all evening.'

'The cheek of her barging in like that,' said Dianne crossly. 'You'd think she'd be able to find a man of her own without coming on to yours.'

'So you think she's after Eddie? That's what I've thought all along.'

'Damn right she is. And you're a fool, Tanya, if you let her swipe him from under your nose. Toughen up, hun. You better put up a fight if you want to get rid of her for good. I know women like that. They know every trick in the book. She's out to steal somebody else's man. You just make sure she doesn't steal yours.'

'This wine is going down very nicely, I must say,' Alice said appreciatively to Eddie, glad that Tanya had left the room to take the phone call. It was so much nicer when she was out of sight. 'Where did you get it?'

'Oh, I just picked it up in O'Brien's off-licence. They recommended it. It's a South African.'

'Really? You must write down the name for me. I'm always on the lookout for a decent wine.'

'I will, remind me before you go.'

Alice stood up to stretch her legs and wandered over to the mantelpiece. 'And have your folks been in touch?'

'Yeah, they usually ring every second day or so. They love everything over there from the food to the weather to the golf. Green fees are much cheaper out in Spain than they are here. In fact, everything's cheaper. I'd be almost tempted to move out there myself.'

Alice laughed and then noticed something. 'I see they took that photo of you and me at your debs away with them.'

She saw Eddie frown. 'No, I don't think they did. They didn't actually take that much stuff with them because they're only renting a one-bedroom apartment over there.'

'That's funny, it was definitely here the last time I was round talking to your mum.'

'It's always been there,' Eddie confided, blushing slightly, which made him look cuter than ever. 'My mum loves that picture.'

'Well, then, maybe she took it with her.'

But Eddie shook his head, looking decidedly puzzled. 'No, I could have sworn it was here a few days ago. I must have a look for it.'

'Yeah, well, it could hardly have been stolen,' Alice joked. 'I mean nobody would want it for sentimental reasons apart from your mum . . . or maybe you or I?' she added, giving him a deliberately coy look.

Eddie shrugged. 'I must have a root around tomorrow and see where it got to. You might want to make a copy of it.'

'Oh yes, that's such a good idea. I'd love to do that.'

Their conversation was halted by a mobile phone ringing on the coffee table.

'Is that yours?' Alice asked.

'No, it's Tanya's. We'd better leave it.'

But the phone rang and rang and then it rang again.

'Maybe it's Elaine or one of her clients. Just take a message,' Alice urged.

'Okay then; I can't be listening to that thing going all evening and Tanya can't have two telephone conversations at the same time,' Eddie said, picking up Tanya's mobile phone.

'Hello?'

Alice watched Eddie's usual easygoing expression change.

'Eh . . . she's on another call at the moment. Is, eh, is this a client? Can I take a message? Okay, David, she'll know who you are? Right then, will do. Bye.'

As he ended the call, Alice noticed that he looked very put out. Hmmm. Very interesting indeed. Who on earth was David? Why was he looking for Tanya? And why didn't Eddie seem to have a clue who he was? The mind boggled . . .

'So who's this David chap?' Eddie asked his girlfriend once Alice had gone home and was safely out of earshot.

Tanya slowly drained her glass of wine and stared back at him blankly. 'David? I don't know any David.'

'Funny, that's not what he seems to think,' Eddie retorted, sounding decidedly miffed. 'When you were on the phone earlier some guy called David rang your mobile and asked to speak to you. I don't think he was too thrilled to hear my voice instead.'

And suddenly it dawned on her with a thud. David? The guy she'd met in Samsara? What on earth was he doing phoning her? Would he not have just given up by now? Oh God! And why did Eddie, of all people, have to answer the phone? She swallowed awkwardly. How on earth was she going to explain this one away?

Eddie looked at her expectantly. 'Well?'

'Oh, I remember now. David's just some guy I met when I was out with the girls a few weeks ago. There's nothing going on there,' she added flippantly.

'Nothing?' he said sounding astonished. 'You gave your number to some strange guy out on the town and you're telling me not to be worried?'

'It wasn't like that,' she said, moving in closer to him and placing a hand on his thigh which he swiftly pushed away.

'What was it like then? Go on, I'm listening.'

Tanya explained the whole story about Rose getting manky drunk and how David had seen them all home safely and had even paid for the taxi.

'Sounds like quite the knight in shining armour,' observed Eddie, laden with sarcasm.

'Listen,' she snapped. 'I tried calling you several times that night but some woman answered your phone instead.'

'I just think it's a bit strange that he should be calling you, that's all. Did you not tell him you were attached?'

'Of course I did. I made that perfectly clear to him. I always make it clear to men from the start when I'm out.'

'So he was coming on to you then?'

'Well, I suppose he was just taking a chance. Most men will.'

'But why did you feel the need to hand your number out to him?' Eddie persisted, refusing to let the matter drop.

'He just wanted to make sure I'd got home okay.'

'How nice.'

'Eddie, can we let it drop?' Tanya pleaded with him. 'I've got a headache now and just want to go to bed. Please don't let us fight over something so insignificant.'

She stood up as if to make a point. She didn't want to pursue the conversation. Yes, she had led David on more than she'd intended, but she'd been tipsy that night and hadn't meant any harm. Now she simply wanted to forget the whole incident. Just as she reached the door, Eddie spoke again.

'Tanya, do you know what happened to the photo that was on the mantelpiece?'

'Which photo?' she said, feigning innocence but feeling herself go red, much to her annoyance. She knew exactly which photo he was talking about.

'The one of me and Alice at my debs?'

'So you noticed I took it down,' she answered coolly.

'*She* noticed, actually. I think she was insulted when she saw that it had been removed.'

'I put it in one of the drawers, Eddie. Obviously I hadn't realised how much it meant to you,' she added acerbically before walking out and closing the door firmly behind her.

32

Alice woke to the sun streaming in the windows. She sat up in the bed and stretched, feeling decidedly pleased with herself. Last night had been a resounding success and she had even got to talk to Eddie alone for a little while when Tanya was off talking to her friend on the phone. The evening had certainly taken a surprising twist as well. Eddie's face had been a tonic to see when some guy called David had phoned looking for Tanya. Whoever this David guy was, Eddie didn't seem to know anything about him or the reason he should be calling Tanya's mobile. What a spot of luck it was that Alice had been sitting in the room at the same time. This could provide her with much ammunition on her quest to take Eddie back from Tanya. Alice had noted that Eddie didn't mention the phone call when Tanya eventually came back into the sitting room to join them. Obviously he was waiting for her to leave before he blew his top. Oh God, what she wouldn't have given to be a fly on the wall when that had happened. Alice almost hugged herself with glee at the thought of it all. Things were far from hunky dory in the love nest next door and Tanya was playing right into her hands. Give her a few more weeks and Alice would make sure she was gone altogether. This time for good.

She jumped out of bed and pulled back the curtains. What a glorious spring morning it was. She looked out the window to see if any cars were parked in the driveway next door as was customary for her to do every morning. The drive was empty though.

She threw on her dressing gown and pottered downstairs barefoot to make herself a strong black coffee.

She noticed her dad in the back garden busy with the hose and she waved to him from the kitchen window. Her father loved that garden. He was always pottering about in it. Just like the Toners next door, his garden was his pride and joy. When Mr and Mrs Toner lived next door he was forever exchanging plant names with them and talking about shrubs and flowers. God, somebody kill me if ever I become that boring, Alice thought, popping a piece of bread into the toaster. Mind you, the Toners certainly seemed to derive a great deal of joy out of their garden. She had noticed Tanya had taken an interest in the garden too, of late. She'd seen her out at the crack of dawn some days digging and weeding as if her heart depended on it. Huh, she obviously thought playing the green-fingered goddess would keep her in the Toners' good books. And then Alice had another brainwave. The toast popped up but she ignored it. She no longer felt hungry. Instead she went out to the garden to her dad.

'Good morning, love,' he greeted her enthusiastically. 'Isn't it a lovely morning?'

'It is indeed, Dad,' she said, pulling her dressing gown around her. 'I must say the garden's coming along nicely. It's a real credit to you.'

'Thank you. Did you see the lupins there in the corner? They really love this weather.'

'Aren't you killed though, getting rid of all those damn weeds?'

'They're a pain, all right.' He nodded. 'But I've got some weed killer now that the fellow at the garden centre recommended. You need to be careful with it, though, as it'll kill everything in sight.' He pointed out the big white plastic bottle a couple of feet away.

'It wouldn't kill a dog, though, would it?' Alice frowned.

'No, it won't harm animals but it'll destroy any living plant. You have to dilute it first with a good bit of water.'

'I see.'

'You're not thinking of taking up gardening, are you, Alice? I've never seen you take an interest before.'

'Ah no, I'm not that old,' she laughed. 'But I have to say it's very pretty out here with all the different colours and everything. You must be really proud of all your hard work.'

She remained chatting for a while in the sunshine about the different flowers her dad had planted and tried her best not to keel over with boredom. Eventually he looked at his watch and said he had to get going to the doctor as he had an appointment at 12 p.m.

'What's the appointment for? There's nothing wrong, is there?' she asked, feeling mildly alarmed. Although her dad had reached the ripe old age of seventy he'd always been fit and healthy. Hopefully there was nothing wrong.

'Ah no, pet. Just a routine check-up. I've been feeling more tired than usual recently and my energy levels are a bit low so your mother made an appointment for me.'

'Oh, okay.'

Once her dad was gone, Alice quickly got dressed and popped around next door where Prince joyfully greeted her by putting his paws on her waist, wagging his tail furiously and trying to lick her face.

'Get down, you big lump, will you?' she snapped as she noticed the two paw prints he'd left on her pristine white top.

She went out to the garden and Prince was very disappointed to realise that he wasn't allowed to follow her. Then, after looking furtively around her and deciding that the coast was well and truly clear, she opened the canvas Dunnes Stores bag that she'd brought with her, retrieved the white plastic bottle of weed killer, and did what she had to do.

She was going soft in the head, she really was, Alice thought as she tried to keep Prince still so that she could put his lead on him. She hadn't had any intention of bringing him for a walk today but he had this way of looking at her with his big mournful eyes that would gladden the hardest of hearts. Finally, Alice had given in and agreed to bring him for a short walk to stop him from whining.

First of all, she left the weed killer back next door in her dad's shed and then decided to bring the dog to the shops to buy herself a packet of cigarettes and a can of Diet Coke. That's what she was practically living on these days: tar and caffeine. Well, she had to go to drastic measures to try and keep her weight down. Her phone wasn't exactly hopping with clients trying to book her, was it? She must ring the agency later and find out when the press call for that new airline would be. For some reason she'd thought it was this week but when she'd heard nothing she supposed they'd probably changed the date. Still, that job would pay good money and she needed it badly. The credit card company had sent her a nasty threatening letter just the other day and she was determined to pay off all she owed and then cut it in two for ever. She'd begged her dad for the loan of five hundred euros which was the last minimum payment on the card. If she could pay that then she could bide for a bit more time and when her payments from the modelling agency finally came through she could start paying him back. He'd been a bit reluctant at first because he'd said he'd been planning on buying a new set of golf clubs but eventually she had persuaded him. After all, once she got paid by this new airline for promoting it she'd be laughing all the way to the bank.

Outside her local Spar she tied Prince to a lamppost and then ran into the shop to buy her stuff. It was only when she was in the shop that she absent-mindedly started flicking through one of the tabloids to see what trouble Britney Spears and Amy Winehouse had recently got themselves into. Then her heart hit the floor flying. She was so shocked she could hardly speak. There was a huge picture of her rival Sadie on page one promoting the airline which she herself had thought was in the bag. She felt like vomiting. How could they treat her like that? Did her agency not even have enough respect to ring her and let her know that she had been replaced? God, a year ago

Sadie wouldn't have been within a hair's sniff of landing a big campaign like this. Alice felt her head begin to spin.

Was she past it after all?

Was it really all over for her already?

33

Tanya woke up alone on Saturday morning. Eddie's side of the bed was empty. It had been her birthday yesterday and he had treated to her to dinner last night in the fabulous La Mer Zou restaurant on Stephen's Green. Although they'd both made an effort to keep the conversation light and breezy, Tanya felt it was a bit strained. His mind seemed to wander when she was talking to him and she wondered whether he was stressed at work at the moment. When they'd arrived home last night there had been a message from Eddie's parents wishing her a happy birthday and Mr Toner had thanked her for keeping up the good work in the garden. She'd been pleased that Eddie had obviously told them how hard she'd been working to keep it looking in tip-top shape.

It was a nice sunny morning and she found Eddie downstairs in the sitting room sipping orange juice and watching Sky News.

'Morning, love,' she said to him, planting a kiss on the top of his head. 'We're taking Prince to Killiney Beach, remember?'

'Oh yeah sure,' he said with none of his usual

enthusiasm and Tanya worried that he might be trying to shut her out. It wasn't usual for him to be this cool towards her. She didn't feel very positive going off to Kerry for a few days when things weren't going smoothly for them.

'I'm going to make myself a cup of coffee,' she said, trying to sound bright and breezy. 'Would you like a cup yourself?'

'Oh, yes, that would be great,' he said, his eyes never leaving the TV screen.

Tanya wandered into the kitchen in her dressing gown but as she pulled up the blinds to let the sunlight filter in through the window nothing could have prepared her for the shock that beheld her. The garden looked like a patch of barren waste ground. Everything was dead. She blinked in disbelief and rushed to open the back door. Prince was sitting on the doorstep and she nearly tripped over him. He looked up expectantly, wondering if she was going to feed him. But she barely registered him. Instead she walked out to the garden, dazed, as if in a trance. The grass was covered in rough brown patches and there wasn't a plant or a flower alive. Tanya thought she was having a nightmare. She felt her head spinning like a waltzer. How on earth could this have happened? How would she tell Eddie, never mind his parents?

'Hey? Are you making the coffee or are we waiting on Starbucks to make a special delivery?' Eddie called from the sitting room. Tanya was back in the kitchen now but found herself too shell-shocked to speak. How could she explain this?

On hearing no answer Eddie made his way into the kitchen. 'Tanya, you look like you've seen a ghost!'

'Look out the window,' she said, now feeling and sounding numb. He did as he was told.

'Jesus Christ,' he muttered, his face visibly falling. 'What the hell happened?'

'I don't know,' she said, her voice catching in her throat.

Eddie's face had turned ashen. 'What do you mean, you don't know, Tanya? The garden was your responsibility. You promised my parents . . .' he trailed off.

The look of disappointment in his face wounded Tanya. 'You don't think this has anything to do with me, do you?' she gasped. 'I know who's behind this, Eddie.'

He raised an enquiring eyebrow.

Tanya was shaking now. 'This is Alice's doing. I know it is. That girl is warped.'

Eddie looked shocked. 'Listen to yourself, Tanya. I don't know what's got into you lately. You're obsessed with Alice. It's not normal. I don't know what you did to the garden but you'd better find a way to make it all right again.' He shook his head in despair. 'Mum and Dad would be devastated if they were here to witness this. They'd be absolutely crushed. This is your fault and you should grow up and accept responsibility for it. You obviously watered the garden with weed killer instead of water. How else could you have killed every single plant or flower? It's insane. I need to get out of here and clear my head. I'll bring Prince to Killiney. You'd better stay here and figure out how to make this mess right again.'

Five minutes later Tanya heard the front door slam. Eddie hadn't even bothered to wait for his coffee. She was furious at Eddie's reaction. Couldn't he see that it was crystal clear that Alice was behind this? Tanya was sure their neighbour was vindictive enough. If she could do this to somebody's property what else was she capable of? She clearly had a screw loose and couldn't be trusted under any circumstances. Would Tanya and Eddie come home one day to find the house burned down? God, it didn't even bear thinking about. And now she was going to Kerry this evening. Her flight was at 6.40 p.m. Would Eddie even be prepared to drive her to the airport? Things seemed to have gone from bad to worse in the last twenty-four hours. She could never remember a time when Eddie was so distant with her. She almost felt like cancelling her trip to Kerry at this stage. Which was more important – her career or her man?

34

Mrs Adams was at the Aga stirring a pot of stew as Alice sat at the kitchen table, leisurely flicking through the pages of *Grazia* magazine.

'Alice, there's been something I've been meaning to ask you.'

'Oh?' Alice didn't like the tone of her mother's voice. She sounded terribly serious. She hoped her mother wasn't going to start asking her for rent or suggest that she should help out more with the household chores. After all, it wasn't exactly her choice to be living at home with her parents at her age. In fact, it was stifling. As soon as Alice had enough dosh she'd be moving swiftly on. Still, it was very nice to be in such proximity to Eddie . . .

'You know it's your father's birthday next week?'

'Oh, is it? I forgot. Thanks for reminding me so. I'd better go and get him a card.'

'Actually I was thinking that we'd go away for the occasion. Just the three of us?'

Alice looked at her mother as if the woman had suggested she join them in a group suicide. She opened her mouth to say something but then thought better of it. Maybe if she said nothing then her mother would just forget about it. Imagine the three of them going away somewhere? She wasn't ten years old any more and the idea was simply preposterous.

'I was thinking of Galway, maybe?' her mother continued.

Alice closed over her magazine. Galway? What the hell was her mother suggesting? That they go back to that dreadful caravan camp where they'd made her spend all her insufferable childhood summers? Is that what she was thinking? Alice could hardly believe her ears. Did her mum honestly think that she would agree to something so horrible? There was no way in hell that she would. Absolutely no bloody way.

Alice finally found her voice. 'You mean to the caravan site?'

Mrs Adams laughed as she turned down the heat of the cooker. 'No, of course not, darling. I was thinking of somewhere nice for your father's birthday and a friend of mine suggested the House Hotel just off Eyre Square. It's supposed to be a gorgeous boutique hotel and it would also be nice and central. We could stay a couple of nights there and maybe tour some of Connemara during the day. You know that's where your grandparents come from and your father loves the peace and quiet of the place.'

Alice thought about it for all of two seconds before she made her mind up. The answer was a firm no. She didn't care how nice the hotel was. She didn't want to be carted off to Galway in the back seat of the car like she was a schoolgirl again.

'I'm sorry, Mum, but I've been booked for a couple of

important modelling jobs next week and I can't cancel at this late stage.'

Her mother looked deeply disappointed but Alice didn't care. Wild horses couldn't drag her to the West of Ireland to endure a cosy little get together *en famille*. Tanya had now gone off to Kerry for a few days and if her parents went off on a little trip at the same time, well that was just great timing, as far as she was concerned. With Eddie alone next door and her parents safely out of the way Alice was going to make sure she finally had some fun.

35

Tanya looked out the window as the small plane landed with a thud at the tiny Farranfore airport. The sun had gone down now and it would be dark soon. This really was such a beautiful part of the world and she should really be so excited about spending the next three days filming in such stunning surroundings. But given recent events and Alice's bizarre behaviour towards her recently, she couldn't shake off the niggling doubts that were in her head. She'd briefly considered cancelling the trip especially since Eddie hadn't come home from his walk on Killiney beach in time to give her a lift to the airport. Instead she'd had to ring for a taxi. She'd worried throughout the flight about leaving Eddie alone in the house, knowing full well that that vixen Alice would be up to all sorts of tricks in her absence. But this type of job only presented itself once in a blue moon and she couldn't afford to turn it down. She just had to trust Eddie, that was all there was to it. After all, if she couldn't trust her boyfriend, who might one day be her husband, what hope was there for the two of them? However, those doubts still niggled at her when the taxi picked her up outside the airport and drove her to the luxurious

Aghadoe Heights Hotel which was to be her home for the next few days.

Thankfully the next couple of days were so hectic that Tanya didn't have much time to be negative. She threw herself into her work with gusto in order to keep positive and found herself enjoying doing the make-up on this film. Although she worked long hours and had to be constantly around to powder the actors' noses when required, she had to admit that you just couldn't pay for this kind of experience. The cast and crew all behaved like one big happy family and even the extras, who were mainly local people, were all very nice and welcoming.

The hotel room that had been booked for her was the height of luxury although sadly she didn't get to spend much time in it due to the insanely early starts and late finishes. However, it boasted the most perfect view she'd ever seen, looking out on to the magnificent Ring of Kerry and she was truly grateful to be part of something so exciting. It was hard to believe that only a short couple of months back she'd been waxing irate women's bikini lines and doing make-up for sulky brats going to their debs' dances.

She didn't miss Eddie as much as she'd initially thought she would, mostly because she was working so hard and at night she was so exhausted she just flopped into her big double bed. Of course she phoned him each evening to let him know how her day had gone and he was always polite to her even though the one time she finished the call with 'I love you', he didn't respond.

On the first evening most of the cast and crew

members went to bed but some diehards made their way into Killarney, which was buzzing. Tanya had got talking to a lovely American girl called Amy who was associate director on this movie. The two of them had got along like a house on fire and they'd both been the last to leave the pub.

She'd asked Amy if she planned on spending any time in Ireland after filming.

'Well, yes, actually,' the girl had replied. 'Would you believe I've just got hired by a US firm to direct my own commercial here in Ireland next week?'

'Wow, that's amazing. You seem so young.'

Amy was flattered. 'I know, I'm delighted but I've got a big problem on my hands. Maybe you could help me out?'

Tanya was intrigued. But perhaps the girl was going to offer her the chance to do the make-up for the ad. Apparently it was to advertise a new Irish brand of tea and it would be launched here in Ireland and the UK as well as in the States.

'Well, anything I can do of course . . .'

'We were supposed to fly a top American model over for the commercial but she's just cancelled on us. It's such a headache. We're holding a casting in Dublin in a couple of days but as a make-up artist you've probably already worked with all the top Irish models, so maybe you could recommend somebody?'

Tanya was hugely flattered to be asked for her opinion. Amy must have great faith in her as a professional and it looked like all her hard work over the last few days would pay off.

'What kind of girl would you have in mind?'

'Ideally we're looking for a slim dark-haired girl with sultry good looks but not too dark. We'd like her to look realistically Irish, if you know what I mean. But we're steering clear of the stereotypical red-haired girl with freckles as it's so obvious and unoriginal.'

Tanya frowned, deep in thought. A dark-haired model? Hmm. Suddenly an unwanted image of Alice flashed momentarily into her head but she banished it immediately. Not if Alice was the last brunette in Ireland would she recommend her for the job after all she'd put Tanya through. And suddenly an idea struck her.

'Listen, I hope I'm not being cheeky but, em, my little sister is thinking of going into modelling. She's tall and slim with shiny dark hair and she really is a beauty. I hope I'm not being biased when I say so. I'd love to recommend her for the job.'

Then Tanya felt herself flush. Oh God, Amy must think she was terribly pushy. Maybe she shouldn't have opened her mouth at all.

'Listen, I'm sorry if I—'

'Oh no, don't apologise,' said Amy, patting Tanya's upper arm. 'Your sister sounds really great. Just what we're looking for, in fact. What a stroke of luck. Um . . . I'd have to see a picture of her though, just to be sure. Has she a Facebook page or anything?'

'Actually she does. But even better, I happen to have a picture of her on my mobile phone,' said Tanya, enthusiastically whipping it out. 'It's not the best quality photo ever but it'll give you an idea.' Tanya flipped open her phone at a rare smiling picture of Elaine taken on her twenty-first. Amy scrutinised it for a few seconds before nodding and smiling at Tanya.

'Well, what do you know?' She beamed. 'I think you've just found me my girl.'

36

No sooner had her parents taken off for Galway than Elaine appeared on the step of Alice's house. She was feeling very happy with herself after Tanya had excitedly phoned her from Kerry to tell her she'd just secured her the booking of a lifetime. Imagine! Her first ever modelling assignment and it would apparently pay enough to completely clear her student loan. That would mean she could chuck in the job as sales assistant in the shoe shop. Tanya had warned her not to tell a single soul, however. Since Elaine hadn't yet signed with any agency she wouldn't have to give anybody any commission for the job so it was imperative to keep this bit of good news to herself for the time being.

'Once you've completed this job, you'll be hot property, Elaine, so then it'll be up to you to select the agency of your choice.'

Elaine felt bad keeping this bit of good news from Alice who was being so kind to her and had offered to help style her for the following day's shoot. She had even organised her photographer friend Mike to take pictures for her portfolio at half his usual fee. Then again, her sister was older and wiser and she had made Elaine promise not to breathe a word of this to anybody, not even to her best friend. Elaine, thinking of that student loan she so badly needed to pay off, had agreed to keep schtum.

'Come on in, you look fab,' said Alice, opening the front door wide. She had to admit that Elaine looked particularly nice today with her hair blow-dried and her make-up looked great too.

'Tanya couldn't do it 'cos she's in Kerry so her old colleague Rose did it for me. I feel like a completely different person.'

'What time is the photographer arriving at your house?' Alice asked.

'Three.'

'Right then, we've got no time to lose. Come on up to my room and you can pick out some dresses from my wardrobe and then we'll go next door and see what Tanya has in her wardrobe. She did agree that you could borrow some of her clothes for your test shoot, didn't she?'

'Of course she did.'

Alice smiled to herself. Everything looked like it was going to plan. She really needed to get into Eddie and Tanya's bedroom no matter what.

They went upstairs and Elaine was deeply impressed with Alice's wardrobe. Every label under the sun was here. Her eyes were almost out on stalks at all the clothes. Elaine had never worn anything designer in her life.

Alice limited Elaine to strictly three dresses only, however. She was worried that Elaine might see so many things she liked here that she might not bother to go next door to check out what Tanya had to offer. But once Elaine had her dresses picked out Alice frogmarched her into the Toner home.

Alice followed Elaine up the stairs with Prince bounding excitedly alongside them. Although Alice had the keys to the house, she'd never ventured upstairs before. She just didn't have the bottle to do that. Imagine if Tanya or Eddie unexpectedly came home and caught her in one of the bedrooms! She'd never be able to explain that one away. No. That's why today was the perfect opportunity to take her game to the next level.

There were two wardrobes in the room. Elaine opened the first wardrobe.

'Oh, this must be Eddie's,' she said spying the shirts, ties and suits. She shut the doors again and went to the other wardrobe.

'Now this is more like it,' she said, picking out an armful of dresses and placing them in a heap on the bed.

'That's a lovely one.' Alice picked up a black chiffon minidress with gold beading on the bust line. 'It's really glam.'

'Yeah, I like it. And I love this one too. It's one of Tanya's favourites,' Elaine said, picking up a navy and white Diane von Fürstenberg wrap dress that her sister had spent almost a month's salary on last summer.

'It's stunning,' Alice agreed. 'Now you go on into the next room and try them on for me one by one. There's no point in you taking a load of them with you if they don't even suit you.'

'True.' Elaine gathered up the dresses in her arms and moved to the door. There she halted momentarily and turned around. 'Alice, I just want to let you know how much I appreciate you doing all this for me. If there's anything I can do . . .'

'Not at all.' Alice waved her off. If only the silly girl knew exactly how much she'd helped her already.

Elaine came back into Eddie and Tanya's room moments later having changed into the Diane von Fürstenberg dress.

'I really like it,' she said, doing a little twirl.

'Yeah, it looks good on you. It really accentuates your figure and will look good in the photos. But you can see your bra.'

'Oops, can you?'

'Yeah, take it off and I'll see if you'd get away with not wearing one.'

Elaine obeyed and threw the bra on the bed.

'That's much better,' said Alice with approval. 'Now try on the other dresses quickly. We don't have all the time in the world,' she added, glancing at her watch.

Once Elaine had disappeared out the door, Alice waited a few seconds before picking up the other girl's discarded lacy black bra and hiding it under the double bed.

37

A lice thanked the young man at the garden centre for all his help as he filled her mother's car boot full of unusual and exotic-looking plants. Thankfully her mother had agreed that she could go on the insurance of her car while they were in Galway, otherwise Alice wouldn't have had a chance in hell of carrying all this stuff home with her.

She'd finally got rid of Elaine at 2 p.m. by telling her she had to drive to Wicklow to pick up some shrubs and stuff. Elaine had thought it was quite funny.

'I wouldn't have put you down as a keen gardener,' she'd laughed.

Yeah, well, that's because you don't know anything about me, Alice had privately thought but had decided to keep her mouth shut instead. She wanted to keep Elaine on her side for the moment.

She drove back to Dublin as the sun was fading, the boot of her car resembling something like the Chelsea Flower Show. She really couldn't wait to see Eddie's face later when he saw the garden with a new lease of life. She had hoped to get back to Dublin earlier and plant everything before Eddie got home from work as a nice surprise but now it looked like she wouldn't have the time. Damn that silly Elaine for delaying her earlier.

She decided to ring Eddie when she was stuck at the traffic lights of Foxrock church.

'Hey, Alice,' he said, answering the call.

'Hi, you. Listen, I'm just wondering if you're home from work yet?'

He sounded surprised by the question. 'Actually I have to stay late to go over a case due in court in the morning. Why? Is everything okay? Is Prince okay?'

'Oh yeah, everything's fine. It's just that I have a boot full of plants here with me and I wanted to plant them in your garden before night falls.'

'Alice, you shouldn't have . . .'

'Ah listen, I was getting stuff for our garden anyway as a birthday present for Dad so there was no problem picking up some extra plants for you. It makes me sad seeing your garden the way it is now. Even Prince seems sad when I call over to take him for his walk. Maybe a bit of colour in the back garden would cheer him up.'

'Alice, do you ever just think of yourself instead of always doing things for other people?' he asked, his voice full of warmth.

'Ah, stop making me out to be a saint,' she said airily. 'I enjoy making other people happy.'

'So I see. Well, listen, I'll be home around eightish. I can't wait to see the garden. Is there anything I can do to thank you?'

'You could offer me a glass of wine to enjoy in the new garden?' she suggested flirtatiously.

Eddie hesitated. Would that really be such a good

idea? Tanya would probably kill him if she found out. Then again, it would be rude to turn Alice down. And she was great company, not to mention exceptionally attractive. And he was lonely. He was missing Tanya. But was she missing him? he thought darkly as he remembered David's call.

Alice, at the other end of the phone, found the silence almost unbearable. Oh God, maybe he thought she'd been too forward.

'Eddie, are you still there? Listen, it's okay about tonight if you're not up for a drink. You're probably tired and—'

'I'd love to,' Eddie answered in a definite tone of voice.

Alice punched the air with joy.

Then very calmly she rang 11811 and asked to be put through to Interflora.

'Hello, yes, I'd like to order one of your biggest bouquets of flowers please . . . yes, roses sound lovely . . . great, carnations would be lovely too . . . no problem, I'll just give you my credit card details . . . message? Oh um. Let me think now . . . I'd like something simple . . . With lots of love, Dave . . . yes, that sounds perfect.'

I t was ten past eight and Eddie's car had been parked in his drive for the last twenty minutes. He would be well and truly showered and freshened up by now. Alice poured another splash of vodka into her glass and swirled it around. It wasn't like she really needed the Dutch courage but it might help all the same. This was the first time in years herself and Eddie would be in the same room. Alone. Just like old times.

She took her drink into the hall and took a long, hard critical look at herself in the full-length mirror. She hoped her pink baby-doll dress wasn't a bit OTT for just a friendly drink. Then again she couldn't think of anything else to wear and it was imperative that she wore something Eddie hadn't seen her in before. And he definitely hadn't seen this because she'd never worn it before. However, worried that Eddie might think she was making too much of an effort, she nipped upstairs and borrowed her mum's good grey cashmere cardigan to wear over the dress. She could always slip it off later as the night progressed.

Alice rang the next-door bell nervously, but her nerves soon vanished as Eddie opened the door.

'Wow!' he exclaimed in open admiration. 'You look hot.'

'Thanks.' She beamed and brushed past him, dangerously close so that he could benefit the full whiff of her Chanel No. 5 perfume. 'Inside or out? Oh, nice flowers,' she added, nodding at the enormous bouquet on the sideboard. 'Somebody obviously has a secret admirer!'

Eddie conveniently ignored her comment. 'I think we'll stay indoors. You've got to remember you're not in LA any more. Go on into the sitting room and make yourself comfortable. I've got the champagne chilling in the fridge.'

Alice did as she was told, feeling decidedly pleased with herself. Champagne, no less? Somebody was going to great efforts!

She sat down on the sofa and the first thing she noticed was that Eddie's debs' photo was still gone. Oh well, she thought, the photo may have disappeared but she certainly hadn't. It would take a hell of a lot of effort to banish her to oblivion.

Eddie soon joined her. He looked relaxed and undeniably sexy in a light blue shirt, open at the collar, and a pair of Levi's. She was sure she could smell a delicious aftershave off him too. How nice that he had gone to so much trouble on her behalf.

He poured the Veuve Cliquot into two flutes and they clinked glasses. Instead of sitting opposite her as she had expected, Eddie slipped on to the sofa beside Alice.

'It's good to see you,' he said, looking her directly in the eye.

She didn't flinch. 'Just like old times,' she said boldly.

Suddenly he looked away. 'Yeah, just like old times,' he said in a much quieter tone of voice. 'Those were the days when we didn't have a care in the world.'

Alice crossed her legs and toyed playfully with her champagne glass. 'Do you remember when we used to sneak off down the garden and drink cider without our parents knowing?'

Eddie smiled. 'How could I forget? I could never get served in the off-licence 'cos I used to look too young, whereas Johnny never used to have a problem so he'd buy the booze for all of us. He used to fancy you too, as far as I remember.'

'He did?' Alice twirled a strand of her hair, feigning innocence.

'You know he did. We all used to fancy you. Even *I* did.'

'Really? I never knew,' said Alice coyly.

'Of course you knew. It's not like I didn't make it obvious.'

He looked up at her again and she felt her heart beat faster. She hadn't thought this would be so easy but he was like putty in her hands. He obviously still fancied her.

'More champagne?' he offered, noticing that she had already drained her glass.

'That'd be lovely, thanks. I must say this champagne is going down a treat.'

'Yes, we've come a long way since our cider-drinking days.'

'Have we?' She pondered his statement. How far had they really come? Eddie had moved on. With somebody else. And Alice had foolishly let it happen. But all wasn't lost of course. She had to remain positive now. This was a crucial moment. There was still time for new beginnings. Eddie wasn't married and didn't have children, thank God. Neither did she. Maybe they had always been meant to be together but she had been too blind to see it.

'Well, you certainly have done well for yourself. I've got used to seeing your picture in the paper all the time looking ridiculously glamorous. Sometimes I ask myself, is that really the same girl I used to play hide and seek with as a kid? Is that the same girl I used to write love poems to and make a total idiot of myself for?'

Alice cleared her throat to interrupt him, lowering her eyes at the same time. 'I am still that same girl,' she insisted. 'I might not look the same as I did then but deep down nothing has changed. That girl you see smiling out at you in the papers is just an image I portray. It's just my job, not me.'

'Do you remember I used to be mad about you?' he ventured, his voice softening.

Alice struggled not to show the delight in her face. The champagne was obviously lowering Eddie's inhibitions. This was working. It was really working!

She lowered her eyes again. It was important that she dealt her hand carefully. 'You say that in the past tense.'

'Yeah,' he sighed. 'Well, everything's changed now.'

'You mean your feelings for me have changed,' she said tentatively.

Eddie looked away. 'I try not to think about that any more.'

'Think about what?'

Eddie seemed a bit uncomfortable. 'I suppose I don't like to be reminded about how I used to chase you around the place. I put it down to a crazy infatuation. I suppose everyone goes through it when they're young.'

'Can I have some more champagne?'

'Sure.'

He topped up her glass again. She could feel the bubbles going straight to her head but inside she had a nice warm feeling. Eddie and herself had never really had an intimate conversation like this before. Then again, there hadn't really been the opportunity, what with Tanya always hanging around like a bad smell. And it might just be the last opportunity they'd have to be together. She didn't want to let it slip through her fingers.

She moved closer to him on the couch. 'Did you ever think that the two of us might end up together?'

'Well . . . at one stage I had hoped but . . .'

'. . . we drifted apart,' she finished for him.

'How can we have drifted apart when we were never together in the first place?'

'I thought we were too young back then,' said Alice. 'I had a lot of growing up to do.'

'So did I. But it's great that we've remained friends.'

Alice sat up straight. Friends? Hmm. This wasn't exactly what she wanted to hear. She didn't want to be Eddie's friend. She wanted to be his lover. She'd never been as sure about that as she was now. She just couldn't afford to let him get away. She could feel herself begin to panic slightly.

'Do you think if Tanya wasn't on the scene we could be . . . I mean, more than just friends?'

She reached over and touched his arm. He didn't move away.

'I can't even think about that,' he said in a quiet voice. 'It would only be fruitless to go down that route.'

'Would it?'

He looked at her now, his face a mask of confusion. 'Am I not getting something here? You're not telling me you have feelings for me, are you?'

Alice put her glass down deliberately and her eyes never left his as he placed a warm hand over hers. 'How did you guess? Is it that obvious?'

'I don't know what to say.'

'Well, then,' she whispered, 'don't say anything.'

She leaned towards him very slightly as he squeezed her hand.

'Alice, I don't know if this is right . . .'

'. . . it feels right though,' she interrupted. 'To me anyway.'

Her heart almost stopped when he placed his other hand under her chin and lifted it slightly.

'You are so beautiful.'

'Kiss me then.'

He moved closer to her and stroked her hair. She then leaned forward but suddenly he drew back, shaking his head.

'Don't pull away,' Alice begged. She couldn't afford to let him out of her grasp now. Finally, finally she had got Eddie exactly where she wanted him. She didn't want this opportunity just slipping away for ever.

But at that moment, Alice's mobile phone rang in her bag, making her start. God dammit! Why hadn't she switched the blasted thing off? It rang off and then started ringing again.

Eddie turned away, suddenly looking guilty.

'I won't answer,' she said huskily. She didn't want to ruin this perfect moment. But the blasted phone kept ringing and eventually she opened her bag. It was her mother's mobile number flashing. What on earth did she want? Trust her mother to wreck everything. She switched off her phone altogether.

'It's just my mum,' she explained. 'I'm sure it's nothing. Now,' she said, wrapping her arms around Eddie's neck and inhaling his strong masculine aftershave, 'where were we?'

But the moment had indeed been lost as Alice had feared it might. Eddie got to his feet. 'This is all so confusing, Alice. I'm really sorry. My head is just spinning. I had no idea you had feelings for me but I have to think of Tanya. She's my girlfriend. I can't cheat on her.'

'But there's a connection between us, a spark,' Alice pleaded with him. 'You can't deny that. I've never felt it with anybody else. I suppose . . . I suppose you're feeling guilty?'

Eddie exhaled slowly. 'Yes.'

'How do you feel about Tanya?' Alice asked, even though it killed her even to mention her love rival.

'I don't know. Things have been a bit awkward the past few weeks but I know that I love her and that she has changed my life for the better.'

Alice sat rooted to her chair. She felt like a dagger was being pushed straight through her heart. This was excruciating. 'I see,' she said in a small voice.

'But that doesn't mean I'm not attracted to you. You're a beautiful woman. I'm sure you could have any man you want.'

Alice stood up and gave a wry smile. She knew that she had lost this game. 'How ironic,' she said. 'That's what everyone always says to me. They always say I can have any man I want. But that's obviously not true. I have to go now. Thanks for the champagne.'

Eddie reached out to hug her. 'I do care for you,' he said.

But Alice spurned his touch. She didn't want to hear any more. She picked up her bag and saw herself out.

Alice woke with a hollow heart. She felt so empty and unwanted. The memories of the night unwittingly flashed in her brain. She'd been a fool. Eddie didn't love her after all. He had made that perfectly clear. But what had she been expecting? For him to drop everything and throw Tanya out just because he'd once had a childhood crush on her? Of course he didn't have any intention of doing such a thing. The curtains were drawn and the room was dark. Alice didn't even know what time it was. Eventually she leaned over the side of her bed and retrieved her mobile from her bag. It was nearly eleven. Somebody had left a message on her phone. Her heart leapt. Maybe it was Eddie wanting to apologise. Maybe he'd thought things over and realised he'd made a huge mistake letting Alice walk out his door for good. But her hopes were dashed as she saw it was just a message from her mum telling her to phone her urgently.

Wearily Alice dialled her mother's number.

'Oh Alice,' he mother cried down the phone before dissolving into floods of tears. 'Thank God you've called. Your father has had a heart attack.'

Mrs Adams was hysterical. Her husband had been

taken ill on the golf course and had been rushed to Galvia Hospital in Galway where he was currently undergoing tests.

'I'm sick with worry,' she said down the phone as Alice listened, numb with shock. 'He's had a bad night. At one stage the doctors feared we were going to lose him.'

'I'll drive down straight away, Mum. I should be at the hospital in less than four hours. Everything's going to be okay, do you hear me?' she added with an air of confidence she didn't feel.

The journey from Dublin to Galway seemed to take for ever. Alice was still in shock. She was wracked with guilt. Suppose her father had passed away during the night? Suppose he had died without her saying goodbye to him? She had ignored her mother's call last night and hadn't phoned her till this morning because it had seemed insignificant compared to her quest for Eddie's affections. Now she felt like the worst daughter in the world. Her dad was seriously ill and it looked like she hadn't given a stuff about him. Passing Athlone, halfway to Galway the reality of the situation had finally hit her. She was her parents' only daughter and she was a crap person. They deserved better. Had she really thought a cheap fling with Eddie was worth more than her parents? And that's all it would have amounted to. Eddie didn't love her. Sure he found her attractive but that didn't matter. She'd wasted so much time and energy trying to win his love, and for what? Now she felt like a complete idiot. As she drove towards Ballinasloe, light raindrops hit her windscreen. Alice had never felt so depressed in her life. Her parents were all she had left and were always there for her no matter what. She hadn't given them back anything in return. She'd spent most of her life resenting them for not giving her enough. She'd pushed them to the limits and they still loved her unreservedly. She kept driving through the rain. Please, please, Dad, hang on till I get there, she begged silently. Please hold on so that I get to tell you that I love you.

As Alice passed through the town of Ballinasloe in County Galway it continued to rain. She was tired now and feeling hungry. She stopped the car. She needed a little rest or else she was in danger of falling asleep at the wheel. That was the last thing she needed to do. Maybe she should get herself a can of Diet Coke to perk her up? Then she spotted SuperMacs. Wouldn't it be nice to go in and sit down and order a large portion of fries for a treat? It had been so long since she had eaten anything naughty that she'd almost forgotten what it was like to pig out. To hell with her miserable diet, she thought, getting out of the car and locking it. She'd always starved herself and it hadn't made her happy. Now that she realised how short life could be, it was time to start living like a human being again. A large bag of hot chips smothered in ketchup wouldn't kill her. And for pure devilment she was going to have ice-cream for dessert.

When she finally reached the hospital, her tummy nicely full, a nurse brought her to her father's bedside where he looked tired and old.

'Dad!' she cried, taking his hand, the tears streaming down her face. 'Oh Dad, I got here as quickly as I could.'

'I'm going to be okay.' He smiled weakly, closing his

eyes. 'I'm tired now but the hospital staff have been very good to me. I need you to look after your mum for the next few nights. She's had an awful shock.'

'I know. We all have. But you're going to get through this, Dad,' she urged. 'You're so strong.'

'You're strong as well, my love. That's what I love so much about you. But you need to be even stronger for your mother right now. She needs you. In the meantime I need to get back to my old self. The doctor said my collapse has been a warning to me to slow down. They want to keep me here a few more days as a precaution. But there's nothing to worry about.'

'I was so terrified I was going to lose you,' she sobbed.

She sat with him for almost an hour, holding his hand and then he insisted that she should go off with her mother to get some dinner and a rest back at their hotel as he was fading and needed some sleep.

Alice promised to spend the next few days in Galway to keep him company.

'Everything will be fine in Dublin . . .' she said. 'I alarmed the house before I left.'

'I'm a bit worried about the plants though,' he said. 'Maybe Eddie next door could water them for me? Could you phone him and ask him to do that?' He looked his daughter directly in the eye. 'I don't want my precious garden to go the same way as the one next door.'

Alice gulped. She looked away, riddled with guilt. She knew that her father knew what she had done.

'I'll ring him,' she said. 'And I'll ask him. I think I'll stay away from gardening from now on. I need to think about what I'm going to do for the rest of my life now. Thinking

I might lose you has made me re-evaluate everything.' She kissed her father's frail cheek. 'I'll be back again in the morning,' she said and made to leave. But at the door of his room she paused and turned around. 'And Dad? I just want you to know that I love you.'

His eyes lit up and she smiled back at him. She hadn't told him that since she was a little girl. But it was better late than never.

40

Tanya was relieved to be back in Dublin. Those few days away had taken their toll. It was tough living out of a suitcase and working all the hours of the day but she was proud of herself for all that she had achieved in the short time and now knew that it had been the right decision to venture out on her own. But now it was crunch-time. She'd have to face Eddie to see if their relationship could be saved.

As Tanya's taxi pulled into the drive she noticed that the house next door was in darkness. Hmm, the Adams family must be away. She was relieved that they were. She just couldn't face Alice calling around again tonight under some other silly pretence. Honestly, she was a thorn in Tanya's side. Why couldn't she just leave them in peace? And why did Eddie seem to encourage her? Did he genuinely like Alice or was he just trying to keep Tanya on her toes? There was nothing that boosted the male ego more than attention from the opposite sex. She let herself in and turned on the hall lights. She spotted the flowers in the hall. How sweet of Eddie, she thought. It was nice to know she was obviously back in the good books. She dragged her case into the kitchen as she was too tired to carry it upstairs. She heard Prince barking in the back garden. He was obviously hungry. After feeding him, she flopped down on to the sofa in the sitting room and poured herself a generous glass of red wine. Hopefully when Eddie came home he'd share the bottle with her or else she'd probably end up drinking it all by herself. She had to admit it was good to be home. No matter how fabulous hotels were it was always nice to get back to your own familiar surroundings.

Twenty minutes later, Tanya heard Eddie put his key in the front door and her heart soared. She had missed him so much. But would he feel the same way? This had been the longest they'd ever been apart since becoming a couple.

She stood up and rushed to greet him. He threw his arms around her and kissed her fully on the lips. 'I can't tell you how glad I am to see you.' He grinned. 'You should have texted me to say you'd landed. I would have collected you.'

Tanya visibly felt herself relax. Eddie took off his shoes and followed her into the sitting room, gratefully accepting a glass of red wine.

'Do you fancy a Chinese?' he said, picking up his mobile.

'Oh Gosh, yes. You've read my mind,' she said, snuggling in beside him. 'So, did you miss me?'

'I did.'

'Well, I missed you too,' she said and then filled him in with all the news of the past few days. She was still talking when she was interrupted by the sound of the delivery man ringing the front doorbell.

'That must be our food. Oh God, for an awful second there I thought it might be Alice at the door to welcome you back,' she laughed.

She noticed her comment failed to raise a smile on Eddie's face. What was going on? Eddie went out to the door to pay the deliveryman. He came back in with the food but although Tanya had been ravenous, her appetite was beginning to disappear. What had happened in her absence? Had Alice called around? As she ate her vegetable curry and egg-fried rice she wondered whether Alice had indeed been meddling in their lives again. No doubt she had. She wouldn't have been able to help herself.

After they had eaten, Tanya cleared away the rubbish and commented that the Adams family must have gone away.

'Have they? I hadn't noticed,' Eddie said vaguely.

'Well, their house is in darkness. Prince mustn't have got his walk today. Maybe we should bring him around the block.'

Eddie sighed. 'I'm tired now and I want to watch the match. We'll bring him for an extra long walk tomorrow.'

Tanya toyed with her wine glass, deliberating what she should say next. After all, she didn't want to keep harping on and on about Alice but deep down she really had to know whether the other girl had called around.

'Was Alice here when I was away?' she asked suddenly. She might as well be blunt about it. No point beating around the bush at this stage.

Eddie gulped and looked decidedly uncomfortable. He averted his eyes and Tanya's heart sank. She began to imagine the worst. Oh God, what had happened now?

'She just popped over for a drink.'

Tanya's face clouded. She looked at her boyfriend stonily. 'Just a drink? You mean she invited herself around again?'

'Well, actually, I invited her around.'

Tanya tilted her head in disbelief. 'You did what?'

'It was all very innocent,' he insisted. 'She brought around some plants for the garden and to thank her I invited her in for a drink. I felt I had to do something.'

Tanya felt the room begin to spin. She felt utterly betrayed. Eddie had just gone and confirmed her worst fears. And what was more he was acting like it wasn't even a big deal. To think she'd been off in Kerry working flat out while he'd been boozing it up. With a supermodel. And his ex no less. She thought she was going to be sick. 'I don't believe this,' she muttered.

Eddie looked wounded. 'Don't you trust me?'

'Trust?' She uttered the word as though she didn't understand it. She was in a daze now.

'Say something, Tanya.'

She drained her glass before putting it firmly down with a thud. 'I don't know what to think any more, Eddie,' she said, before standing up and going to bed.

'I've decided to move home,' Tanya tearfully told her mother the following morning. 'I just need some time to get my head sorted. I'd really appreciate it if you didn't ask me any questions for the time being.'

After a night of tossing and turning Tanya had woken up and decided that she had no choice but to leave. Eddie had slept in another room and had left for work this morning without even saying goodbye. Tanya couldn't take it any more. How could she possibly forgive Eddie for entertaining Alice behind her back like that?

'Of course,' her mother had assured her. 'You know you're welcome to come home. We'd be glad to have you back.'

And so she spent the rest of the morning packing. It didn't take very long to fill her two suitcases. And then just to be sure, she looked under the bed to see if she had left anything behind. It was then she discovered the strange bra. She knew it didn't belong to her and that she had never seen it before in her life. That was the final straw to break the camel's back. Once home she took to her old bed and refused her mother's offer of a cup of tea. She didn't want tea or sympathy. She just wanted to be left alone. She had never felt so distraught in her whole life. How could Eddie have treated her so badly? She hadn't deserved it. She hadn't deserved a bit of it. She had adored him and had presumed he'd felt the same way. Eventually Tanya cried herself to sleep. It was dark when she woke up again. Dark, dreary and depressing. She turned on the bedroom light and checked her phone. There had been several missed calls from Eddie but she couldn't even bring herself to check her messages. She didn't want to hear any pathetic excuses. Too late for that now. It was over, completely over. There could be no going back.

A light knock on the door made her jump.

'It's Elaine, Tanya. Do you want to talk?'

'No, I don't.'

But Elaine being Elaine, she came in anyway. 'Do you want me to help you unpack?'

'I just want to be left alone.'

'Are you sure you don't want to talk about things?'

Tanya shook her head resolutely. 'No.'

'It might make you feel better.'

'Nothing could make me feel better at the moment,' Tanya sniffed before breaking down and telling Elaine exactly what she had found under the bed.

Her younger sister put her hands on her hips and frowned. 'So *that's* where it got to!' she exclaimed. 'I've been racking my brains for the last couple of days trying to figure out where I'd left that damn bra.'

Now it was Tanya's turn to look confused. Why on earth would Elaine have been in the bedroom she shared with Eddie?

'Oh, no, it wasn't like that,' Elaine explained hurriedly, sensing her sister's bewilderment. 'I was just over there trying on clothes. You said I could, remember?'

And then the penny dropped. Everything made sense now. Oh God, she had completely forgotten that she'd given Elaine permission to raid her wardrobe. But this was a disaster! What had she done? She'd mistrusted Eddie and had stormed out in protest. He would never, ever forgive her for walking out on him without so much as an explanation. Tanya sat up straight in the bed, sweating, as wave after wave of panic washed over her.

'What time is it, Elaine?'

Her sister glanced at her watch. 'Almost midnight.'

'Oh God, it's too late to call around to Eddie now, isn't it?'

Elaine shook her head, looking much wiser than her years. 'It's never too late', she said, 'to try and save a relationship that's worth saving.'

The sitting-room light was on. Good, Tanya thought, parking her car in the drive. Thank God Eddie hadn't gone to bed yet. She had left her set of keys on the kitchen table before leaving the house earlier on so now she had to ring the doorbell.

Eddie answered almost immediately. He looked tired and dishevelled and pain was etched in his handsome face. 'You're back?' he said, almost whispering.

'I've made a mistake,' she said tearfully. 'I'm so, so sorry.'

'Come in.'

She followed him into the sitting room and they sat on the sofa together, neither of them quite knowing what to say. It was then that Tanya noticed the huge bouquet of flowers on the table. Eddie must have brought them in from the hall.

'They're beautiful,' she said. 'A lot of thought must have gone into those flowers.'

'Indeed.' Eddie grimaced.

'I forgot to thank you for them last night.'

'Oh? Didn't you read the message that came with them?'

Tanya looked puzzled. 'I didn't see a card. You old romantic, you. How could I have ever thought of leaving you?'

'I think you should read the card,' said Eddie, without feeling, pulling away as she tried to kiss him.

None of this made sense. Why was Eddie being so cool with her? She stood up and walked over to the flowers. A small card lay beside them. She read the words aloud. 'With lots of love, Dave.'

'Who's Dave?' She shook her head in wonder.

'That's exactly what I was trying to figure out myself,' said Eddie. 'But then of course I remembered. He was the guy you met in the club, the guy who was phoning you . . .'

Tanya suddenly saw red. This was a trap. David didn't know where she lived. He had no way of knowing. This was just another well-thought-out set-up by a scheming arch-enemy. 'You know,' she said, 'I bet Alice sent these.'

'Alice?' Eddie looked astonished.

'Seriously. I wouldn't put anything past her. She was here the night David phoned. She has done everything in her power to try and split us up. Right from the very beginning.'

'But why would she do that?'

Tanya sighed. 'Because she's in love with you, Eddie. Or obsessed with you anyway. Even a blind man would be able to see that. But what I really need to know is whether *you* are still in love with *her*.'

Eddie took her hand and squeezed it. 'Still? Tanya, I was never in love with the girl. It was a childhood crush, nothing more. Years and years ago. Another lifetime ago.

How many times do I have to tell you that you're the only one I love? I love you, Tanya, and I want to spend the rest of my life with you.'

She stared back at him, numb with shock. What was he talking about? What did he mean? Had Eddie just said he wanted to commit to her for ever?

'I think you're just saying that,' she said, trying to keep her voice from shaking. This was all too much to take in. Her emotions were all over the place and out of control.

'I'm not, Tanya,' he pleaded with her, taking both her hands in his. 'Listen to me and don't say anything till you've let me say my piece. I've known since the night I met you that you were the woman I wanted to share the rest of my life with. You mean the whole world to me. I wanted to propose to you before but I was so afraid you'd turn me down. That night I asked you to move in with me? Well, I actually had a ring in my pocket but I bottled out at the last minute because I couldn't face the rejection if you said no. In the end I asked you to move in because I thought that if we lived together for a while you would eventually come around to the idea of being my wife.'

Tanya opened her mouth to speak but found herself unable to say a word. She'd wanted to hear this for so long and now that it was happening, she just couldn't get her head around it.

'If you don't believe me,' he continued, 'go upstairs and look under the bed. You'll find a ring there gathering dust. I had decided to propose last night because I missed you so much when you were away but you were acting like a stranger. And then this morning you just left. No explanation, nothing. I thought I'd lost you for ever.'

'I was just worried that you still had feelings for Alice, that's all,' Tanya said, feeling almost ashamed now.

Eddie gently put his arm around her and she could see he had tears in his eyes. 'You still haven't agreed to marry me yet.'

Tanya melted. He looked so cute and vulnerable and at that moment she realised that she could never ever live without him. He was her soulmate, now and for ever.

'Okay. I will marry you,' she said eventually with a smile, 'but only under one condition.'

'What's that?'

'I'd like us to move out of here into our own house.'

'Done,' he said, hugging her. 'I'll do anything for you now, anything at all. Because you've just made me the happiest man alive.'

'And Eddie?'

'Yeah?'

'Maybe we could get a nice detached house to live in. Maybe in the country somewhere. I'm kind of done with having next-door neighbours right now.'

little black dress

brings you
fantastic new books like these
every month - find out more at
www.littleblackdressbooks.com

And why not sign up for our
email newsletter to keep
you in the know about
Little Black Dress news!

Pick up a *little black dress* – it's a girl thing.

THE UNFORTUNATE MISS FORTUNES

Jennifer Crusie, Eileen Dreyer, Anne Stuart

PB £3.99

Ever wanted a charmed life?

Three is supposed to be lucky but the Fortune sisters – Dee, Lizzie and Mare – are about to have the worst weekend of their lives. Unless they can figure out how the hell to work their magic powers . . . and their hearts.

978 0 7553 4191 7

CONFESSIONS OF AN AIR HOSTESS

Marisa Mackle

PB £3.99

Air hostess Annie's life takes a serious nosedive after her boyfriend dumps her but with a plane full of passengers to look after she'll just have to keep on smiling. And you never know, the departure of Mr Wrong could mean the arrival of Mr Right . . .

978 0 7553 3989 1

We hope you relax and enjoy your trip

Pick up a *little black dress* – it's a girl thing.

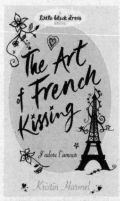

THE ART OF FRENCH KISSING
Kristin Harmel
PB £4.99

When Emma lands her dream job in Paris, she starts to master the art of French kissing: one date, one kiss and onto the next delectable Frenchman. But what happens if you meet someone you want to kiss more than once . . .

A très chic tale of Paris, paparazzi and the pursuit of the perfect kiss

978 0 7553 3828 3

THE CHALET GIRL
Kate Lace
PB £4.99

Being a chalet girl is definitely not all snowy pistes, sexy ski-instructors and a sensational après-ski nightlife, as Millie Braythorpe knows only too well. Then handsome troublemaker Luke comes to stay at her chalet and love rages, but can he be trusted or will her Alpine romance end in wipeout?

978 0 7553 3831 3

You can buy any of these other
Little Black Dress titles from your
bookshop or *direct from the publisher*.

FREE P&P AND UK DELIVERY
(Overseas and Ireland £3.50 per book)

Risky Business	Suzanne Macpherson	£4.99
Today's Special	A. M. Goldsher	£4.99
The Trophy Girl	Kate Lace	£4.99
Truly Madly Yours	Rachel Gibson	£4.99
Right Before Your Eyes	Ellen Shanman	£4.99
Handbags and Homicide	Dorothy Howell	£4.99
The Rules of Gentility	Janet Mullany	£4.99
The Girlfriend Curse	Valerie Frankel	£4.99
A Romantic Getaway	Sarah Monk	£4.99
Drama Queen	Susan Conley	£4.99
Trashed	Alison Gaylin	£4.99
Not Another Bad Date	Rachel Gibson	£4.99
Everything Nice	Ellen Shanman	£4.99
Just Say Yes	Phillipa Ashley	£4.99
Hysterical Blondeness	Suzanne Macpherson	£4.99
Blue Remembered Heels	Nell Dixon	£4.99
Honey Trap	Julie Cohen	£4.99
What's Love Got to do With It?	Lucy Broadbent	£4.99
The Not-So-Perfect Man	Valerie Frankel	£4.99
Lola Carlyle Reveals All	Rachel Gibson	£4.99

TO ORDER SIMPLY CALL THIS NUMBER

01235 400 414

or visit our website: www.headline.co.uk

Prices and availability subject to change without notice.